THE LATE BR

The Late Breakfasters

ROBERT AICKMAN

FABER & FABER

This edition first published in 2014
by Faber & Faber Ltd
Bloomsbury House
74–77 Great Russell Street
London WC1B 3DA

Typeset by Faber & Faber Limited
Printed in England by CPI Group (UK) Ltd, Croydon, CR0 4YY

A CIP record for this book is available from the British Library

ISBN 978-0-571-31684-7

I dedicate this book to
HERBERT VAN THAL
Magician

Part One

I

Griselda de Reptonville did not know what love was until she joined one of Mrs Hatch's famous house parties at Beams, and there met Leander. Her brief and blighted association with Leander led rapidly, as a reaction, to her marrying the unsatisfactory Geoffrey Kynaston. After Kynaston's death, she took up with an unpopular baronet, and lived with him very happily. There may have been one or two earlier episodes, none of them important. She is now twenty-five and has never wholly forgotten Leander; their ecstatic community of thought and feeling is something she fears she has lost for ever. She knew its worth at the time; she never for a single moment doubted it: but society was inevitably too strong for her, and ate her improper passion at a gulp. Leander doubtless never expected anything else, and therefore possibly suffered less, but of this there is little record.

A woman of less spirit would have blushed at being named de Reptonville; wearied of being called patient, and of the remarkably general assumption that by reason of her name she would always be so. De Reptonville, when Mr Repton assumed the name (early in the nineteenth century), was quizzed as the apogee of unwarranted pretentiousness; now it is written off as a meaningless relic of conquest feudalism. Griselda, however, merely smiled sometimes when she looked at her visiting card, newly printed in flawless italics by Parkin and Gotto. The repetitive jokes about her patience only led her to think that in the absurdity of human nature lies much of its charm.

Beams was not an enormous house but it was approached from the insanely noisy main road through Hodley village by a drive two miles long. There had been a car to meet her and the other guests at Hodley railway station; but the season had called to Griselda, and the other guests alarmed her. She had sent on her suitcase, and was now following on foot. As the weather looked settled for an hour or so, her jacket and handbag had gone on with the luggage: she was now wonderfully unencumbered. She wore a white silk blouse, a short skirt of black linen, and substantial shoes. She walked fast, swinging her arms and singing 'Now that I have springtime.' This song came from The Three Sisters by Hammerstein and Kern, which she had seen at Drury Lane the previous evening with a girl whom she had known since childhood. The drive was lined with poplars, slightly discoloured with dust from the new works of the North Downs Cement Company, which now gave good employment to the village.

Beams had a glorious situation (once or twice a year it was possible to see the English Channel from the top of the tower); but as architecture it was unremarkable. Run up by the Duke of St Helens, owner at that time of Hodley Park (since demolished), to provide accommodation for a great Belgian actress named Stephanie des Bourges, whom he had loved frenziedly until her premature death, it was soon acquired by Mrs Hatch's grandfather, a rising merchant banker, called Eleutherios Procopius. His son John Procopius represented the Division in Parliament for the remarkable period of sixty-one years. At his death he left Beams to his only child Melanie, together with more than three million pounds, which would at that time have enabled either of them to live in something larger. The Procopiuses had never, it seemed, been lucky in love: of Mrs Eleutherios there is no record at all; Mrs John died in childbirth the year after her marriage to a man aged nearly sixty; Melanie married during the Boer War a certain Captain Hatch of the CIVs, who almost immediately proceeded to drift away from her and in one way and another to resist recapture during a period of time not expired at the date now under construction. Beams, none the less, had eighteen reasonable bedrooms and was a wonderfully comfortable place to visit. It was, however, haunted: quite seriously, even, on occasion, dangerously, by the apparition of Mademoiselle des Bourges, beautiful even in death.

After glancing at the view, which only burst upon the visitor as he or she reached the lovely gravel waste before the house, Griselda pulled the elaborate bell handle. Though apparently designed to operate an old-fashioned bell wire, the handle proved, in fact, to have been connected with a modern electric system. Before the servant could reach the door, it opened and an elderly gentleman passed out of the house into the garden. He was wearing rather shabby tweeds, leggings, and a black homburg hat. On seeing Griselda he jumped considerably, and nervously raised his black hat; then, without a word, linked hands behind his back and shambled off towards the rose garden. Griselda noticed that he was still shaking perceptibly with the shock of their encounter. By now a middle-aged footman had arrived. Griselda had never before seen a servant in appropriate livery except in musical comedy.

'Good afternoon, miss.'

'Good afternoon. I'm Miss de Reptonville. Mrs Hatch is expecting me.'

'I'm sorry to have kept you waiting, miss. It's the new bells. The Prime Minister got to the door first, I'm afraid.'

'Was that Mr Leech?' Griselda had thought there was something familiar about the quivering figure.

'Regular visitor, miss. In office or out. Mrs Hatch makes no distinction. Would you care for me to show you to your room?'

'Thank you.' The front door closed behind her. 'I sent on my luggage in the car. Also my handbag and jacket.' After the spring sunshine, the house seemed cold.

'They have been taken to your room, miss. This way please.'

The large hall, though filled with comfortable armchairs and sofas (a little like a furniture shop window, Griselda thought), was completely empty. She followed the footman up the wide staircase. A royal blue carpet completely covered the shallow risers. The mahogany balusters were expensively hand-carved. After the soft spring tumult outside, the house seemed silent.

'We've only just ceased the central heat,' remarked the footman over his shoulder as he trudged before Griselda down one of the passages which radiated from the gallery encircling the hall.

Griselda noticed the gilded pipes at frequent intervals.

'You've got the Newman Room, miss.' He opened the door.

'Why is it called that?'

'Cardinal Newman used to sleep here when he came to stay.'

'Was that often?'

'Often, they say. To write his books and that. Mr Cork's got many tales of him. He's our Head Gardener. You must get him to tell you.'

'I'll remember. Thank you.'

'Thank *you*, miss.' He withdrew.

The Newman Room was large, square, well-lighted by windows in two walls, well-heated by a coal fire in a modern grate of patented design. Neither beautiful nor particularly ugly, it had recently been entirely refurnished by a contractor. It had no atmosphere whatever; of its eminent former occupant, or of anybody or anything else.

Griselda began to unpack. The drawers slid on stainless steel runners; the innumerable hangers in the

7

wardrobe rattled together like the bones of a dancing skeleton. In the corner of the room was a cabinet, which proved to contain a shower, with a bath adjoining. Griselda turned the tap: the water cascaded downwards with terrifying force, far exceeding the capacity of the wastepipe in the floor. It was difficult to imagine anyone standing beneath that cataract and emerging undrowned. The water began to flow out of the cabinet and soak the bedroom carpet in a rapidly expanding black blot. Griselda rotated the tap (it seemed to be geared very low, she thought); but all that happened was that the downpour suddenly became scalding hot. A great cloud of steam filled the bedroom, like a geyser suddenly blowing off.

'Don't mind my interrupting your bath,' said a firm voice behind Griselda's back.

Griselda rapidly rotated the tap in the opposite direction. It was difficult to see who had entered the room.

'I'm Melanie Hatch. Just thought I'd say How d'you do?' With a spasmodic crash of plumbing, the water stopped. It was as if it had been intercepted in the pipe.

'How d'you do? I've heard so much about you from Mother.'

'How is she?'

'Still suffering rather a lot, I'm afraid.'

'Bad business about your father.'

'Yes.'

Mrs Hatch was a woman of middle height, considerably more than broad in proportion, but very healthy and active. Her chestnut hair was excellently dyed; but

8

it had never been very beautiful hair. She was the kind of woman whose appearance, for better or for worse, changes surprisingly little with the years. Her expression indicated that a deficiency in imaginative understanding of the problems with which she had been faced, was so far as possible made good by conscious will to face them. She wore an extremely well-cut and expensive tweed coat and skirt; finely made woollen stockings; and a grey sweater with a polo collar enclosing her large neck.

'Do go on with your bath.'

'I wasn't really having a bath. It was just curiosity.'

'Well, have one now.'

'I don't think I want one. I might have one tonight.' Griselda, as in the matter of her name, never lacked for spirit to resist attempts to order her doings.

'I shan't be here then to talk to you.'

'I can't talk and scrub at the same time,' said Griselda smiling. 'I'm a perfect simpleton by your standards.'

Mrs Hatch looked at her. 'Do you mind if I sit down?'

'Please do.' Mrs Hatch seated herself in a large Parker-Knoll armchair at the foot of the bed, and watched Griselda putting away her stockings and underclothes in the ample drawers all lined with paper which smelt of a specially perfumed disinfectant.

'You know your Mother fagged for me at Wollstonecroft?'

'She has always told me how fond she was of you, I hope you'll go and see her one day.'

'Poor old Millie,' said Mrs Hatch crossing her legs,

'I easily might. In the meantime I expect to prefer your company.'

'Thank you,' said Griselda, hanging up her mackintosh. 'It is very kind of you to ask me.'

'Not really. I can always do with young girls about the house. The great men who visit me expect it. It helps them to relax. I'm very calculating.'

'I see. I'll try and do what is expected of me. It's nice of you to ask me.'

'I've got Austin Barnes here this weekend. In fact he should have come on your train. You must have met him in the car.'

'I walked from the station. I couldn't resist the weather.'

'So you like walking?'

'I love it. Particularly by myself.'

'You must come for a walk with Austin and me. We're both good for twenty or thirty miles still. Austin's an old flame of mine, you know.'

'I only know about his public life. And not very much about that. I didn't know that Cabinet Ministers had any other kind of life nowadays.'

'As far as I'm concerned, Austin hasn't. Though he's still game enough, I believe, when circumstances are more propitious. But let me see your dress. The one you've brought for tomorrow night.'

'I haven't brought any particular dress for tomorrow night. Should I have done?'

'Didn't your mother tell you?'

'I don't think so.'

'My dear. Millie must have told you about the All Party Dance tomorrow. It's the main reason I asked you – asked you now, I mean.'

Griselda had not been told and the reason was clear. Griselda so detested dancing that, had she been told, she would have declined Mrs Hatch's invitation altogether, thus possible alienating a friend from whom Mrs de Reptonville hoped for much.

'I'm terribly sorry. I don't dance.'

'Why not? Are you crippled?'

Griselda felt disinclined to explain.

'Shall I go home?'

Mrs Hatch considered the proposal for a moment. Clearly she was much disturbed. 'No, no . . . No, of course not.' Then, taking control of the situaltion, she returned to her previous demand: 'Let me see your dress.' She added: 'I do think Millie might have warned me.'

With some reluctance Griselda took from the mechanized wardrobe one of the two evening dresses she had brought. 'I must clearly tell you: I won't dance.' The dress was made of coffee coloured taffeta and very simple. She held it up.

Mrs Hatch seemed surprised. 'It's far too old for you, of course, but delightful. Where did you get it, if I may ask a plain question?'

'Nothing very distinguished. A friend of mine works in a dress shop. I think she has very good taste.'

'Improbably enough, she has. My friend Louise will help you put it on.'

11

'Thank you very much, but I don't need help.'

'You don't know how much Louise will do for you. I'll send her along. Now then.' Unexpectedly Mrs Hatch smiled.

'Yes?' said Griselda, unexpectedly smiling back.

'Before tomorrow night you must learn to dance. Oh yes you must. I positively owe it to Millie. In the meantime I'm glad to have met you, Griselda, and tea will be ready when you are. In the Hall then.'

And suddenly she had left the room, leaving Griselda rehanging her dress.

II

The party in the Hall had grouped themselves round an electrical space-heater, which raised the temperature of the atmosphere without anybody becoming aware of the fact. Mrs Hatch was manipulating a vast and heavy teapot, apparently without effort. As Griselda descended the stairs, two men rose to their feet.

'This is Griselda de Reptonville,' said Mrs Hatch, recharging the teapot from a silver kettle which must have held at least a gallon. 'Her mother used to be my greatest friend at school. Griselda, let me introduce you: Pamela Anslack, you two should be great friends; George Goss; Edwin Polegate-Hampden, he runs the St James's News-Letter, which tells us what is really happening in the world; and Doris Ditton, who lives in Hodley. Now let me give you a crumpet. There's room for you on the sofa next to Pamela. You two must make friends.'

Griselda was rather regretting she had not put on her cardigan, but Pamela was wearing a slight (though obviously exorbitant) afternoon model and seemed perfectly warm enough. A wide diamond bracelet encircled her left wrist; a diamond watch, her right. She was indeed about Griselda's age, but her perfectly made-up face was singularly expressionless, her dark hair like a photograph in *Vogue*.

She said nothing at all: not even How do you do?; and Griselda biting into her crumpet, stared with furtive curiosity at George Goss. The famous painter looked much older than he did in the newspapers; but his hair and beard, though now more grey than black, were impressively unkempt, his face exceedingly rubicund, and his general bulk prodigious (though augmented by his unyielding green tweeds). He drank, not tea, Griselda noticed, but something in a glass; probably brandy and soda, she thought, as it sparkled energetically. He drank it noisily; and even more noisily devoured huge sections from a lump of rich cake which lay on the plate before him; while he stared back at Griselda, delighting massively in the thrill his presence gave her. He was like a very famous hippopotamus.

Edwin Polegate-Hampden was discoursing upon the inside politics of Morocco. He had paused to greet Griselda with significant courtesy, even, it seemed, cordiality. About thirty-five, and beautifully preserved for his age, he was dressed equally beautifully in a black jacket, cut rather fancifully after a bygone sporting original, yellow trousers, a mauve shirt, a silk tie with large spots, and a beautiful rose from Mr Cork's smallest and private conservatory. His hair was treated with a preservative pomade from a shop in New York.

He resumed.

'But all I have been saying is of secondary importance. Quite secondary. What really matters is that the Atlas Mountains are entirely made of tin. You appreciate what that means in the modern world?'

George Goss nodded heavily, as painters do when interesting themselves in politics or sociology. Griselda looked bright and interested. Mrs Hatch looked from Pamela to Griselda, and back to Pamela. Doris Ditton continued looking into her empty teacup. Possibly she was reading her life's pattern in the leaves.

'The Sultan himself told me the inside story of the concessionaires. I won't tell you the full details, but it comes down to a fight between Meyer Preyserling of Wall Street and a London firm of bankers whose name I can't pass on. I've known Meyer for years, of course, and when I heard that he was interested, I at once flew over and had a talk with him. As a matter of fact, I stayed with him a week. To cut a long story short, he told me that Washington is behind him – secretly, of course, but up to the hilt; so that he has all the gold in Fort Knox to play with. Naturally the London people can't compete with that. So you can take it that all the tin will go to America, as they can exchange it for gold. And that will mean new labour troubles in Bolivia, possibly even a revolution.'

George Goss nodded again. Mrs Hatch was lighting a cigarette. Pamela, Griselda noticed, was one of those girls whose mouth is seldom entirely closed.

'So if you have any Bolivian investments, you'd better think carefully what to do. Of course, it may all blow over. The output from the Bolivian tin mines largely goes to Germany anyway, and I think the market may hold up for some time yet. But we must find out what the French are going to do about it all.'

'Why the French?' asked George Goss. His voice reminded Griselda of a porpoise.

'Morocco.'

'Oh yes,' said George Goss like an undergraduate convicted of inattention. Noticing that his glass was empty, Mrs Hatch passed him a bottle, and added soda from a syphon behind him.

'I've an engagement to talk matters over with Derrière in Paris next week.' Edwin's French accent was incredibly good. 'Derrière is the one man who really counts in France at the moment, and, after all, the Moroccan business may easily end in a world war.' He subsided affably.

'Have some of our fruit cake, Griselda?' said Mrs Hatch. 'It's one of our traditions. No other cake for tea but our very special fruit cake.'

'Thank you very much.'

'Have some more tea, Pamela?'

Pamela merely shook her head.

'You're not sulking are you?'

Pamela shook her head again.

'What about you, Doris?'

'Thanks, Mrs Hatch.' Pamela looked at Doris scornfully; Griselda with some curiosity. Edwin handed her cup with precise courtesy.

'You've had five cups already.'

'I'm afraid I'd lost count, Mrs Hatch.' Doris was a pale little creature, with intermediate hair and wearing a cotton frock, obviously her best but somewhat crumpled.

'I just thought I'd tell you.' Mrs Hatch had refilled the

cup and Edwin returned it to Doris with pale hands.

'The arranging must have made me thirsty.'

'Doris has been helping with the preparations for to-morrow night,' explained Mrs Hatch to Griselda. 'The balloons haven't been used for some time and a lot of dust had been allowed to collect. And that,' she continued firmly, 'reminds me.'

'Must I?' asked Griselda, rather charmingly, as she thought.

'Would you believe it, Edwin? Griselda thought we could do without her at the dance.'

Pamela's mouth opened another half-inch.

Edwin replied: 'I do hope not.'

'I can't dance,' cried Griselda a little desperately.

Pamela's large eyes opened to their utmost.

'Please permit me to teach you,' said Edwin. 'It would be delightful.'

'Thank you. But, as I've explained to Mrs Hatch, I don't really like dancing.'

'Let *me* teach you,' suddenly roared George Goss. 'You'd like it well enough then.'

'Neither of you will teach Griselda,' said Mrs Hatch. 'It's much too important a thing to be left to amateurs. You'd be certain to start her on entirely the wrong lines. She's a job for Kynaston.'

'Who's Kynaston?' asked Griselda fearfully.

'He's a somewhat neurotic young man who none the less dances like a faun. He makes a living teaching dancing in Hodley.'

'Only until he establishes himself as a poet,'

unexpectedly interjected Doris.

'Doris is in love with Mr Kynaston,' explained Mrs Hatch. 'But it's quite true that he writes poetry as well. Very good poetry too. If you spend the whole day with him tomorrow you should pass muster as a dancer by the evening.'

The project appalled Griselda, but to continue in her refusal seemed somehow gauche, and not only in the eyes of her hostess.

'Doris will speak to Mr Kynaston to-night and you can go down in the car at ten o'clock tomorrow morning.'

'And I very much hope,' added Edwin as epilogue, 'that when the time comes you will give your first dance to me.'

Griselda smiled at him rather uncertainly.

'I wish Leech would come in. The tea's cold.'

'Let me go and look for him, Mrs Hatch.' Edwin had sprung to his feet and was making for the door.

Pamela was staring at Griselda's uncoloured finger nails.

'And where's Austin and the Ellensteins?'

Griselda supposed these to be the terrifying figures whose company she had evaded in the car from the station.

'Send Monk upstairs,' said George Goss. 'Don't look at me.'

'Doris,' said Mrs Hatch, 'would you mind ringing for Monk?'

Doris rose and rang. The footman appeared who had

shown Griselda to her room. Mrs Hatch despatched him to enquire after the missing guests. Soon he was back.

'Mr Barnes asks you to excuse him, ma'am. He is lying down in his room. Their Highnesses are coming directly.'

'Thank you. We'd better have some more hot water. I don't imagine their Highnesses will require crumpets, or Mr Leech either. Though you never know.'

'No ma'am.' Monk departed with the vast kettle.

A fat elderly man was descending the stairs, followed by an equally fat woman of similar age. Both were immaculate; she in a dress younger than her years, in which, oddly enough, she looked much more attractive than she would have done in a more appropriate garment.

'This is Griselda de Reptonville,' said Mrs Hatch, 'The Duke and Duchess of Ellenstein.'

The Duke clicked his heels and kissed Griselda's hand; the Duchess, even more to her surprise, kissed her lips.

'You two are late,' said George Goss. 'Tea's over.'

'For some time now it is during the afternoon that I make Odile mine,' explained the Duke, in a high gentle voice with only the slightest of accents, and that adding greatly to his charm. 'We both of us find it best at nights to sleep.'

'I'll look in tonight and see if Odile will change her mind.'

'We make love while the sun shines, George,' said the Duchess.

'Only during the wretched war have we missed a

19

single day,' said the Duke, putting a piece of cake on his wife's plate, and then taking a larger piece himself.

Monk returned with the recharged kettle, sustaining with difficulty his dignity and its weight.

'Bring Miss Ditton's bicycle round to the front door, will you. Monk?' said Mrs Hatch. 'Now Doris, don't forget. Mr Kynaston is to set aside the whole of tomorrow for Miss de Reptonville's tuition.'

'Tuition?' said the Duchess. 'In what, my dear?'

'Griselda is learning to dance, Odile.'

'But that is impossible in England. I learned for years when I was a girl and not till I met Gottfried was I anything but a carthorse. Believe me, my dear, I was mad to dance, just like you, but you cannot dance until you love.'

Monk's liveried figure passed the window pushing Doris's rattling bicycle. She slipped away.

'It would be a weight off all our minds if Doris married Geoffrey Kynaston,' observed Mrs Hatch.

Pamela took the opportunity to retire upstairs. The Ellensteins, George Goss, and Mrs Hatch were engaged in animated conversation about experiences they had shared in the past. Their memories seemed excellent; their relish for detail almost unlimited. No reason was apparent why they should not continue for days or weeks; and then start again at the beginning like a film programme. Necessarily, little attempt could be made to include Griselda. Though she did not much care for George Goss, she noticed even that he had ceased to look at her and was gazing instead at the Duchess's fat but still not ill-proportioned legs. (He resembled, she thought, an inquisitive elephant.)

After about an hour and a half of it, Edwin returned and said that he had been having a really valuable talk with the Prime Minister upon the Indo-Chinese problem; and that Mr Leech had made his tea of a biscuit or two he had brought from his pocket. 'I'm so sorry, Mrs Hatch,' concluded Edwin. 'I just couldn't persuade him to leave his beloved roses.'

There were a number of cold dead crumpets on the occasional table in their midst, and some dregs of tea in the cups; but, Griselda noticed, the Ellensteins and George Goss had eaten the entire famous fruit cake among them.

'Thank you, Edwin,' said Mrs Hatch. 'I quite understand. You'd better go back and pump the old man until dinner time. We're perfectly happy without you.'

'I'm sure you're divinely happy every single hour of the day, Mrs Hatch,' replied Edwin. 'But I must admit I should be glad to have the true story of the railway strike. I have a great responsibility to my readers. They do trust me so completely.'

He was gone.

'Is there a railway strike?' asked Griselda. 'I didn't notice it.'

But the Duchess was recalling the night the four of them (and several others) started a bonfire in Leicester Square.

'Do you remember?' said the Duchess. 'It was Austin Barnes's idea.'

III

Dinner was not until 8.30; but Pamela gave the impression of having spent the entire interminable interim changing for it. Griselda, plainly debarred for tonight from the coffee-coloured taffeta, had put on her other dress, of pinkish organdie and very nice too; only for Pamela to make it immediately though silently obvious to her that the proper style for the occasion was that followed by herself, a blouse and long skirt. Mrs Hatch, when she appeared was similarly dressed; as, to Griselda's complete dejection, was the Duchess, who came down last, skilfully made-up, with the Duke in a beautifully fitting dinner jacket. Edwin's dinner jacket was of very dark red velvet; and his rose had been changed by Mr Cork for an even larger one in a more suitable colour. Mr Leech looked rather nondescript by comparison.

'Where is Mr Barnes?' asked Mrs Hatch when they were seated.

'Mr Barnes asks me to present his compliments,' replied Monk, 'and to say that he is so fatigued that he has thought it best to retire completely to bed. I am to bring him a boiled egg later.'

'There is nothing the matter with Mr Barnes, I hope?' asked the Duke anxiously.

'I understand nothing, your Highness. Mr Barnes did mention to me that his present condition was nothing out of the ordinary. Shall I request Mr Brundrit, ma'am, to serve Dinner?'

'Please do,' said Mrs Hatch; and under the super-intendence of a tall, wasted-looking butler, Monk and a pretty parlourmaid called Stainer served the most portentous meal Griselda had ever attended. There was paté: there were truffles; there was a sorbet. There was a blanc-mange-like pudding with angelica and an under-tone of rum insufficient to offset the otherwise total lack of flavour; which in turn was followed by a savoury (called Tails in the Air), and a choice of stilton cheese or dessert, or both for those (like the Duke and Duchess and George Goss) who wished. There had been no al-coholic preliminary, but, accompanying the food, four successive wines and a liqueur with the wonderful strong coffee. Mr Leech ate very little, but at the end brightened up enough to express a preference for brandy if any was available, and Mrs Hatch joined him. Pamela found tongue enough to indicate her various gustatory preferences; though even then appearing to force out words like stones from her mouth, and as if each single word was a disgusting thing to be shunned when uttered. Griselda did the best she could, seated between the Duke, who occasionally said something pa-ternal to her, and Mr Leech, who showed little sign of the taste for young girls which Mrs Hatch had plainly implied to be his; but by the end she felt a little sick.

During dinner there were more reminiscences.

Griselda noticed that the endless stories tended to begin admirably and to hold out real promise; but after a time it always became apparent that there was to be no climax, point, or even real conclusion. The stories were simply long rakes, designed to turn over as many memories as possible. There was little nostalgia, however, about the reminiscing quartet, Griselda observed with pleasure; they all in their different ways seemed as full of gusto as ever, especially the Duchess, in whom gaiety seemed positively a normal mood.

Replete, they migrated to the Drawing Room; an apartment of which the faultless and spotless comfort fell just short of elegance. There were a rosewood grand piano of German make; a white mantel some way after the Adam Brothers; and a number of French eighteenth century pictures, well and harmoniously selected. The general colouration was pink; which, as it happened, excellently set off Griselda's dress. There was a real Aubusson carpet, like the cloths of heaven to walk upon. All that fell short was individuality, and perhaps vitality, however controlled.

Edwin at once suggested bridge. Mrs Hatch agreed with appetite; and the Ellensteins also volunteered. Mr Leech asked if anyone would mind his sitting quietly in a corner with an excellent book he had found in the library. He then half sank into an elaborate illustrated manual of horticulture, sitting semi-submerged for hours, every now and then turning the volume round and round on his knees the better to penetrate the botanical detail. Griselda noticed, however, that much of the time his mind seemed to be wandering and his expression strangely blank. He turned the pages much too infrequently and irregularly. Occasionally he could be heard sighing, almost groaning. It was remarkable how little any part of him moved: even the occasional blink of his eyelids seemed consciously decided upon and consciously executed.

The Duchess being occupied, George Goss seated himself on a sofa upholstered in *couleur de rose* flowered silk, beside Pamela. Pamela immediately moved to an armchair next to Griselda; whereupon George Goss making the best even of adversity, placed his feet on the sofa where Pamela had been seated, and lay bundled together like a giant chimpanzee in a dinner jacket. He continued smiling blandly before him, and soon, without asking Mrs Hatch's permission, fired and began to draw on a huge inefficient pipe which had recently been presented to him by an admiring young woman. Later, again without enquiry of his hostess, he managed to reach a bell with his long arm, thick as the branch of a tree; and, when Monk answered, ordered a bottle of brandy to be brought to him with a syphon. Having appeased his thirst, he fell asleep and began to snore. Bridge had gripped the players into its own distinctive delirium; so that none of them noticed George Goss, still less Griselda and Pamela.

To Griselda's surprise, Pamela, upon escaping from George Goss, spoke to her.

'Are my eyes all right?'

Griselda looked at them with conscientious care. As

well as being large, they were yellowy-green and ichthy-ological.

'I think so. They're lovely.'

Irritated with the familiar compliment, Pamela replied: 'The mascara, I mean. It's new stuff. Daddy brought it back from B.A.'

Griselda looked again. 'It looks all right to me.' A question seemed expected. 'What was your Father doing in South America?'

'You know that Daddy's Chairman of Argentine Utilities. We practically own the country. You don't use mascara much, do you?'

'Not much,' said Griselda.

'I can tell by the look of the lashes. You're probably very wise.' The tone of the last observation suggested that the speaker thought the opposite. 'Mascara's frightfully bad for the eyes.'

'Like staring too long at me,' said George Goss.

'Shall we look at this together?' said Pamela to Griselda, ignoring George Goss, who continued smiling all over his face.

It was the latest issue of *The Sketch*. Griselda was not particularly interested, but something had to be done to pass the time, and Mrs Hatch had told her to make friends with Pamela. Moreover, Pamela was used to getting her way.

'Where do you live, by the way?' asked Pamela.

'About twenty miles outside London.'

'I thought I was the only one to do that. But perhaps *you* don't mind?'

'I haven't much choice really.'

'Daddy thinks the country air's good for me and Mummy. It's hell having to motor out after parties and having no friends.'

'It's surely easier to make friends in the country than in London?'

'It depends what you mean by friends.'

Pamela began to explain the scandalous circumstances and backgrounds of the various people whose photographs appeared in *The Sketch*. The explanations were rendered lengthy by Pamela's lack of vocabulary; and complex by her lack of all standards of references beyond her own changing impulses. Griselda noticed however, that Pamala was as much interested in the financial as in the sexual history of her friends, and as well informed upon it; also that she appeared as strongly to disapprove of homosexuality as if she had been an elderly pillar of some Watch Committee.

When they had finished *The Sketch*, Pamela produced *The Tatler* from the same heap; and before she had finished explaining *The Tatler* (her opinions of various current plays and films being now involved, and of certain recent Rugby football matches at Twickenham), George Goss had ordered his bottle and fallen into a slumber, and the bridge players had entered upon their inevitable row. It seemed to be mainly Mrs Hatch setting upon the Duchess (her partner). The Duke (though, of course, on the other side) loyally backed his wife (to whom, indeed, he seemed utterly devoted in every way), wheezing with exasperation and becoming much more Teutonic in delivery. Edwin was trying very hard indeed to smooth things over, so that the game could be resumed. When one expedient or line of argument was obviously unavailing, he never failed to produce another, surprisingly different. Griselda had noticed for some time that the partnership of which Edwin was one, seemed usually to win. The combatants stabbed their fingers at selected cards among the litter on the green topped walnut table.

Absorbed in an account of how well she knew Gladys Cooper, Pamela ignored the row as long as possible. When it became necessary almost to shout above the raised voices, she switched to details of the similar scenes which commonly attended the frequent bridge parties organised by her parents. 'I can't be bothered with the game myself,' said Pamela, 'though I've quite broken Daddy's heart by not playing with him.' An achievement of some sort seemed implicit in her words; a triumph of righteousness in some inner conflict. George Goss's mouth had fallen wide open, but he was snoring less loudly in consequence.

Griselda looked at her wrist-watch.

Suddenly with a high-pitched squeal, the Duke had overturned the card-table, the top of which struck Mrs Hatch sharply on the ankle. 'We are misbehaving ourselves' cried the Duke, 'let us kiss and once more be friends. I appeal to your warm heart, Melanie.'

'I really think that would be better.' It was Mr Leech who spoke 'Of course I take no sides in the matter under dispute. But I do warmly endorse the Duke's appeal.'

His finger remained fixed to a point in a large diagram of corolla structure.

Mrs Hatch had lifted her long skirt above her knees, and was rubbing her ankle while the blood rushed to her head. 'I think you've broken a bone, Gottfried,' was all she said. She certainly seemed more chastened than aggressive.

Griselda hurried forward. 'Perhaps I can help. I've had a little first-aid training.'

The Duchess, absolved from offering succour beyond her competence, smiled gratefully at Griselda, and began carefully to attend to her heavy make-up. Edwin rushed to bring a cushion to support Mrs Hatch's back.

Griselda began to take charge. 'May I remove your stocking?'

'Please do.'

Griselda undid the suspenders and rolled off the stocking.

'Nothing's broken. But it's an exceedingly nasty bruise.' The swollen place was already turning the colour of cuttlefish ink.

'If that's all, I'll say no more about it,' said Mrs Hatch.

'Melanie, you are magnanimous,' exclaimed the Duke. 'I knew you had a great heart.'

'You'd better put your leg up, and not take much excercise for a day or two.' Griselda placed the injured foot on the chair vacated by Edwin, who immediately ran to fetch another cushion, to place beneath the foot.

'My dear Griselda, what about the dance? What about the preparation for the dance?'

Griselda felt most strongly tempted to reply that the dance might have to be cancelled, when George Goss, whom she had not seen wake up, cried out:

'Melanie won't miss the dance. Melanie won't miss a dance when she's in her grave.'

In some ways it seems uncharacteristic that Mrs Hatch should be so fond of dancing; but all the evidence seemed to suggest that such was the case.

'I'll be there, George,' said Mrs Hatch. 'Gottfried has failed to break my leg.'

'The idea!' said the Duke tearfully. 'It was only a gesture for peace between us. My very dear friend.' He placed a plump hand on the shoulder of Mrs Hatch's evening blouse.

Pamela was reading about Longchamps in *The Bystander*.

George Goss lumbered round to look at the bruise. 'It's like the night Austin Barnes gave Margot two black eyes.' They laughed. George Goss subsided on a Pompeian red pouffe and sat leering at Mrs Hatch's expensive underclothes still visible inside her lifted skirt.

'Have you any liniment?' enquired Griselda.

'You shall apply it in my bedroom,' said Mrs Hatch, rising to her feet and letting her skirt drop. She staggered and Edwin supported her. 'You and Pamela shall help me to undress. The rest of you can stay here if you want to. Monk has gone to bed, but you're at liberty to forage if you wish, so long as you conceal the traces from Brundrit and Cook, and don't leave masses about for the mice. Come along, Pamela, you can't read all night.' Reluctantly Pamela let *The Bystander* fall upon the floor. George Goss remained seated, but the others grouped themselves solicitously. 'Good night,' said Mrs Hatch.

The Duke clicked his heels. Edwin said: 'There must be something I can get for you.' Mr Leech said: 'I am so relieved that things are not worse.' The Duchess kissed Mrs Hatch on the mouth; then said to Griselda and Pamela 'I suppose I shan't be seeing you two again tonight either,' and kissed them also. At the moment of Mrs Hatch's departure, George Goss floundered vaguely upwards; but his intentions had not been made clear before she had left the room with one arm round Griselda's neck, and the other round Pamela's. Edwin went before them and opened the door of Mrs Hatch's bedroom.

'Good night, Edwin,' said Mrs Hatch, and he retired downstairs, having said Good-night to the girls in a tone which at once commended their charitable helpfulness and conveyed his own deep regard for them.

The bedroom was stuffed with clothes and lined with photographs, many of them signed ones of celebrities, with pleasant words of gratitude adjoined. A real fire burned in the grate, making the room close (the Dining Room and Drawing Room had been impalpably warmed by further space heaters). The single bed was white and simple. In the corner of the room was a large green safe.

Pamela's assistance proved fairly useless. Not only had she become silent once more, but she more than once knocked something over, and even tore Mrs Hatch's slip while trying to extricate her from the garment. Not unreasonably, Pamela seemed to fear the effect of the heat upon her complexion, and carefully kept away from the large fire. Griselda could have wished for the presence of Louise, that expert in putting on clothes: but in the end, and despite Pamela, inserted Mrs Hatch, masterful to the last, into her pyjamas, and was rubbing her leg as she lay sprawled on the bed. Pamela was now yawning ostentatiously.

Griselda rubbed diligently for what seemed at least ten minutes.

'That'll do,' suddenly said Mrs Hatch, and began to roll down her pyjama leg. 'But I may want you to do it again tomorrow.'

'I shall be dancing,' said Griselda, almost maliciously. The exertion and the rubbing against the bed had not improved her beautiful fragile dress.

'So you will. But I expect you'll be back for tea. People usually are. Tea at Beams is a daily event, you know. You can massage me, if necessary, between tea and dinner. I usually lie down before a dance anyway.'

'I'm not really a masseuse, you know. It's quite easy to do the wrong thing, I believe.'

'You won't do the wrong thing. Would you please give me my book? Over there on the banker.'

In the corner of the room was a big cabinet, with long shallow drawers.

Griselda brought the book. It was entitled 'Warlock on Comparative Agriculture.' Mrs Hatch was hanging from the other side of the bed and opening the door of the commode, apparently to confirm the presence of its contents. It was a distance to stretch and Mrs Hatch, at the very end of her reach, had to shut the door with a slam.

'Thank you, my dear Griselda, for all your help.'

Griselda smiled.

Mrs Hatch opened the book at page 601. Griselda was about to say good-night and depart, when Mrs Hatch looked up.

'Pamela is very pretty isn't she?'

Griselda started. It was an extraordinary thing but she had not noticed Pamela's departure.

'Where is Pamela?' Griselda felt she must be very tired to be so unobservant.

'She slipped out while you were kindly attending to my injury. Never mind. She's in the room next to yours. The Livingstone Room, we call it.'

A big brass clock above the large fire struck two. Griselda was surprised it was not later.

IV

Trouble began almost as soon as Griselda was back in her bedroom.

The house, formerly so quiet, not unlike a specialist's waiting-room, now seemed full of noises. Nor was it only the noise of Pamela snoring like an ox and perfectly audible through the substantial wall, or that of some unknown making periodical clattering trips down a distant passage (could it be Austin Barnes? Griselda wondered). There were constant small disturbances which seemed in her own room, or at least only just outside the door: creaks and jars, of course; but also sudden sussurations, in among the window curtains, near the cabinet containing the shower, or under the bed. To Griselda, overtired as the incident in Mrs Hatch's room had suggested she must be, it was almost as if some small animal were loose in the apartment. Rats and mice seemed extremely improbable in such a carefully ordered house. Griselda, used to living out of London, wondered whether some small creature could have entered during the day. She had removed her charming dress and was vaguely endeavouring to fluff up the organdie, flattened and pulled while she had worked on her hostess's leg: it was certainly true that the garment no longer looked new, as it had looked so far every time she had worn it. Laying

34

down the dress, she began to investigate the room, half-heartedly examining corners and peering into the angles of the ceiling, not very well illuminated by the conceiled lighting. Even a small bird was not out of the question, she thought. As the idea came to her, a screech owl cried very loudly outside her window. Griselda found that she was shivering, slightly clad as she was, and away from the excessive heat of Mrs Hatch's bedroom. She drew her dressing-gown from the wardrobe and put it on. It had once been the colour of dying peonies, but Griselda had owned it since her last disastrous year at school.

Griselda hung up her dress, assumed her pyjamas, and faithfully removed her make-up. She cleaned her teeth, carefully and thoroughly as always, for she regarded her teeth as attractive. Then, still shivering excessively, she drew back the curtains, opened the window at top and bottom, and leaped from her familiar dressing-gown into her unfamiliar bed. Outside there was a misty moon, predicting, as usual, a change for the worse in the weather. Inside, the little noises had not abated, but Griselda resolved to ignore them.

The noises were difficult to define. Nor was it easy to know whether or not any particular one of them was a new noise. One of the worst, and surely a new one, however, was like that of voices muttering. It came and went like a radio set out of order and turned very low; with long pauses of silence. Another was like long nails destructively scratching at smooth hard paintwork. Once a silent bird struck the window very hard, so that Griselda felt surer than ever that another had flown in during the day and was now in the room with her, probably lying exhausted behind a piece of furniture. The sussurating noise was still audible from time to time: it rustled for seconds or minutes in one place, then was long silent before starting elswhere.

Griselda slept intermittently until she reached a condition of uncertainty whether she slept or waked. She continued disagreeably cold until she was merely shivering without any distinctive consciousness of being cold at all. At one moment when she was nearer waking than sleeping, she heard the sound of tears, a high-pitched sobbing, somewhat petulant it seemed, but distant and subdued. It was possible, she thought, that Pamela wept in her sleep. Before long the noise, which from the time she first heard it had been growing less and less, died away.

Several times during the later part of the night Griselda woke from nightmare; but not a detail could she remember even in the first moments of consciousness. She might have been dreaming of things so horrible that the mechanism of repression was forced to clamp down once more on her consciousness in the very instant of waking. But the nightmare had each time seized and penetrated her whole body and mind; it was as if she had been twisted into another identity, mysterious and horrible, which, when she returned, there could be no question of remembering since the two beings had no capacity for memory in common. She shuddered to reflect that this second identity, totally unreachable lay always behind her face and beneath her thoughts. The strain of having perpetually to maintain the ascendancy over it weighed upon her.

Now that she no longer loved her Mother, perhaps it was getting possession of her mind and affecting her gait. In the end none the less, she returned to slumber.

The worst occurrence of the night was perfectly natural and commonplace. Griselda woke to hear a dog howling. It howled on an unusually shrill whining note. It continued howling for a very long time; for long after Griselda was fully and entirely awake. She lay with her back towards the window listening to the distressing sound and unavailingly searching her memory for a dog in the house. In the end, she was almost reduced to leaving her bed and investigating; but desisted when she saw that the dawn was near. This circumstance, she felt, might be related in some way to the unknown dog's behaviour; moreover, she had once more started to shiver and shunned the silent chill of the large room. She was uncertain whether the dog had ceased to give tongue before she once more fell asleep.

With the first symptoms of daylight, the tension in the room melted into appeasement. Griselda subsided into deep quiet sleep, the little noises ebbed, a measure of warmth returned.

Griselda slept steadily for the time which remained. At the last moment before waking, she seemed to have a dream of a different order. The earlier dreams she never remembered; this one she never forgot. She dreamed of a strange perfect love; a great good, unknown to the waking world; an impossibly beautiful happiness. The rapture of her dream was something new to her. It stayed with her while she rose to wash and dress; and longer.

V

A housemaid brought her tea and two rusks on a tray.

'Pity it's raining. It'll spoil tonight.'

Filled with her dream, Griselda felt happily combative.

'I don't see why it should.'

'All the lovely dresses'll get sopping wet. And lots won't come at all if it's raining.'

'Perhaps it'll stop. Rain before seven. Fine before eleven.'

The housemaid laughed. 'Not round 'ere.' Then, looking at Griselda accusingly, she said, 'Will I run a bath for you?'

'No, thank you. I'll manage it myself if I want it.'

'The shower's tricky.'

'I'll risk it.'

'Just as you say.' She went.

Without resorting to the shower, for she hated getting her head wet, Griselda washed carefully all over. She felt that there was no knowing where the day's events might take her. To meet the changed weather, she put on her coat and skirt, and a woollen jumper.

Mrs Hatch was already seated at the head of the breakfast table, dressed precisely as on the day before; but there was no sign of any of her other guests. Monk and Stainer were both in attendance. Before Mrs Hatch was an enormous congregation of eggs, all so green that they looked as if disease had struck them.

'Good girl,' said Mrs Hatch. 'Up in proper time and prepared for the weather, I see. You sit next to me. Pamela can sit the other side of me when she chooses to appear. Have some eggs? At Beams we have duck eggs every morning for breakfast. It's one of our traditions. Take as many as you like. And have some cocoa. We don't rot our guests with tannin or caffeine until later in the day.'

'Thank you,' said Griselda. 'I'm hungry. May I take two?'

'For breakfast at Beams no one ever takes fewer than four. Except Mr Leech, perhaps. I'm sure you don't want to follow after him. Take another two.'

Monk raised a huge bowl-like cup containing about half-a-pint of cocoa and conveyed it to Griselda.

'I think I'll eat these two first, if I may.'

'Afraid for your liver?' enquired Mrs Hatch. 'You needn't be, you know, if you make sure of enough exercise. That reminds me, I plan to take Austin for one of our walks tomorrow. It'll set him up and blow away all the fug from the dance as well. As you're a walker too, I'm sure you'd like to join us.'

'Thank you,' replied Griselda, battering her second egg. 'If I'm not too tired after dancing.'

Mrs Hatch glanced at her, but at that moment one of the windows was raised from the outside, and Mr Leech entered over the sill. He looked very tired and dingy.

'Good morning. I trust I'm not late. I've been trying out my old limbs on the trapeze in the garden.'

'Fine exercise for men,' said Mrs Hatch. 'Useless for women, unfortunately. Help yourself to eggs.'

With a hand which trembled slightly, Mr Leech took a single egg.

Monk, who had departed for the toast, now returned bearing also an armful of mail. He proceeded to sort it and to distribute it among the various places. Most of it seemed to be for Edwin: a vast heap of letters in flimsy envelopes with foreign stamps, and large official packets. The correspondence for the Ellensteins seemed mostly to bear penny and halfpenny stamps. George Goss received a single letter: in a very thick violet envelope, bigger and more massive than usual, and threaded down one side with a fragment of carmine ribbon. The handwriting of the superscription, Griselda could not but observe, was proportionate in size to the envelope. Mrs Hatch received a few nondescript items, all of which she opened voraciously with the bread-knife before reading any. Griselda, to her surprise, received a letter from the girl she had known since childhood, and who liked to write to someone sojourning at so distinguished an address as Beams. She had nothing to say and Griselda felt faintly bored by the obligation to reply. Pamela received nothing. Probably, Griselda felt, Pamela never replied to letters, so that people gave up writing. More surprisingly, Mr Leech seemed to receive nothing either.

'Mullet is taking Mr Barnes's letters up to his room,' remarked Monk.

Mrs Hatch said nothing.

Soon Edwin appeared full of apologies and newspapers. At least six of the latter were under his arm in various stages of mutilation and decomposition.

'I do hope you will also forgive my taking the liberty of cutting up all your morning papers. I shall, of course, replace the copies later, but Miss Van Bush, my secretary, will be calling immediately after breakfast, and it is best if I can pass the really relevant items on to her right away.' He flourished a little packet with a large red seal. 'Clippings. The result of my labours before breakfast. Ah, how really wonderful to see a Beams breakfast again. There is nothing quite like it anywhere else.' Edwin wore a brand-new light grey suit, a dark grey silk shirt, and Old Etonian tie, and an orchid. He began to wade through the expected clutch of eggs.

George Goss entered in his hairy green tweeds.

'Good morning, Melanie. Gottfried and Odile ask me to tell you they won't be down until later.'

He put his letter to one side unopened, and began to smash away at a bevy of eggs. Immediately he had entered, Monk, Griselda noticed, had slipped away.

'George,' said Mrs Hatch. 'Would you please put that billet-doux in your pocket or somewhere? No one cares for a good scent more than I do, but that isn't a good scent. It makes the whole room stink.'

'The poor little thing hasn't the cash for the sort of stuff you'd go in for,' remarked George. Inserting a thick finger, he rather clumsily ripped open the envelope.

41

Monk returned with a bottle of brandy, about two-thirds full, which he passed on to Mrs Hatch. Taking a syphon from the sideboard, he placed it on the table next to George. This seemed the usual method, Griselda observed: Mrs Hatch normally maintained control of the bottle.

'Why do you keep her so short?'

'My dear Melanie, now that I've got on in the world, so to speak, I don't have to *keep* anyone. There's always a long line eager to take care of me.'

He began to read the letter, looking, Griselda thought, like a monstrous sheep which had been dyed green.

Edwin was working methodically through his heap, opening the letters neatly with an ivory and gold paper-knife which had been given him by the King of Roumania, and making three piles, one of matter to be handed over to Miss Van Bush, one of items to be answered in his own holograph, and one of empty envelopes.

A number of the packets containing whole newspapers, often with marked passages. Glancing at one of these, Edwin suddenly rose, and saying to Mrs Hatch 'Excuse me. Something rather unexpected,' bore it round the table to Mr Leech, pointed out the significant passage, and said something quietly in Mr Leech's left ear. The Prime Minister, who had apparently sunk into a light coma (he had not even finished his egg), stirred very slightly and began to read. After some time had passed with Mr Leech staring unwinkingly at the paper, Edwin spoke again in his ear.

At last Mr Leech slowly nodded twice. 'I suppose there's no help for it,' he said.

'I imagine that a couple of divisions would suffice, sir,' said Edwin. His voice was still low, but this time fully audible. All of them could appreciate the urgency of the matter.

'I don't really know,' said Mr Leech, still without blinking.

'Better make it three, perhaps,' said Edwin as before.

'I'll consult Mr Barnes,' said Mr Leech almost in the tone of one nearing a decision. 'Can't be swayed by the press, you know,' he added roguishly.

Edwin returned to his place, looking as if a weight had been lifted off his mind. 'Sorry Mrs Hatch,' he said. 'So many things happen at the most inconvenient moment.' He began to assault his fourth egg.

'Melanie,' said George Goss. 'Could I have a drink?' He was still less than half way through the prodigious letter. Mrs Hatch passed him the bottle. He looked round for a tumbler, and, when Monk had brought him one, filled it liberally, passing back the bottle. He resumed reading the love letter, belching every now and then as food reached his empty stomach.

'Do have some more to eat, Griselda?' said Mrs Hatch.

'No thank you very much.'

'How is Barnes this morning, Mrs Hatch?' enquired Mr Leech.

Mrs Hatch looked at Monk.

'Mr Barnes asked for his breakfast to be taken to his room as you know, madam. Also his letters. Beyond that I know nothing, madam. Shall Stainer ask Mullet?'

The parlour-maid glowered. Mrs Hatch turned to the Prime Minister.

'Would you like that to be done, Mr Leech?'

'Please do not go to any trouble,' replied Mr Leech. 'I'll find my way to his room and enquire myself later. I must consult him on some business; urgent, alas!'

George Gobs looked up. 'Never could see why Austin gave his time to politics at all. Should have thought he had too much red blood in his veins if you know what I mean.'

Mr Leech stared at him. 'That is just why, Mr Goss,' he said with unusual fire. 'I believe you once painted Barnes's portrait. You cannot have overlooked the main fact about your sitter: that he is a patriot.'

George Goss chuckled gutturally. 'Poor old Austin,' he said.

'Austin Barnes is also a magnificent administrator,' said Edwin reprovingly. 'A first class man to put in charge of any Department in the Government; is he not, Mr Prime Minister?'

'A leader,' replied Mr Leech, 'Certainly a natural leader of men.' He discarded the remains of his egg and began to look round for the marmalade.

Pamela arrived. She was wearing a simple white silk nightdress and a lilac satin wrapper. The large yawn with which she entered suggested, however, that this costume implied less of coquetry than of the possibility that she had only just awakened. Then Griselda noticed that Pamela was made up with her usual time-consuming elaboration. At her entrance George Goss had actually dropped the letter (he was still far from having completed reading it). Mrs Hatch was also staring at Pamela, though less noticeably.

'Don't want anything to eat. Just a cup of coffee.'

Mrs Hatch seemed alarmed. 'Are you ill?'

'Slept too long. I'm always doing it.'

George Goss guffawed.

'Sit in your place,' said Mrs Hatch, 'and see what you can manage.'

Pamela subsided into her seat and silence. Monk brought her the usual bowl of cocoa. Edwin began to converse with her on subjects suitable to one who has overslept.

There was a knock at the door which gave access to the kitchen, and the head was poked in of the house-maid who had awakened Griselda.

'What is it, Mullet?'

'Maghull waiting for 'is orders.'

'Good gracious!' cried Mr Leech. 'It's no business of mine, I know, but I do think it rash of you still to retain in your employ a man who played such a catastrophic part in the Irish disorders. You will recall that I thought it my duty to warn you on a previous occasion.'

Edwin tried to indicate that this topic should perhaps be left until the servants were absent.

'Common enough knowledge,' muttered Mr Leech,

45

subsiding considerably, however. 'But no business of mine, I know.'

'Tell Maghull,' said Mrs Hatch, 'that he is to take Miss de Reptonville to Hodley immediately, to Mr Kynaston's. Then he is to return for further orders. I expect we shall all be very quiet today, preparing for the dance.'

Mullet went.

George Goss flipped a fragment of eggshell across the table to Pamela, who was looking particularly disagreeable.

VI

It was an unremarkable speculative builder's two-bedroom bungalow; one of about a dozen lined up along the fiendishly noisy main road through Hodley. Geoffrey Kynaston himself opened the door, explaining that though he called upon a certain amount of casual assistance, it had at the moment all failed him, so that he was alone in the house. He closed the front door, thin, narrow, ugly, and with small panes of glass at the top to light the little hall; and suggested coffee. It was early and Griselda had just swallowed an excessive quantity of cocoa; but she offered to make it. Kynaston thanked her pleasantly, but said that that would be unnecessary as he had some just off the boil awaiting her arrival. This statement did not increase Griselda's inclination.

'Come into the studio.'

It was what the builder of the bungalow would have called the lounge: in fact, the only sitting-room. Now the floor was bare; a bar extended round the walls; and there were photographs of Karsavina, Lifar, and Genée. There was also a rather larger photograph of Doris Ditton in a white shirt and black tie, the walking-out uniform of some women's organization.

'It's not very much,' said Kynaston, glancing round. 'I'll talk about myself over our coffee.'

'It looks very interesting.'

'Sit down.' With his foot he pushed towards her a small round stool covered in scarlet artificial leather. He departed for the coffee.

Griselda soon rose and began to examine the photographs. Lifar, every feather in position as the male Blue Bird, particularly took her fancy. Doris Ditton also, she thought, looked more self-sufficient than at the tea party the previous day. There was a heap of copies of a paper she had not previously heard of. It was called The Dancing Times

'Do you read poetry?'

This was something Griselda had forgotten about her teacher.

'Not as much as I should.'

Kynaston had returned with two large mugs and a small dun-coloured book.

'I don't know about that. But some of these might amuse you while I fill the jug.'

He departed once more. The book was entitled *Days of Delinquency* by Geoffrey Kynaston. It contained about thirty short poems. Somewhat to her surprise, Griselda seemed quite able to understand them.

Incubus

Can you hear my feet approaching?
Can you bear my heart encroaching?
No hope to hide when I am coming
Straight into your soul I'm homing.

There were about twenty more lines but Kynaston had returned with a steaming jug and a milk bottle.

'White, I imagine?'

'Please.'

The mug was very heavy and very hot. It was in peasant ware and bore an inscription in Breton.

'What are you making of your own life?' He sat on the floor at her feet.

'Very little.'

'Good. I dislike womanly women. They're the only ones who make a success of it. Of being a woman I mean. It's hell, isn't it?'

'It varies.'

'Do you read Rilke?'

'Yes.'

'I don't altogether care for his work but he had a lot in common with me as a man. I have the same utter dependence on a strong woman.'

Griselda looked up at Doris's photograph.

'I didn't mean Doris. Though she can look rather splendid, don't you think?'

'Very attractive.'

'It's only skin deep, though, or clothes deep. She lacks guts, little Doris.'

'I rather liked her.' This was not true, but Griselda disapproved of Kynaston's comment.

'Of course. Don't misunderstand me. I adore Doris. She's the sweetest girl in Hodley.'

'How long have you lived in Hodley?'

'Eighteen months. Ever since I left the Shephard's

Market Ballet. They chucked me, you know. After that I was done. You don't get another shop when you've been chucked for the reason I was.'

Griselda thought enquiry was unnecessary.

'I refused to go to bed with Frankie Litmus.'

'Oh.' Griselda took a resolute pull at the interminable coffee.

'I'm not that way at all, believe it or not. And look what's become of me in consequence! Let that be a lesson to you. Ditched in this pigstye teaching the lads of the village to caper. Have some more coffee? It's actually Nescafé, as you doubtless perceive.'

'No thank you.' The vast mug was still more than half full.'

'Pupils like you are rare. Do you mind if I make the most of you?'

'I hope you will.'

'We've got all day. Will you come for a picnic with me?'

'I'm under orders to learn to dance.'

'That won't take you all day. By the way, why can't you dance?'

There was something about him which enabled her to tell him.

'I dislike being held.'

He rose dangling his empty mug.

'Even by someone you're fond of?'

'I've never been fond enough of anyone.'

He considered. 'In that case clearly, I must first win your confidence.'

She smiled.

'More coffee?'

'No thank you.'

'Do you think the preparations for a picnic are the best or the worst part? Cutting the sandwiches. Filling the thermoses. Counting the knives.'

'The worst part.'

'In that case we'd better not set about it until later. I haven't told you much about myself yet. That'll fill the gap. Or better still I'll read you some of my poems. I've given up serious dancing you know and am trying to establish myself as a poet.' Griselda noticed it was the phrase Doris had employed the day before.

'I shall be sent home if I don't dance.'

'If they are cruel to you at home, you can always come and live here. But more of that later. And, by the way, I'm coming to the Ball myself, you know.'

'Mrs Hatch didn't mention that.'

'I'll be able to keep an eye on you. And hands off you, so to speak. Other hands than mine, of course. Apropos of which—' He began to read aloud.

'*Disclaimer*

Other loves than mine may kill you;
Other hates than mine fulfill you;
Other saints through grief atone you;
Other sinners crowd to stone you—'

He continued through the poem, then read several others. Griselda, a fair judge of verse, was not very much impressed by Kynaston's poesy, but more than a little charmed by his excellent delivery. His attractive voice and skilful accentuation made far more emerge from the verses than had ever entered into them.

'I won't ask you what you think,' he said at the end. 'A poet I believe must heed only his inner voice.'

This, on the whole, was a relief.

'May I say,' enquired Griselda, 'how very much I enjoyed the way you read?'

'I was taught by Moissi,' replied Kynaston. 'And much good has it done me.'

'That was before you took up dancing?'

'I have many gifts,' he answered, 'but none of them has come to anything at all. I need a suitable woman to manage my life for me. Without that, even my poetry will be still another dreariness and misery.'

'You've at least achieved publication. Many poets don't.'

'True. And against really passionate opposition by Herbert Read. Still, fewer than a hundred copies have sold. Well, well. Before we pack the picnic basket, will you help me with the washing up?'

There were not only the coffee adjuncts, but the remains of Kynaston's breakfast and of another vague meal which had seemingly involved the consumption of some very fat ham or boiled bacon. Griselda hung her jacket on the door of the little kitchenette and applied herself, while Kynaston dried on a small, discoloured tea-cloth. The tiny room became hot and steamy.

When it was all over, Kynaston, from a box-like cupboard in the hall, produced a large wicker picnic-basket.

'Now for the awful preliminaries.'

'Must we have the basket? Are there going to be enough of us?'

'If we don't take the basket, the picnic will turn into a walk, and with you, I couldn't stand that.'

From the dilapidated meat-safe he produced the knuckle end of a Bath chap, a bottle of French mustard, and half a stale loaf. 'Better than no bread,' he remarked. 'Will you please do your very best with the ingredients provided? Here's a knife. I'm going to pack the tinned apricots and the opener.'

Griselda began to make sandwiches. Kynaston hurried about packing the basket with heavy, and, in Griselda's view, superfluous objects. 'I'll just get the stove for coffee,' he said.

'What does Doris do?' enquired Griselda at one point, for something to say, and in the capricious and destructive spirit in which women ask such questions at such times.

'Part time nursing,' replied Kynaston, packing plates. 'She's no use at the bedside, but the clothes are good. Mostly, she's waiting of course. Waiting for experience of the male. Shall I put in some bottles of beer?'

'I dislike beer.'

'You sound as if you dislike me too? Would you rather not come on the picnic? I can always go unaccompanied.'

'I have to stay here until it is time for tea. You're supposed to be teaching me dancing, which I don't want to learn. We'd better use up the time somehow.'

'Yes,' he said, lining up the cutlery they were to take. 'You're at my mercy, aren't you? I should so much prefer the situation to be reversed.'

After a round of complicated preparations, remarkably onerous in view of the smallness alike of the bungalow and of the undertaking before them, they at last found themselves on the doorstep.

'Forgive me if I double-lock the front door,' said Kynaston. Griselda reflected that the whole woodwork would yield like cardboard to any housebreaker.

They set out along the distractingly noisy main road through Hodley, carrying the ponderous basket between them. The traffic made conversation impossible, and the preservation of life, weighed down as they were, a matter calling for constant attention. After about a hundred yards Griselda wished she could change hands with their burden. After about a hundred and twenty-five yards she arranged with Kynaston to do so. After about a quarter of a mile Kynaston shouted: 'Up there for the Woods. Up the steps to your left.'

Griselda was realizing that her left arm was by no means as strong as her right, and she transferred the basket once more as she struggled up the steps ahead of Kynaston. Hodley Woods, though a well-known beauty spot, were neither as extensive nor as dense as Griselda had expected from the descriptions she had often read of them in advertisements; but they appeared unpopulated, it being a time of the day and week when all but the anti-social were at work. The road now ran in a cutting which much diminished its uproar. The sun, moreover, had begun to shine, falsifying Mullet's forecast; and among the undergrowth Griselda noticed a yellow-hammer.

'Places like this are only beautiful when they're near a town,' remarked Kynaston.

'I don't think I follow.'

'When there's no town, the landscape should be more startling. Miles of this sort of thing and nothing else, would be intolerable.'

'It's what I'm used to. I haven't travelled much. Where do we settle?'

'What about here? You can just see the main line through that gap in the trees. At least you will be able to, when there's a train. I like trains.'

It was a spot where several trees had been cut down. Generations of pine needles warmed and cushioned the dead roots. Griselda began to convert one of the stumps into a table. Kynaston lay on his back.

'I suppose you work.'

'Not at the moment. Or not in the way you mean. I had to give it up owing to troubles at home.'

'You mean they took exception to the nature of your employment?'

'No. I had to return home and help.'

'Why? What happened?'

'Things went wrong. Have a sandwich?'

Still regarding the tree-tops he reached about with his arm. 'You're not very informative. Never mind. It's

55

unlikely that I'd be able to assist much. Even with advice.' His hand, roving through the air, struck the arm of her jacket. He took her arm between his fingers and thumb and followed it down to the wrist. Then he took the sandwich. 'I detest mustard, by the way. I should have mentioned that.'

'There's no mustard. I forgot to ask you. I don't like it either.'

He began to drop bits of the sandwich into his up-turned mouth.

'As we've carried plates all this way, perhaps we'd better use them,' said Griselda.

'Am I eating swinishly? After all, it's swine I'm eating.'

'Here you are,' said Griselda firmly. 'Take it.' She held a plate before his face.

Kynaston sat up. He placed the remains of the de-composing sandwich on the plate. 'I am a creature of moods,' he said. 'As you see. But I like women to know their own minds.'

For the remainder of the meal his behaviour was irre-proachable.

After they had consumed the final tinned apricot, Kynaston busied himself making Nescafé on the little stove. The stove was slow to light and laborious to sus-tain. 'It's getting old,' he remarked. 'I've had it since I was at school. I was at Stowe, you know,' he added, as if alluding to a matter of very common knowledge. 'It's supposed to be better than the usual reformatory. We were allowed to have a few possessions of our own. This was mine. I used to make Bantam in the grounds. Nescafé hadn't been invented, I think, at that time.' He was striking matches and blowing the minute flame. 'Don't get me wrong all the same,' he went on. 'At the best Stowe's only a vulgar makeshift. It was built for another purpose.'

'Wasn't it the house of the Duke of Buckingham?'

'It was, Griselda. May I call you Griselda? I think one should ask. Oh, curse.' He had burned himself rather badly.

'You may call me Griselda. I like you to ask. Can I do anything helpful?'

'Nothing.'

'Cold tea would be good for that burn.'

'We've only got Nescafé . . . How did you know about the Buckingham's?'

'I read.'

'About the history of architecture?'

'Family histories.'

'What else?'

'Almost everything else. You can't define. You know that.'

'I know that. I was trying to trap you into an admission.' The stove was now flaming merrily; almost hysterically, Griselda thought. 'I was trying to trap you into an admission of anything.'

'I have little to conceal.'

'Are you awakened? I think not.'

'You think the same of others, I notice.'

'Doris, you mean? It's true. Have you read Casanova?'

'Yes.'

'Oh, You have. Then you'll recall his remark to the effect that most people never receive the initial jolt which is required to bring the mind to consciousness.' The water boiled over, extinguishing the long yellow flames. There had been a good blaze and little of the water was left.

But they made the best of it and somehow began a conversation about books and the psyche which continued until Griselda noticed that her wrist-watch showed half-past three.

'What about my lessons?'

'You've too many brains to make a good dancer, but I'll do what I can in the time.'

'Whose fault is it about the time?'

'Blame it on life. It's hard to know where to begin else. Living in Hodley I cannot be expected to regard someone like you only as a source of income.'

Griselda wondered what there was about her to elicit a compliment from a man who, however irritating in his habits, yet undoubtedly had seen much of the world. She wondered but smiled. Then she thought of the ordeal before her.

They returned with the picnic basket to the bungalow. Entering the studio immediately, Kynaston put a record on the gramophone.

'Leave that outside,' he said, referring to the basket. 'Anywhere.' Soft music trickled forth.

'There's a note for you,' cried Griselda, staving off events. 'It was behind the front door.'

'Read it. Out loud.'

'"I have put your shirt in the top left hand drawer on top of the others."'

'For tonight. Doris has been washing it. She has to wash her own shirts the whole time and she's become very good at it.'

'I'm looking forward to meeting her again tonight.' This remark could hardly do more than gain time.

'Doris won't be coming. I'm asked only for professional reasons.' The music was murmuring on. Kynaston was in the centre of the room. He spoke with a touch of impatience. 'I'm ready.'

There seemed no help for it.

VII

Immediately Griselda re-entered Beams, the Duchess clutched her by the arm.

'You have returned at the right moment, my dear,' she said. 'I have something I want to ask you. Tell me the truth. Did you hear Fritzi last night? Were you awakened?'

This last question seemed to recur.

'I don't think so,' replied Griselda, courteously but cautiously. Could the Duchess be referring to the noisy frequenter of the distant passage?

'I am so very glad to hear it. The lovely Pamela was not awakened either, and, of course, George it is always utterly impossible to awake. But everyone else, it seems. Even that Irish assassin, who sleeps outside above the motor-cars. And poor little Fritzi he could not at all explain to me what was the matter with him.'

Griselda realized that Fritzi was the Duchess's dog. She remembered. She was a little frightened.

'Have you no idea yourself?'

'No idea at all. Gottfried and I woke up together. There was little Fritzi crying his poor heart out. We could not see him as there was no light. Gottfried, you know, will never allow there to be a crack of light in the room when we are in bed. I clutched Gottfried very tightly. What could it be? Gottfried kissed and caressed me. Then he got out of bed and turned on the light. Fritzi was standing up in his basket, quite erect and stiff as a statue. I got out of bed too. I went to Fritzi and asked him why he was crying. And do you know, my dear, what happened then? He growled at me as if he didn't know me. Fritzi has never growled at Gottfried or me in all the eleven years we have had him. But Gottfried made it better for me again and in the end Fritzi stopped crying and fell asleep quite suddenly. I asked him again in the morning but he couldn't tell me what it all meant.'

Palpably the Duchess had related the story many times, presumably at intervals throughout the day. None the less, Griselda for some reason was not surprised that she still seemed much upset. The Duke came to her, and, saying nothing, put his arm round her shoulder. Suddenly Griselda realized that the dog was dead. She recalled that the Ellensteins had not appeared for breakfast; and, with unreasonable shame, her own confident inner explanation of their absence.

'How perfectly dreadful!' she said to the Duchess. 'I am so very sorry.'

The Duchess kissed her gratefully. 'Thank you, Griselda,' she said. 'Fritzi was only an animal, but the death even of an animal that has been a long time—' She left the sentence unfinished, as the Duke led her to a sofa. She looked up brightly, and the more engagingly for what had gone before. 'I am absolutely determined not to spoil the dance.' The Duke kissed her left hand.

Griselda was pleased that the Duchess had remembered her Christian name aright and called her by it.

The others present, Mrs Hatch and Mr Leech, had doubtless, with the rest of the house, expressed their grief already. Mr Leech none the less looked exceedingly distressed as he nibbled at a chunk of the unique cake.

'Come and have your tea, Griselda,' said Mrs Hatch. 'I shan't require massage, after all, but I daresay you could do with a short rest before you change. Pamela has gone up already.'

Griselda advanced and sat down with an enquiry after her hostess's affliction.

'I've been so busy all day that I've not had time to think of it. In consequence it has now quite ceased to trouble me.'

'How splendid!' said Mr Leech quietly, 'Would that all our ills could be cured so readily.' He sighed.

'Several men have already asked me for dances with you.' remarked Mrs Hatch to Griselda, 'and I've booked some of them on this card.' She took a dance programme from her handbag. 'Only some of them, of course.' She passed the programme to Griselda. 'I won't ask whether Geoffrey Kynaston was pleased with your progress; but I'll ask whether you were. Were you?'

To her alarm and mortification Griselda felt that her brow and neck were hot.

'I did my best,' she answered. 'But Geoffrey tells me I'm too much of a bluestocking to make a dancer.'

'You're starting late. But you're starting under excellent auspices. It's much too soon to despair.'

'Of course it is,' said the Duchess, 'Griselda may meet her affinity this very night. Then she'll dance better than all of us.'

'I don't know about that,' said Mrs Hatch. 'But the All Party Dance is certainly going to be an occasion. We shall be making history tonight.'

Griselda felt very ignorant. 'Is it such a very special dance?'

Mrs Hatch looked at her. 'You cannot have been reading the newspapers lately.'

'Not very much, I'm afraid. I prefer books.'

'Good thing too. Provided you choose the right books. Millie always had dreadful tastes: Tolstoy, von Hügel, and rubbish like that. Still you ought to know about tonight.' Mr Leech nodded gravely several times.

'The country's on the rocks,' continued Mrs Hatch. 'That I'm sure you *must* know.'

'More than usual?' asked Griselda.

'Much more. You've heard about the Roller Report?'

'I've seen the name on the newsbills.'

'The Roller Committee has presented a Report showing that we're bankrupt.'

'And after sitting for only six months,' interpolated Mr Leech. 'That's where much of the seriousness lies, you know. Mrs Hatch. Things are really urgent.'

'Well, you know what that means?'

'Not a revolution?' This was the Duke.

'I suppose it means we must all make some more money,' suggested Griselda rather wildly.

'It means a coalition.'

Mr Leech nodded again more gloomily than ever.

'I see. The dance is to celebrate?'

'Certainly not.' Mr Leech almost snatched the words from his hostess's mouth. 'I will explain.' It was clear that his life mainly consisted in explaining the same thing to a succession of careless audiences. 'When Lord Roller came to me, my first thought, after consulting my colleagues, was to get in touch with Mr Minnit, though it's never pleasant to have to ask favours of the Leader of the Opposition. Still one must put the country first, of course. After we had talked things over, Minnit said that he and some of his people would come in with us; but we both thought that something more was needed than a merely administrative change of that kind. After all, Miss de Reptonville, not everybody nowadays even knows who is or who is not in the Cabinet at any particular moment.' He smiled. There was a complete silence. Mrs Hatch was wriggling her foot in the thick carpet. The Duke's arm was still round his wife's shoulders, his hand on her breast. 'Something more seemed to us to be needed.' repeated the Prime Minister, blinking. 'Something more – so to speak – emotional. In a popular sort of way. Something which appealed to the underlying unity of the nation, the readiness of the people to make sacrifices for patriotic reasons. For sacrifices will certainly be called for. A heavy burden. Oh yes—' He paused again, then pulled himself together. 'My first thought was a Mass Meeting in some suitable place, to be addressed by Minnit and myself in turn. Considering the country's need, I thought we might prevail upon the L.C.C.—'

'Then fortunately Mr Leech consulted me,' interrupted Mrs Hatch. 'I happened to be calling in at Downing Street for tea. I saw the answer at once. I offered Beams for an All Party Dance. The press response has shown how right the idea was. Everyone is coming. Not only Minnit and all of them, but representatives of the splinter parties too. Half way through the evening Mr Leech and Mr Minnit are going to make their speeches – short speeches, of course – as hostess I insist on that; and everyone will think well of the coalition from the outset, instead of the whole thing falling flat.'

'Will there be enough people to listen to the speeches?' asked Griselda. 'I don't mean to be rude. I'm sure there'll be everyone there's room for. But will there be quite enough to achieve national unity?'

'People don't actually need to *hear* the speeches on these occasions,' replied Mrs Hatch. 'In many cases it is better if they do not. All the press will be coming, and, of course, the speeches will be broadcast. Those are the things which matter nowadays.'

'I was more than a little doubtful myself at first.' remarked Mr Leech, 'whether we should avail ourselves of Mrs Hatch's wonderfully generous offer. But she soon quite won me over.'

'Melanie,' observed the Duke, tightening his hold upon his wife, 'will persuade the Recording Angel to let her organize a dance at the Day of Judgement.'

Monk entered and began to pound with a gong in the sight of them all.

'The dressing gong,' said Mrs Hatch, rising smartly. 'Dinner will be in exactly an hour.'

VIII

In her bedroom Griselda found a tall thin girl seated in one of the armchairs, who rose as she entered.

'Who are you?'

'Louise. If you like, I'll help you to dress.'

She was wearing a costly dress of pale grey silk, which tightly fitted her long neck up to her chin and ears, and was buttoned with many small buttons from the waist to the top of the collar, and girdled with a shiny black belt. Her long hair, the colour of smooth water under a grey sky, was drawn into a tight ballet-dancer's bun. Her face was exceedingly pale, and made paler with a suggestion of powder almost green in tinge; but her features made an unusual blend of resolution and sensibility, a large nose and small firm chin combining with a slightly sensual mouth and huge dark-brown eyes, full of life and beauty, behind very large and expensive black-rimmed glasses. Her voice and accent were contralto and cultivated.

Griselda recalled her hostess's words: 'You don't know how much Louise will do for you.' To have Louise about one, would, she thought, be charming and beautiful. It was the first luxury she had really desired.

'Hadn't you better help Mrs Hatch first? She'll have to be down to receive people, I expect.'

'No one outside the house party will be here until nine. Mrs Hatch particularly wanted me to help you.' Louise smiled delightfully.

'Thank you.' There was a silly pause. Griselda had placed her handbag on the bed. 'I must tell you I've never met a lady's maid.'

'I'm not *exactly* a lady's maid.'

Griselda blushed. 'I'm so sorry. Mrs Hatch—'

Louise waved away her apologies. 'We'll have to learn from one another. About each other, I mean.'

They were standing in the middle of the floor, looking at each other, about three feet apart.

'Are you coming to the dance?'

Louise shook her head. 'Political dances are not my thing. Not that kind of dance. Therefore I'm not asked.'

'What do you do?'

'Various things. But now it is time that I help people to dress.'

'For dances you don't go to?'

'And for some I do.'

'Do you like the work?'

'I have a certain natural apptitude, I think,' Louise answered solemnly. 'And little alternative. I am destitute and unqualified. But I don't give satisfaction, I'm afraid.'

'I think that Mrs Hatch might be hard to please. From what little I've seen of her, of course.'

'It's I who am hard to please. At least, harder to please than Mrs Hatch.' Again she smiled.

'I see.'

'Shall we begin?'

Louise helped Griselda remove her jacket, and pulled her jumper swiftly over her head.

'I expect you would like a bath?'

'I'm afraid of the machine.'

'I'll try to protect you from it.' Louise began to operate the formidable equipment, while Griselda removed her remaining garments.

In a remarkably short space of time Louise was announcing that the bath was ready. 'Hot,' she added. 'And deep. We've won. It's a beautiful bath.' She stared for a moment at Griselda's naked body. The steam of the bathroom had made her face glisten very slightly, despite the careful make-up. 'Given the right dress, you will be the belle of the ball,' she said.

For the second time that evening Griselda felt herself blush; this time, it seemed, all over her body, making her look absurd.

'Fortunately,' she replied, 'I have exactly the right dress.'

Likewise the bath was the right temperature, the right depth, accompanied with the right accessories, a new cake of heavily scented soap and a huge white bath towel. Griselda entered it, letting the water rise above her shoulders.

'Which dress?'

Griselda shouted back. 'The taffeta.' It was wonderful.

Louise appeared in the bathroom door, which Griselda had left open. 'Your dress is good. Really good.' Griselda felt flattered and pleased that Louise did not seem surprised, she whose taste, it was obvious, was unapproachably high.

'I told you it was.'

Louise was withdrawing to the bedroom, but Griselda stopped her.

'Come and talk to me.' She had never spoken like that before. 'Or is it too hot and steamy?'

Louise shook her head and sat on the bath stool, an inappropriate throne.

'Undo the collar of your dress. Make yourself comfortable.'

Louise shook her head again. 'My dress must be worn severely.'

'It becomes you.'

'I have no wish to look like everyone else. It is one thing about my life here that it enables me not to. Soon even nuns and nurses will be wearing little cotton frocks from Marks and Spencer.'

Griselda remembered what Kynaston had said about the photograph of Doris. She thought for a moment.

'Cotton frocks are comfortable.'

'But do they appeal to the senses? Are those who wear them satisfied?'

'Does what one wears affect that?'

'Very much indeed. One's body needs to be always conscious of its clothes. One reason why there are so many more unsatisfied women than there used to be, is that they have forgotten that.'

'I fear my clothes are very commonplace. Except that dress.'

'I will help you to do better if you like.'

'Thank you. But I have very little money.'

'That matters more than it should, but less than you think.'

'Then I should like you to help me.'

'Of course there are limits to what I can do. But if you are seriously interested, I might later introduce you to Hugo Raunds. He lives entirely for clothes. He designed this dress. You've probably heard of him. As it happens, his father, Sir Travis, is coming tonight. Not that all this matters much, as I'll be leaving here at any moment, and that will be that.'

'Where will you go?'

'I shall try to find someone amenable to my ways.'

Griselda began to fill the bath with strongly smelling soap.

'I know so little of life. Oh, curse.'

A sud had entered one of her eyes. Louise rose and carefully removed it with a handkerchief, which she took from a pocket in the skirt of her dress. It was a silk handkerchief and soothing: though the pain remained, therapeutic in sensation, but curing nothing; probably, in fact, Griselda feared, damaging slightly the conjunctiva. Louise had resumed her seat. She was wiping her large glasses on the handkerchief.

After thanking Louise, Griselda continued: 'All I know comes from books. It's a wonder I keep my end up as well as I do.'

'Books are better, I think, most of the time,' replied Louise. 'The more you know of life outside them, the less it's like them. But there's one problem that you have to solve if you're to go on profiting from books, and books won't help you much to solve it.'

'And that is?'

'The problem of finding someone, even one single person, you can endure life with. To me it's acute.'

Inadvertently Griselda knocked the large slippery cake of soap on to the floor, where it slid out of sight.

'I always thought *that* difficulty was peculiar to me,' said Griselda.

Louise had laid her glasses on the stool and was groping for the soap.

'Please stop,' cried Griselda. 'I should be getting out anyway. It was selfish of me to ask you to sit in all this steam.'

Louise returned the soap to its lair and resumed her glasses.

'I'm not all that short-sighted,' she remarked. 'Though I am, of course, a little short-sighted I don't have to wear glasses. It's just that glasses suit me. We may as well get *something* from modern inventions.'

Griselda was out and towelling.

She found that Louise had laid out new underclothes for her.

She submitted to being dressed by Louise, to having Louise brush her short hair, even to being made up by Louise; all with a strange remote pleasure, possibly recalled from childhood, though certainly not consciously, for Griselda could recall little of her childhood that was pleasant, except books.

It all took a long time, and as they worked, they talked.

The remarks they exchanged became shorter and rapider; varied with occasional longer passages such as in normal converse no one listens to. They began, without any feeling of guilt, to talk about the people in the house.

'Have you ever set eyes on the mysterious Austin Barnes?'

'No.'

'Why does he never appear?'

'The coalition. He hates it.'

'Oh yes. I heard about the coalition during Tea.'

'Also he thinks he ought to be Prime Minister and not Leech.'

'I see.'

'Also he's afraid of Mrs Hatch.'

'I like the Ellensteins.'

'Yes,' said Louise. 'The Ellensteins are good. One could not endure living with them, but they are really good. And that is most unusual.'

'What about the Duchess's dog?'

'It was Stephanie.'

'Who's Stephanie?'

'Stephanie des Bourges. She's a ghost.'

'So the house is haunted?'

'Only occasionally. Stephanie comes only at certain times.'

'I could wish the times weren't the present.'

'I could not. Stephanie was my only friend until you came.' This now seemed to Griselda not even to call for acknowledgement. 'In fact she came because I was here.'

'Do you talk to her?'

'Oh yes, often. She's a lonely ghost.'

'When did you last talk to her? Last night?'

'This afternoon.'

'Where?'

'Here. I was talking to Stephanie just before you came in. I talked to her here yesterday too.'

'Do you mean that I've been given the haunted room?'

'Dear Griselda, you couldn't expect a beautiful woman like Stephanie – for she *is* beautiful, fortunately – to come to my little turret and probably wake up the servants below into the bargain? Now could you?'

'I suppose not,' said Griselda. 'But it explains why I slept badly last night.'

'I don't think so,' said Louise. She was drawing on one of Griselda's stockings and now paused for moment, kneeling at her feet. 'It is not that this is the haunted room or anything so vulgar, if you will forgive me putting it so. You think of it like that because you think a ghost must be bad. This is merely the room where Stephanie and I meet because, being at the end of the corridor and usually unoccupied, it is quiet and seldom disturbed. And you mustn't think of poor Stephanie as bad either. Ghosts only harm those who fear them. Stephanie is one whom I find it easy to love. And you must do the same, Griselda.'

'I'll try.' Louise began attaching the stocking to its suspender. Griselda felt curious. 'Do you *see* her by daylight?'

'No. It is true that you can only see her at night. But I can talk to her sometimes by day.'

'Could I?'

'I don't know. It depends.'

'On what?'

But Louise was reflecting and did not answer directly. 'Yes, Griselda,' she said. 'I think that *you* could see and talk to Stephanie. It occurs to me that it may have been because you also were here that she has come at this time. She hadn't been seen or heard of before, they tell me, for more than twenty years. Not since the time something happened during that bloody silly war. I don't precisely know what.' She was on her feet again.

'I'm afraid,' said Griselda, 'that nothing you say makes me very much less frightened of Stephanie. I'm not sure that I shall find thought very enjoyable – I mean, even after the dance, to which I'm not looking forward at all. She was even responsible for the poor Duchess losing her dog,' added Griselda as an afterthought.

'It's difficult about animals,' replied Louise. 'But you can't say that ghosts really treat them worse than we do.'

'What colour is her hair?' asked Griselda.

'A gorgeous golden red,' answered Louise. 'And her eyes are, of course, green.'

'I have never seen really green eyes outside a book.'

'I think that Stephanie must be a mixture of races,'

said Louise. 'Probably she has some Jewish blood. I should say quite a lot.'

She lifted Griselda's dress from the bed where she had laid it. 'Now for it,' she said.

It was done.

'You are truly beautiful,' said Louise.

'The girl who designed the dress should get most of the credit,' said Griselda, looking away from Louise, and into the mirror.

'What was her name?'

Griselda told her.

'I might have known it,' said Louise. 'In fact, I really did know it. One of Hugo's.'

'I haven't heard her mention him.'

'No. Hugo is a very secret man.'

'Oh. Anyway I don't know her very well. I wish I were a better dancer.'

'Don't worry about that.'

'I wish something else. I so much wish, Louise, that you were coming to the political dance with me.'

Stretching out her hand, she touched Louise's grey silk neck.

'Yes,' said Louise gravely. 'To my utter surprise, I wish that too.'

IX

'We mustn't let things go to our heads,' remarked Mrs
Hatch as she seated herself at the dinner table. They
settled to a substantial meal.

Griselda, for some reason, had come down rather
late, and Mrs Hatch, whose practice as hostess it was always to appear for dinner last, had entered the dining
room only just behind her. The absence of Louise might
in any case have retarded her preparations.

Griselda, to whom Louise's good opinion of her dress
had given more confidence, carefully examined the
company. The Duchess, in a very tight dress which,
it had to be admitted, suited her much better than
something looser would have done, was certainly the
most striking; but Mrs Hatch, in a sense (not a sense
that Griselda particularly cared for), ran her close, wearing a dress after the style favoured by Madame
Récamier, but dark blue, and elaborated, perhaps somewhat inappropriately, with a full display of the famous
Procopius jewellery, a fabulous, multi-coloured mêlée.
Pamela, in one of the quieter garments approved by
Vogue, seemed slightly outshone by her seniors; and to
be in a state of sulky suspicion, though her appetite remained good. Altogether Griselda felt rather pleased.

With the men it was simple: the Duke (bearing on

his dress coat a tiny but conspicious token of some ancient chivalrous Order particularized in the Almanach de Gotha), and Edwin (in a dress suit the colour of night on the Côte d'Azur, and wearing a rare flower in his buttonhole, which Mr Cork said grew only on the island of Tahiti and in his conservatory at Beams) were well-dressed; Mr Leech and George Goss were not. George Goss had not even brought a tail coat.

There was soup with wine in it; a large, but excellent, sole; roast duck, with apple sauce, and salad; a confused but rather rich concoction described as 'Summer Pudding' (though, as someone pointed out, it was not yet quite summer); mushrooms on toast; and dessert. 'No cheese tonight,' announced Mrs Hatch, 'in view of what is before us. Those who are still hungry must make do with nuts; or go and see Brundrit privately in his pantry.'

Pamela had refused to take duck on the ground that her Father had always said that ducks were garbage eaters; and had had to have a small exquisite point steak specially cooked for her. When it came, she ate it, without a word, almost in a couple of mouthfuls.

It was not the gayest of meals. The Duchess, upon whom so much depended in that direction, was cast down by the death of Fritzi, though she struggled pathetically hard with her feelings, and though the slight air of grief (like most things) distinctly became her. The Duke, though he did all that could be expected of him with Griselda, complimenting her upon her dress and describing clothes worn by beautiful women he had met at now extinct German courts, was concerned about the Duchess. Mr Leech was concerned about his speech, apologizing to Griselda for his inattention to her remarks, apologizing to his hostess for making notes during dinner, dropping his food on his clothes, and from time to time muttering a possible rhetorical effect under his breath, then changing it with a stub of pencil and muttering it again. Edwin seemed almost more concerned than the Prime Minister, and his concern seemed more active or transitive; it was not that he deflected in the slightest from his habitual perfection of appearance and behaviour, but that a score of unconscious details disclosed his inner distress, and made him less than a contributor to the sodality of the occasion. Once even he had to ask for a second access to the salad, being unable to eat any more duck. Pamela was as negative as usual: and even Mrs Hatch seemed strung up, in her not very suitable dress and dangerously valuable jewels. It hung over all of them, perhaps, even over Mrs Hatch, dearly though she appeared to love a dance, that the gaiety ahead had an ulterior, and presumably important, end. George Goss merely leered at the Duchess's bare bosom and ate, crouched over his plate like an octopus.

Mrs Hatch left the table early in order to receive the first guests, commanding the others to remain and give their digestions time to work. Edwin, however, sprang up, and, exclaiming 'I am sure there must be something I can do,' followed his hostess, having bestowed a final uncertain glance upon Mr Leech.

'It's bad news about our friend Austin,' remarked the Duke, after a pause.

'I hadn't heard, darling,' said the Duchess.

'Same old trouble,' grunted George Goss.

Griselda had meant to enquire further of the Duke, but after George Goss's remark, felt quite unlike doing so.

'I hope we have a schottische,' said the Duchess, brightly making conversation. 'Mentioning Austin made me think of it.'

'I doubt whether the younger generation have ever heard of it,' said Mr Leech. He was at his very gloomiest.

Griselda had to admit that she had not.

'I've heard of it,' said Pamela, gnawing round an imported nectarine. 'All those Victorian things are coming back in, you know. Chaperones, petticoats, and all that.'

For Pamela it was quite a speech.

X

'Hallo, Griselda. What a dress!'

The first person she had met was Kynaston, and she was not as pleased as immediately after she had last left him, she would have expected to be.

'Hullo, Geoffrey. Don't think me rude, but I'm on my way upstairs.

Probably it was rude, but she could not help it. Her mood was expansive, something she could not recall having previously felt; and about Geoffrey there seemed an enclosed and private air unsuited to a large convivial gathering. Though, she recollected, she did not know him very well; so that possibly this was wrong.

Approaching her room she felt unreasonably agitated; and entering it, much more unreasonably disappointed. The room was empty. From one of the dressing-table drawers she took the dance programme Mrs Hatch had given her; and looked at it for the first time. There were three names inserted in Mrs Hatch's clear handwriting (one of them twice), none of them known to Griselda, except that of Edwin Polegate-Hampden, inserted not, as he had hoped, for the first but for the supper dance. There were no names inserted after supper. Griselda was wholly ignorant of the procedure on these occasions, but had thought that dance programmes were obsolete. She wondered whether it was usual for the hostess, unasked, to arrange in this way partners for her guests. It might be important to ascertain whether it was the custom or merely a peculiarity of Mrs Hatch's. Then Griselda thought of Stephanie des Bourges and hurried from the room, her final preparations abbreviated. This, she felt, was no time to meet a ghost. She wondered where Louise was; and shivered slightly.

Suddenly hundreds of people had arrived. The hall was full and quite a queue extended down the long passage, lined with palms and baskets of flowers, which extended to the resuscitated ballroom, recently the scene of Doris's dusty labours. At the entrance to the ballroom Mrs Hatch was shaking hands with people, and introducing them to Mr Leech, who stood on her right, himself looking rather in need of a dust, and to another man, standing on her left, whom Griselda divined to be Mr Minnit, the Leader of the Opposition. Mr Minnit was a determined-looking elderly man with sparse black hair and a raucous penetrating voice. His evening suit made an even poorer impression than Mr Leech's, because, besides having been worn for longer, it had cost less in the first place. Grouped round the trio were a number of men whom Griselda, identifying one or two of them, took to be some of the new Cabinet. Few of them made a more favourable impression than did either of their leaders.

'I've been waiting for you to come down.' It was Kynaston again. 'I'm quite as terrified by all this as you are.'

Griselda realized that she wasn't terrified at all. She

considered herself much better dressed than most of the other women; and, quite possibly, no less generally attractive. Looking round her, she even began to wonder whether she would show herself much inferior as a dancer. She smiled at Kynaston to give him confidence, and because she still felt she might have been rude to him.

Just then the band struck up. 'You hear that?' said Kynaston. 'You'd better get your hostess's money's worth.'

They began to make their way along the crowded passage. Kynston shook hands with Mrs Hatch, who asked after his poetry. Then they entered the ballroom.

It was a fine large room, though not very inspired architecturally, and expensively decorated not only with vegetation of various kinds but also with a number of patriotic motifs. At one end of the rectangle, the platform occupied by the band was banked with hundreds of carnations which pleasantly perfumed the otherwise already slightly smoky air. At the other end was another, smaller platform, now unoccupied but the purpose of which was clear, as it was swathed in red, white, and blue fabric, and bore an ominous green baize-topped table, with three hard chairs. Above this platform were two oval plaques, edged with laurel, and bearing lively messages from Lord Beaconsfield and John Burns. Presumably many of the guests were not expected to take the floor, as round the walls was ranged a triple rank of gilt chairs with crimson seats, their thin red line becoming disordered as people sat upon them; but already the enthusiastic and the impetuous were in action, their faces settling down to ecstasy or boredom. The long far wall of the room contained a line of big French windows, uncurtained against the chance that later the growing heat might require them to be opened. Griselda wondered who might be without these windows, unseen but all-seeing.

As Kynaston led Griselda on to the floor, they encountered Edwin with a fascinatingly beautiful young partner. Briefly he introduced her as the Marchioness of Wolverhampton. 'See you later,' he said to Griselda, in an accent of warm significance. Griselda watched them glide away. Obviously Edwin's dancing was as flawless as everything else about him. Griselda wondered why he should elect to sup with her instead of with the incomparable Marchioness; or whether this also was Mrs Hatch's doing.

Griselda danced three times with Kynaston, not precisely with elation, but certainly with competence. Her ancient inhibition against being intimately clasped by a little-known male had not disappeared, but was perhaps in abeyance. In practice, the whole curious transaction seemed, at least with Kynaston, unexpectedly impersonal. They said little, the monotonous music thrummed in Griselda's brain, and she felt completely mistress of the situation, while still unclear why such store was commonly set by the pastime. Possibly things would be different in the circumstances advocated by the Duchess; but surely it must be only occasionally that the habitual dancer could dance with a partner whose body inspired to passion? Griselda wondered whether possibly she suffered from some physiological deficiency akin to tone-deafness. She then listened with her conscious ear to the music, and deemed that the matter was not worth undue concern.

The business had its social problems, however. Griselda's fourth dance had been allocated by Mrs Hatch to an unknown named Mr Coote. She did not know who Mr Coote was, but when she announced his imminence to Kynaston, she was startled to learn that Kynaston had taken it for granted that she would be dancing with him (Kynaston) throughout the evening.

'You said you wanted me to ward off other males.'

'Not exactly.'

'You couldn't abide being pawed.'

'Mrs Hatch has arranged the next dance for me.'

'What do you think I'm going to do? I don't know a soul here – if anybody here has a soul; and they're not the kind of people I *want* to know. Not that I'm likely to be introduced. I'm a mixture of a poor relation and the local tradesman.'

'What would you have done, if you hadn't met me?'

'Contrived to bring Doris. Of course, I much prefer you, but I've made a very fair dancer out of Doris, and she's vastly better than having to talk about the state of the nation with a string of politicians.'

The situation was dissolved by Mrs Hatch appearing with Mr Coote.

'Let me introduce Mr Coote, Griselda; your next partner. This is Griselda de Reptonville. I told Mr Coote about you while you were out of the house and he asked me for a dance with you.'

'The reality exceeds the description,' said Mr Coote.

It was a waltz and Mr Coote was heavy on other people's feet. While dancing, however, he maintained a steady flow of conventionally complimentary verbiage, of a type which Griselda was surprised to find still existed, but which began heavily to pall in an astonishingly short period of time. Griselda had always understood that men preferred to talk about themselves and tried to direct the conversation in that likely direction. But Mr Coote was unexpectedly reticent. Griselda could only gather that though not in the political limelight, he occupied an entirely indispensable position far behind the scenes.

'Sort of Chief Foreman, you know. The chap who sees that the roundabout is oiled. Poor sort of job at times, I find it. Let's talk about something pleasanter. Our excellent hostess told me you had short hair but I never knew short hair could be so attractive.'

Suddenly Griselda noticed something odd. Mrs Hatch was dancing with (and much better than) Pamela.

Mr Coote was, Griselda recollected, the one of her three allotted partners who recurred. He was due to re-appear for the next dance but one. Apart from anything else, it seemed poor planning, like selling all the adjoining seats in a theatre, instead of spacing the audience about.

This little trouble solved itself, however, in the very instant that Griselda had thought of it.

As the dance number (it was a bagatelle entitled

'Mooning with the Moon') neared its point of cessation, Mr Coote suddenly crumpled up in the most dramatic possible way. He dropped his partner, clutched the lower part of his belly with both hands, became instantly green in the face, and lurched groaning to one of the gilt chairs which had strayed out among the dancers. There he sat, odd pairs of dancers occasionally navigating round the back of him, until two muscular and efficient footmen assisted him away, their hands under his armpits. Now that the music had stopped, his dreadful groans were clearly audible above the hubbub of talk; but so expertly was the incident disposed of, that few were clearly aware of what had happened, and none sustained any notable setback in jollity.

Griselda had been left isolated not far from the centre of the floor, and, so thick were the dancers, could not reach Mr Coote before he was whisked away.

'If that doesn't teach you, I cannot imagine what will. You see what happens when you try to fraternize with the people.' It was, of course, Kynaston. Griselda could have struck him. Then she saw the large shape of George Goss coming towards her, solitary and menacing.

'Better me, don't you think, after all?' said Kynaston, comprehending the entire situation. Griselda, really furious at his deliberate or careless misunderstanding of the need for her to dance with Mr Coote, placed her hand on his arm; and the music started once more, this time a number entitled 'You Twisted Me Before I Twisted You.'

'You don't have to do this the whole time, of course,' said Kynaston.

'Indeed no. Later I am partnering a Mr Mackintosh, and after that Edwin Polegate-Hampden for the supper dance.'

'To hell with them. I didn't mean that. I meant that we could sit out sometimes.'

Absurdly, Griselda had overlooked this possibility.

Out of the corner of her eye she observed George Goss lumber off the floor disappointed.

'Don't I seem to know your unlucky friend?'

'George Goss,' said Griselda.

'I'm flattered that you prefer me. George Goss is the only really first-rank painter now alive in England. Probably in the world. When I looked at his Holy Family at the Leicester Gallery last autumn. I cried like a child.'

It was by no means the end of George Goss, for immediately the dance was over, there he was again.

'Could we please do what you said,' appealed Griselda to Kynaston, 'and sit this one out?' It was to have been Mr Coote's second dance, and Griselda considered that even he would have been preferable to George Goss.

'Let's look for the refreshments,' said Kynaston. 'I expect there are some.' He put his arm round her waist to lead her away. It was hard on George Goss and Griselda smiled at him as she departed. He stood looking after her, fixed like a toad.

But it was not to be. Mrs Hatch appeared.

'As Mr Coote has been taken away, I should like you

to meet Lord Roller.' Mrs Hatch's memory for the details she herself had organized, was appalling.

The great Lord Roller, whose revelations had just shaken the entire world and lay behind the present festivity, was tall and stout, though dignified and wearing the most perfectly cut clothes.

'Melanie suggests that we should dance,' he said in an attractive cultivated voice. 'But I should prefer to sit and talk for just the few minutes allotted to me.'

Griselda consented with relief. Kynaston prowled away, presumably after liquor.

'It's not that I never dance. On the contrary, twenty years ago I used to be considered rather good. But I've been having a tiring time lately and this evening, as you know, is rather a strain on some of us.'

Griselda said she could well understand. They sat. They had moved round the perimeter of the dance floor looking for two empty chairs and had reached the comparatively inaccessible and deserted window side of the room.

'However, no more of that. Let us talk of something else. What do you do in the world?'

'Very little. For various reasons it's difficult for me to leave home.'

'That's bad. The days when women stayed at home are over. For better or for worse. But over, I assure you. What are the reasons, or ought I not to ask?'

Griselda hesitated. But Lord Roller had achieved his position in the world by being under all circumstances unfailingly reassuring.

88

'My Mother, mainly.'

'Illness?'

'Not exactly. Though she suffers a lot.'

'I won't enquire further.' Changing the subject, he said kindly, pointing out a well-known figure: 'You know that's George Goss the painter?'

'Yes. He's staying in the house.'

'I've known him since we were at Winchester together. Then he was a splendid young chap. Full of life. Quite irresistible. He did a drawing of me a year or two ago and I must say I thought he'd become something of an ox. When I saw the drawing I realized that he thought the same of me.'

'You're not at all like him,' said Griselda.

'Our lives have been different. Mine has been spent in the City, like the rest of my family. I haven't been able to let myself go in the way a great painter can. Despite appearances, I suspect I'm very much the man I was when I was at school. I observe that the Prime Minister hasn't been provided with a water bottle.' He pointed to the bare green table at the end of the room. 'That's bad. Later I'll have to see that something is done about it.'

The Duchess passed dancing with Edwin. Seeing Lord Roller, she smiled radiantly; then, observing that he was in conversation with Griselda, smiled again, a little ruefully.

'I've been in love with Odile for twenty years,' said Lord Roller. 'To attempt concealment would be quite unavailing.'

'You know you said you wouldn't enquire further?'

'Yes. I said that. Do you want me to enquire further? If so, I shall.'

'Am I a pest? I should like advice.'

'I know very little about the world outside business and politics. For that reason I should be honoured to advise you. I have all the confidence of ignorance. What is it about?'

It was the next dance and Griselda looked round for Kynaston, but there was no sign of him. She and Lord Roller went on talking.

'I have decided to leave home. My Mother will have to get on as best she can.'

'I can see that this is an entirely new resolution. I hope it is not based on what I just said. You must not take an old man, ignorant of life, too literally.'

'No, Lord Roller. It *is* a new resolution, but I made it before I met you. The question is what best to do after-wards.'

'I hardly know you well enough to advise you upon that. In any case, it is the most useless thing it is possible to advise upon. If you have no clear and conscious vo-cation in life, I advise you to marry and have children as soon as possible. Of course, I speak as a bachelor.'

'I want your advice on something much more defin-ite. I have few claims to a job of any kind, and, of course, a job I must have. A friend of mine has offered me one in the Secretariat of Sociology. It sounds pretty dull, be-cause all the good jobs go to people with degrees, and I have no degree; but I have to promise to stick to it for three years. I don't want to do that unless the result amounts to something, however small my contribution. I am sure you know all about the Secretariat of Sociology. Does it amount to anything?'

'To save a young woman from the Secretariat of Sociology,' replied Lord Roller, 'I would offer her a job myself. With all the new regulations the coalition will introduce, we shall be able to carry more passengers in the business. I quite understand that you wish not to be a passenger, but that is unusual, and you can take over the work of someone on our staff who does. If you care to write to me, I'll see what can be done. It will at least be somewhere near productive employment.'

'But I have no capacity. I cannot even type.'

'If typing is necessary and you do not learn to type within a month of our engaging you, we shall, of course, engage you no longer. You said you wanted to do work which amounted to something. That is the sort of obligation which work amounting to something involves.'

Griselda said: 'Naturally.'

He rose.

'I have enjoyed our talk. Now I must see that the Prime Minister is given his water-bottle, because the speeches will be soon, I regret to say. Have you a partner for the next dance?'

It was Mr Mackintosh's turn.

'Please do not wait, Lord Roller, if time is getting on. I'll find him myself.'

'We may meet again.'

'Thank you for your advice.'

He bowed and departed. His gait was full of distinction, his expression of confidence. As he passed through the throng, he nodded affably from time to time.

There was still no sign of Mr Mackintosh, and Griselda, feeling isolated, and still fearing George Goss, began, faute de mieux, to look round for Kynaston. Almost at once, she saw him. He was dancing with Pamela. Where previously Griselda had resented his attaching himself so calmly and firmly to her, she now resented his having anything to do with Pamela. In both cases resentment was only one of many feelings jumping about in Griselda's mind, most of them without rising to consciousness: and in both cases she felt that resentment was unreasonable.

Not wishing Kynaston, or Pamela either, to see her sitting by herself, she removed to a less conspicuous chair in the back row near a window. She recalled the term 'wallflower' and wished someone nice would speak to her. She still thought her appearance compared favourably with the appearance of the other women present, but all her immediate neighbours were dull looking people seated in small groups, indifferent to the dancing, but talking among themselves, sometimes acrimoniously. Griselda desperately wished that Louise could be there.

She began to study the scene impersonally. Though there were some beautiful women and distinguished looking men, the majority impressed as rowdy but dreary. They had, of course, Griselda recalled, been largely assembled for political rather than social reasons. There had been no sign of Mr Leech since the fun began and Mrs Hatch had now also disappeared, after a sequence of strenuous dances, doubtless in order to settle final details of the feast of rhetoric which impended. Mr Minnit, on the other hand, was dancing energetically with, as Griselda supposed, his wife. The Duke was now partnering the ravishing Lady Wolverhampton; and the Duchess one of the better dressed among the new Cabinet Ministers. In one corner there had been a minor disturbance for some time. Griselda had been only vaguely aware of the turmoil; now she perceived that it arose from attempts to prevent one of the splinter parties from posting propaganda bills on the ballroom wall. Mercifully George Goss was not to be seen. Possibly he was gone for a drink.

'Do you think it was wise of us to exclude the Communists?'

One of the group around Griselda had dried up conversationally and a member on the outskirts of it addressed her. He was elderly in the extreme and resembled a distinguished nonconformist dignitary.

Griselda considered the question.

'I don't see what else we could have done.'

'I think our appeal should be to *all* groups in the nation: to forget the past and think only of the future.' The speaker's voice and accents were great-grandpaternal. 'I've always been a radical; and what are the Communists but today's radicals? I'd be a Communist myself if I were still a young man.'

'Hardly Zec. Not with your collection of fine old stocks and shares,' said a hard-faced woman in his

93

group, almost Zec's contemporary.

'It's Travis Raunds who's responsible for their not being invited,' Zec grumbled on. 'The man's nothing but a despot. What do you think, young woman? Let us heed the voice of youth.'

'I'd rather leave it,' replied Griselda prudently, 'to whoever issued the invitations. But tell me about Sir Travis Raunds. Is he here?'

'Over there,' said Zec stabbing a desiccated forefinger towards the opposite side of the room. 'The old death-shead to the right of the centre mirror. Most reactionary man in the country. I've fought him all my life and he's fought me.'

'You flatter yourself,' said the hard-faced woman.

Griselda stared at the man mentioned by Louise, father of Louise's friend, Hugo Raunds. Though obviously very old, Griselda found him the most striking-looking man in the room. He had a considerable quantity of white hair, fine aristocratic bones, and a yellowish skin. Despite his years, he sat very upright and his expression was that of a censorious Buddha. His long mouth had finely shaped lips, his nose was magnificently powerful, he was clean shaven, and his eyes, Griselda, whose sight was excellent, could see across the room, were a clear yellow.

'Is his son Hugo here too?' asked Griselda.

The effect was unexpected. Zec stared into Griselda's eyes, his own the colour of granite setts and as unyielding, then said: 'Young woman, it is time you learned that to shock and insult your elders is never amusing.'

'I'm sorry,' said Griselda calmly. 'Hugo Raunds is only a name to me. I know nothing whatever about him.'

'I think,' said the hard-faced woman, 'that you'd be well advised to leave it at the apology.' Clearly she supported Zec in aggression though in however little else.

Griselda was about to rise from her chair and walk away when she became aware of tapping on the high French window behind her.

'I *told* you Hugo was a very secret man,' said the voice of Louise.

Griselda nearly fell off her chair with surprise.

The window had been opened and stood slightly ajar. Louise's pale face and large glasses were just visible through the gap.

'Have you got a partner?'

'No. I'm a wallflower.'

'Come away.'

Louise's hand entered through the gap, took Griselda by the wrist, and with unexpected strength drew her outside into the garden before she had time to consider. Louise shut the window and fastened it as easily as she had opened it. The two of them looked through the glass at the disgusted faces of Zec and his friends. A few of the other guests had noticed the brief draught; and it was clear that already, seconds later, they had forgotten it. Even Zec did not consider the incident worth rising from his seat to investigate.

'Louise, I'll be cold.'

'I think not. If you are, there's a cloak.'

'Where?'

'In the Temple of Venus.'

'What's that?'

'One of the Duke of St Helens's follies. We're going there.'

Indeed it was one of those precocious spring days which anticipate or excel Midsummer. There were stars and a moon. How very wrong Mullet had been!

Louise had changed into a simple but elegant black coat and skirt and a white silk shirt. The night was full of her perfume.

'You can see the Temple of Venus at the end of the vista. But the Water of Circe lies between us and it; so, as we have to go round it, the walk's longer than it looks.'

'Circe lived on an island.'

'There is an island. In the middle of the lake. It's where she's buried.'

'Circe?'

'No. Not Circe.'

'Stephanie?' Griselda almost whispered.

'Of course.'

They set out. It was a broad grassy way, cut wonderfully short. In lines parallel with the grass were beds of flowers just coming into bloom, but drained of what colour was theirs by the moon.

'What about the dew?' Griselda's shoes were for dancing.

'There is no dew. That means it will probably rain tomorrow. We must make the most of tonight.'

'Yes, you can smell in the flowers that rain's coming.'

'This morning's rain also.'

'It would be nice if it sometimes stayed fine for longer on end,' said Griselda.

'Nice. But, like most nice things, probably unnatural,' replied Louise. 'What do you think of dancing?'

'I've never danced before tonight – or rather today.'

'I know.'

'Was it so obvious?'

'It came out. Never mind. How do you like it?'

'I think that much depends on one's partner.'

'When does it not?'

They walked in silence the few more steps which brought them to the edge of the lake.

'Don't look back till we're round the other side and have the lake between us and the house,' said Louise; and Griselda never thought of disobeying.

'Give me your hand,' continued Louise. 'The path round the lake is wooded and much rougher. There are roots.' Griselda placed her warm right hand in Louise's chilly left one.

As soon as they had entered the trees the music from the house rapidly faded away.

'The path twists,' said Griselda.

'The Duke did not intend the shortest way between two points.'

'But the trees grow very regularly.'

'They do not grow. They were planted. This is called the Grove of the Hamamelids because every tree bears a fruit.'

Griselda did not know what Hamamelids were or had been, but the new blossom was ubiquitous, claiming alike the senses of sight, smell, hearing, and touch.

'It's an orchard.'

'No, Griselda, it's a grove. It's believed to be the only grove of its kind anywhere.'

After many swift sinuosities the path reached and crossed a wooden bridge in what appeared to be the Chinese style. The blossom, the moon, and the bridge compounded a scene very like to the Orient before one got there, thought Griselda.

'This is the stream which feeds the lake,' said Louise.

'Where's the path?' asked Griselda, looking round. Beyond the bridge it appeared simply to stop, although hitherto it had been wide enough for the two of them abreast.

'The path ends here. After they crossed this bridge, the Duke and Stephanie had no need of it; nor were others desired to follow them.'

Griselda and Louise found their way hand in hand among the trees along the edge of the lake until they rediscovered the vista.

'Now you can look back.'

Across the water and up the other half of the vista the house, normally a trifle obvious in aspect, appeared unbelievably mysterious. The misty moonlight blurred all detail, but across the line of long lighted windows the keen eyes of Griselda could see the moving figures metamorphosed into beauty by night and distance. Looking at them as they danced, it was impossible to believe they were the people Griselda had just left. At that distance she could imagine herself longing to join them.

'If it were all like that,' she said, 'we would neither of us ever wish to leave.'

Now they were out of the grove, the music just reached them.

Turning their backs on the sound and once more retreating from the populous house, they continued towards the Temple of Venus, now black before them at the other end of the vista.

'I want to see you again, Louise,' said Griselda. 'After I leave Beams.'

'We will talk about that when we get to the Temple. It may not be possible, Griselda.'

If there was any doubt, Griselda did not want to talk about it. She changed the subject.

'Do you often come to the Temple?'

'Only at night, when I can't be seen. I wear black and it is not difficult to remain unobserved.'

'Did the Duke build the Temple for Stephanie?'

'Yes. She lived in the house, but she was happiest in the Temple. She was seldom happy, poor Stephanie.'

'Like you, poor Louise.'

'Like us, poor Griselda.'

'I'm happy tonight.'

Louise did not reply.

They walked the short distance remaining in silence.

At first sight in the darkness the Temple seemed to consist of a portico, surprisingly lofty, and with Ionic columns. Up three broad steps was a chamber open to the garden and appearing semicircular in the moon-light.

'Before you enter,' said Louise, stopping Griselda at the foot of the steps, 'I think you had better put on this mask.' She produced a black velvet domino from a pocket of her jacket. Griselda was about to demur or enquire further, but thought better of it, and consented without a word to Louise putting the mask round her eyes and tying it tightly at the back of her head. Louise knew how to do this so that the wearer had no uncom-fortable sensation that the mask was about to slip.

'I like it,' said Griselda; and immediately ascended the steps.

Inside, a seat ran the length of the curved back wall, broken only by a large door in the centre, which gave access to an inner apartment of the Temple. In the middle of the floor was a huge marble bench, wide and long, and curving up at both ends into Ionic flutings. On the Bench were a number of large cushions, looking darkly purple; over which was spread a huge black cloak.

'Put it on,' said Louise. 'Put it on and sit down.'

Griselda again did as she was told. The cloak seemed the right length, and was a businesslike garment with simple black buttons, which Louise proceeded to fasten, shutting Griselda in. Griselda realized that she was now nearly invisible. For no clear reason she felt a sudden palpitating rush of excitement, bereaving her of all reas-onable thoughts.

'Now sit down.'

Griselda's normally strong legs were weak and she was glad to obey. Louise sat at the other end of the bench, her beautiful neck whiter in the smoky moonlight than her white shirt.

'What about *you*?'

'*What* about me?' Louise's tone was warm but enigmatic.

'You'll be cold.'

'Oh . . . No, I shan't be cold. But we'd better speak softly.'

'Why?' This question Griselda knew to be absurd, but her excitement was such that she had no difficulty in restraining a wild hilarity.

'It's better.' Louise paused, then again began to speak, very low. 'I've kidnapped you and brought you here so that we can make some plans. It was necessary that we could be sure of being alone, and also this is the best place.'

'The best place in which to plan?' enquired Griselda, equally softly. She had either to shout or to whisper. She felt she might easily faint.

'Yes, Griselda. If you wish to plan. I don't know whether you do or not. You said you did, but perhaps it was only the beauty of the night or a reaction from other people.'

'Will it be difficult?' Griselda's voice was barely audible.

'It will be very difficult, Griselda. I love you.'

Immediately Griselda felt completely calm; an entirely and absolutely different person. She would never be the same person again.

'I love you, Louise,' she replied in a level voice, still pitched low.

After a moment's silence, Louise said 'It's a pity that the world instead of being at our feet, has to be about our ears.'

Griselda replied: 'As I said in my bath, I know very little about the world.'

'That, though a good thing.' said Louise, 'is also a bad thing. It makes the next step difficult.'

'No,' said Griselda. 'I think it makes the next step easy. I'm so innocent that whatever the next step is, I'll take it without a second thought.'

'Will you live with me?'

'I've decided to leave home. Where else should I go?'

'We could share a loft.'

'That would be rather expensive for us. I've very little money. At least until I get a job.'

'What sort of job?'

'Lord Roller offered me something.'

'Are you going to take it?'

'If it would enable us to share a loft.'

Louise looked her in the face. Louise's smile was full of tears and anguish: she took Griselda's hand.

'The air is, I am sure, full of nightingales,' she said, 'if only we could hear them.'

'This is their night,' said Griselda. 'Tomorrow it's going to rain.'

'Does that stop them singing?'

'Unless they are very imprudent nightingales.'

'I can't see your face,' said Louise. 'It is entirely over-shadowed by a column.'

'Of course you can't. Am I not totally invisible?'

Griselda thought that when she said this Louise looked round the Temple in a way more anxious than she cared for. Then Louise said: 'For my part I have no money at all. And not only that but I hate work of any kind. I hate not to be free.'

'I've never yet had a real job,' replied Griselda. 'I am not looking forward to that particular part of it at all.'

'I wonder if Hugo would give us an allowance? He understands people like us.'

But Griselda noticed something.

'Look Louise. That door's open. It was shut when we came in.'

Louise started up. The black door interfered with the columnar pattern on the carpet of moonlight.

'And there's someone coming.'

Louise's perfume was suddenly heavy on the air. Louise stood quite upright, her back to the garden and the moon, her eyes on the open door. There were undoubtedly footsteps.

But it became clear that the steps were outside the temple. A figure appeared between the columns.

'What's going on in there?'

It was a policeman. He flashed his lamp, ineffective in the moonlight, upon Griselda's dark figure.

Louise wheeled round.

'Officer,' she said, 'please return to your fireside. No one is in need of help.'

'Sorry miss,' the policeman replied. 'I thought you might be reds.'

'You can see at a glance,' said Louise, 'that we're not.'

'Yes miss,' said the policeman.

'I don't know so much,' cried Griselda, rising to her feet. 'Look at me.' Cloaked and masked, she was the perfect operatic conspirator.

'I can see you're nothing you shouldn't be, miss,' replied the officer. 'Just like the lady said. Still we have to be careful. The whole house and garden's surrounded.'

'Surrounded by what?' asked Griselda.

'By the force, miss. We have our orders. There've been half a dozen of us on duty all the evening not a quarter of a mile from this outhouse. Spread about of course. Well, I must be getting back to them. Good night, ladies.'

At this moment the door of the inner apartment of the Temple banged shut as unaccountably as it had opened. The policeman jumped.

'I'd better have a look round.' The beam of his lamp made a dim circle on the heavy painted woodwork of the door.

'There's no one there,' said Louise. 'It often happens.'

'If you say so, miss – ' He thought for a moment, then looked at Louise searchingly. 'Quite sure, miss?'

'Quite sure, officer. I often come here at night.' Her tone was unbelievably patrician.

'Very well.'

Again he bade them Good-night. They reciprocated;

and this time he departed.

'We must go back,' said Louise. 'Soon they'll be look-ing for you.'

'Shall I leave my cloak?'

'No. When we reach the house I'll take it.'

Silently they returned upon their tracks.

They were only a few paces from the shore of the lake.

Louise remarked. 'I don't know how Stephanie is go-ing to behave about this. She is, after all, a Belgian.'

Griselda shivered inside her warm cloak, but said nothing. They entered the Grove of the Hamamelids.

'You know,' said Louise after a while, 'you know that Stephanie was at the Temple?'

'Yes,' said Griselda. 'I know.'

'It was a mistake. I didn't expect her tonight. But I knew she was there even before we got there ourselves. Her scent is the same as mine. I fear she may go after revenge. Though that would be rather absurd of her.'

'Revengeful people don't think of that.'

'Poor Stephanie! But, after all, Griselda, she *is* only a ghost.' Louise suddenly laughed very musically.

'I don't want at all to be gloomy, but do you think I shall be all right alone in the haunted room?'

Immediately she had spoken, she jumped violently. They had crossed the wooden bridge. The figure of a man was visible among the trees. His back was towards the two women and he appeared much occupied at some labour.

The women stopped for a moment; then Louise held

Griselda's hand very tightly and they advanced together. Not until they were right up to the man, did he learn of their presence.

'Good evening, miss,' he said, seeing Griselda's long cloak. 'Didn't expect any of the guests to walk this far from the house.' His voice was sombre.

'Good evening,' said Griselda.

He was leaning on a spade. He was elderly and enormous.

'For her Highness's dog.' He indicated a pit he had dug. 'The best place for 'im on the 'ole property. And if you listen you can 'ear 'em knocking up the little chap's coffin.'

Through the still moonlight night came indeed a very distant hammering.

'Poor little Fritzi,' said Griselda. Louise was lurking indistinctly among the foliage.

'Dunno about that, miss,' said the Gravedigger. 'Reckon 'e was ripe.' Lifting his spade he plunged it up to the haft into the soft black earth. Though hideous, he was still hale in the extreme.

'Good night,' said Griselda, who found the subject distasteful.

Louise drew further into the bushes.

'Goodnight, miss. I must get on with things.' He was again digging rhythmically.

Louise rejoined Griselda as if she had been her shadow. The coffin makers appeared to be working somewhere in the Grove iself.

'The policeman began it,' said Louise. 'Now the

whole garden is polluted. Let's get back as quickly as possible.' She walked faster.

'But before they came,' said Griselda, 'we were happy.' She remembered her unforgettable dream of the night before.

Worse was upon them. As they left the Grove they saw that the vista up to the house was spotted with guests. Several of the long windows had been thrown open. Through them came a certain sound, not of music Griselda realized. The speeches were afoot and most of the guests had left the ballroom. It was incredible that it was not later and the speeches over. But then she had no idea how long they had been continuing, despite Mrs Hatch's injunction of brevity. After all, she recollected, it was a turning point in history, and enthusiasm might well have carried the orators much beyond the dictates of deference to their hostess.

A man in evening dress seemed in hopeful spirit to be approaching the two lone women.

'The cloak,' said Louise brusquely. 'I shall need it to get away in.' Unbuttoning it, she had it off Griselda's and about her own shoulders before Griselda could utter the enquiry of all lovers.

'When shall I see you?'

The man in evening dress was near.

'I'll contrive. Bless you.' On the words, Louise was gone. Her black figure flitted for a second in the moon-light and had vanished.

'Good evening,' said the man. 'You look very ro-mantic. Can we go further away from the sound of the human voice?' He tried to take Griselda's arm.

'Thank you,' said Griselda. 'But I want to hear the speech.'

'Then what are you doing out here?' Frustration made his tone didactic and patronizing.

'I felt faint and needed some air.' No excuse could be too conventional for the commonplace creature.

'Minnit's hour-long pronouncement of his own right-eousness had that effect upon many of us. His objective, you know, was to cut Leech out of his broadcasting time.' Presumably the man now hoped to gain his end through general conversation. 'Pretty low trick, don't you think? Or are you perchance one of Minnit's supporters?' He smiled; and his tone again reminded Griselda of Stephenson's remark that foremost in the character of every man is the schoolmaster.

'No,' said Griselda. 'I have no politics. Will you please excuse me? I must go back to the house.'

He was so startled by the failure of his charms that, writing Griselda off as in some way peculiar, he did not even propose to escort her. Griselda could not feel that his observations boded well for the new coalition gov-ernment. But possibly he was unrepresentative. Soon she would see. She crept in at the window through which she had joined Louise in the garden.

The scene was transformed. Most of the gilt chairs were ranged in irregular rows across the dance floor in front of the speakers' platform. Though by no means all the chairs were occupied, many of the remaining audience were drooping packed together on their feet behind the backmost row. The emptiness of the chairs and the crowd standing behind them combined to make an effect of desolation. Many of the women looked bored. Many of the men looked aggressive. It was plain why Mrs Hatch had demanded brevity. Amplifiers had been lowered from the ceiling and every now and then emitted a resonant croak as the technicians dismantled the broadcasting aparatus, the end of the time allotted to the feature being long past. Each time the amplifiers croaked, Mr Leech stopped short in his flow of words and glowered momentarily upwards before resuming. Often this resulted in his losing the place in his notes.

Even without foreknowledge, it would have been obvious that the Prime Minister had been speaking for some time. His sparse colourless hair stood straight on end, his face was the colour of cheese, and he was thumping continuously when he had a hand free, in the effort to awake from slumber the long defunct interest of his auditory. 'Time presses,' he cried, 'and the festivities offered by our splendid hostess will soon once more be calling us. We have already addressed you for far too long.' Mr Leech, while one eye roamed from table-top to audience, glared momentarily with the other at Mr Minnit, who sat slumped forward upon the green baize, his head upon his arms. As with Lady Macbeth, it was impossible to deduce from Mr Minnit's eyes whether he slept or waked. He was, Griselda realized, a man of very unusual appearance. 'But,' continued Mr Leech, 'it would be improper indeed were I, for any reason whatever, to bring these remarks to an end before coming to the dire and daunting circumstances which have prompted me to begin them.' This time Mr Leech did not thump, but it made little difference.

'I have spoken,' he continued, 'of our great traditions, our unique heritage, of literature, art, and science, of our public school system, our mercantile genius, our sportsmanship, our village hostelries, our ancient monuments, Magna Carta, the noble City of London, the late terrible world conflict, our aircraft and balloons, our love of animals, and the faith we repose in our young folk. Shining through and igniting the whole splendidly coloured picture is one theme peculiar to our people alone: the theme of initial failure transmuted into ultimate success, immediate disaster into final victory.' There was an unexpected burst of cheering. Not even the prevailing need for food could wholly deaden so conditioned a reflex.

'And what has been the philosopher's stone which has wrought the miracle? Always it has been one thing only: our readiness for sacrifice.' Some of the older people nodded their agreement. 'I venture to say before you all, that no other people has so often had demanded of it so many sacrifices. As page follows page of history we read the same story: the story of final ruin averted by ruinous sacrifice. And on too many of those pages we see that the writing was in sacrificial blood. Tonight it may appear that the need is less; not for blood, but for toil and taxes and toil again, to rebuild the sinews of greatness.'

But, if so, it appeared wrongly. For when Mr Leech came to these words, there was a flash and a detonation;

and the ballroom momentarily took on the aspect of a battlefield. The Communists had contrived to throw a bomb.

A group of about a dozen classless figures had appeared from nowhere, screaming slogans and distributing leaflets. One of them even had a banner, bearing a highly coloured portrait of Engels on one side, and a quotation in German on the other (the article having been salvaged from a sympathetic foreign organization recently dissolved by the authorities).

Griselda, whose first political meeting this was, looked around terrified. Fortunately, however, there appeared to have been no loss of life, or even major injury, and what blood the historian could have drawn upon, had come mainly from noses. There was, however, a terrible smell of poor quality chemicals and burnt cardboard. The victims of the outrage were setting themselves and their chairs upon their feet, adjusting their garments and calling for redress. Those who had not been bowled over, were even more belligerent, having more available energy.

Immediately a flood of policemen armed with batons poured through the french windows, and made a series of arrests. The Communists were borne off into the scented night, twisting and biting. One of them had been standing close to Griselda, screeching out vilifications, his face that of a modern gargoyle. In the rough and tumble with the police he was knocked out and dragged from the ballroom by the legs.

'Ladies and gentleman. Supper is served.'

Mrs Hatch had resumed control. Griselda was startled by the volume of the cadaverous Brundrit's voice, as he stood at the other side of the ballroom, just inside the door from the passage.

For the most part, the guests pulled themselves together smartly, and another long queue began to form. The Communists had provided everyone with something to talk about. A small group, however, remained round the platform, and between the heads Griselda could see that both Mr Leech and Mr Minnit lay recumbent in their chairs. Recalling for the second time during the visit her slight knowledge of first-aid, she was about to go forward and offer assistance, when a handsome figure detached itself from the group and approached. It was Edwin.

'How entirely that mask becomes you.'

Griselda had forgotten. She groped at the knot behind her head.

'No. Don't take it off. Unless, of course, you wish; in which case you must allow me to assist.'

'Clearly it is no disguise.'

'Were you seeking to escape supper?'

Griselda remembered. It was appalling.

'I went out in the garden. I am dreadfully rude.'

'Not at all. The speeches, you know, were to have been *after* supper. The broadcasting arrangements were responsible for the change. It's late, but at least we've now nothing to do but enjoy ourselves.' He offered Griselda his arm. They moved towards the tail of the queue.

'What about poor Mr Leech?' Edwin's lack of concern seemed inconsistent with his usual attitude to Cabinet Ministers.

'He'll be better soon. One becomes used to these things in politics.'

'I didn't know that.'

'They're all to the good really. They bring the sediment to the surface so that it can be skimmed off instead of seeping all through society.'

'How did they get in?'

'In the BBC van. This is going to take a long time.' The queue was advancing at a pace so irksome to the ravening guests that, here and there, some of them had to recall to others the conventions of behaviour. 'If you'll excuse me for just a single minute, I'll see if something can be done.'

With a precise movement Edwin replaced Griselda's arm by her side, then disappeared out of the ballroom and into the passage, leaving her alone in the queue. Shortly afterwards he returned.

'I've made arrangements.'

Ignoring the queue, he took Griselda into a little book-lined study, where the Duke and Duchess, together with a group of elegant people Griselda had not met, were eating and drinking in privacy. Everybody was speaking German, in which language Edwin immediately gave every appearance of being word-perfect, though Griselda could not be sure. He conversed animatedly with her, every now and then throwing out a remark in German to the others; and looked after her needs with delightful punctiliousness. She was introduced to the strangers, who made her welcome in broken English, and complimented her upon her mask. The Duchess, radiant in her tight dress, kept a kindly eye upon her welfare. Though Griselda understood little of the general conversation (Edwin was discussing the year's books with her), the atmosphere was friendly and delightful. Griselda had become very hungry in the night air. She ate happily, and drank luxuriously from a glass with a hollow stem.

Suddenly the Duchess cried out in her attractive voice 'Shall we have a game?' She had been speaking German so much as a German does, and now spoke English so much as does an English-woman long married to a foreigner and resident abroad, that Griselda was at a loss to decide her nationality, whether English, German, or Ruritanian.

Conversation ceased and there were guttural cries of assent. They all seated themselves round a large polished table and the Duchess explained to Griselda the rules of an extremely simple card game. They began to play. The game was neither dependent on chance nor exigent of skill: it demanded a degree of intelligence which Griselda, in the circumstances, found perfectly appropriate and delightful. The language difficulty seemed strangely to vanish once they were all immersed, giving Griselda a dreamy illusion of brilliant communicativeness. Small sums of money continually passed, the women every now and then turning out their gay evening handbags for change. Edwin continued to ply Griselda with champagne, nor were the other players backward in drinking. From time to time Griselda wondered what was becoming of the dance, but decided that if the others were unconcerned, she would be unconcerned also. It had been obvious that the main business of the evening was over by the time she had left the ballroom.

No one had interrupted them, but, at the end of a round, suddenly one of the men, a fair youth, resembling Lohengrin, said something in German, and, rising, locked the door. Several of the women (whose ages were unusually disparate), thereupon embarked on motions apparently preliminary to removing their clothes.

Griselda was a little drunk, but not too drunk to observe that her new friends seemed unanimously to turn to some new pursuit upon a word from one of them.

The women were wearing little and the present process could not last long. Almost before it started, however, the Duchess realized that Griselda, as a stranger among them and of a different nation from the majority, might wish to leave. Probably the young man, in making his proposal, had forgotten about her. But at a word, he unlocked the door, they all ceremoniously bade her Good-night, and Edwin escorted her into the hall. The door shut behind them.

Outside the little room it was cool and quiet. Griselda found that all the other guests had apparently departed.

'I expect,' said Edwin, 'that you must be ready for bed. Or can I do anything further?'

'Nothing, thank you,' said Griselda, drowsy with drink. 'You have been really very kind to me. I enjoyed the Duchess's card game.'

'I think the others have gone up already.' Edwin and Griselda were drifting towards the staircase.

'I am sure they have. Good night. And thank you again.'

'Good night, Griselda.' It was obvious that, in the most considerate possible way, he wished to be rid of her. She ascended.

Even at this distance the air was loaded with the smell of the banked carnations in the ballroom. It had long since overpowered the smell of cordite.

XI

Griselda did not again see or hear of Louise until the following evening. It was a desert of time; and a desert with few oases. However, she had happy thoughts and bright, vague prospects: things often preferable to the presence of the being who inspires them.

Back in her room she felt tired and contented, though her mask would not slip over the top of her head and the untying of the knot proved tedious. In the end, however, the labour was accomplished and the velvet strip lay on the dressing-table before her, loading the air with the smell of Louise. Griselda sat resting her arms, looking at the mask, and thinking. How and when, she wondered, would the late guests return to their homes? How had Edwin, although still quite young, achieved welcome ingress into every single one of the world's innumerable diverse sodalities? Was Mr Leech alive or dead? What would become of her and Louise, once they had left Beams? Louise's scent wafted strongly to her brain: more strongly than the faint vapours from the mask could account for. Either it was Stephanie; or it was Griselda's first experience of a lover's hallucination of the sense of smell. The memory of her ecstacy in the garden swept even fear from her.

She put the mask in a drawer and soon she was in

bed. Immediately she slept. There was no other sign of Stephanie; and the room and the night were quiet. Griselda dreamed of a posse of policemen dancing rapturously with the late guests.

In the morning it was again raining. In the muddy light water slapped against the glass of the windows in frequent protracted spasms. Griselda looked at the wrist-watch on the table beside her bed. Despite appearances, it was half-past nine. There was no evidence that she had been called, but clearly it was time to rise. She lay for a moment remembering her happiness. She saw that there was a puddle on the carpet. The rain had been entering for hours through the window she had carefully opened the night before.

She shut the window and dressed. She put on the clothes in which she had arrived, because she imagined that Louise would prefer them to the only other day clothes she had, those she had worn the day before. The silk blouse and linen skirt, though white and black respectively, which Griselda was sure would be taken as progress in the right direction, were far from warm. It was remarkable that such a morning could follow such a night. But the weather would surely deter Mrs Hatch from the proposed walk of which Griselda retained an indistinct though menacing recollection. Griselda decided to put appearance before comfort for as long as the circulation of her blood permitted. She was sure that Louise would approve of this.

Exactly as on the previous morning, Mrs Hatch was seated at the breakfast table alone. She wore the same grey sweater. She was talking in an unusually low voice to Brundrit and Monk, both of whom were stooping towards her, one on each side of her chair.

'Excellent,' said Mrs Hatch, as Griselda entered. 'You're first again. Sit down and take some eggs.' She went on murmuring to her retainers. Griselda could catch only parts of sentences and thought it would be impolite to occupy her former breakfast seat next to her hostess. Taking two eggs, she proceeded towards the other end of the table.

The conference ended with the retainers straightening up and walking away, one on each side of the long table, looking remarkably gloomy, which came easily to Brundrit, but to Monk only with effort.

'Whatever happens,' called Mrs Hatch in her usual clear tones, 'I cannot be kept hanging about in the house after half-past-eleven. Everybody concerned must clearly realize that this is Sunday.' It was a fact Griselda had forgotten. Tomorrow she was to return.

'I perfectly understand, madam,' said Brundrit, in his reverberating croak. 'We shall see to it that everyone is apprised.'

'Do,' said Mrs Hatch. They departed. The room, for the first time in Griselda's experience, was without a domestic to assist with the eating.

'Good morning, Griselda,' continued Mrs Hatch. 'I should have said that before. Please forgive me and have some cocoa.'

'Good morning, Mrs Hatch.'

'You are somewhat distant.'

Griselda started; then realized that the allusion was spatial.

'Shall I move?'

'I think that would be better. Come and sit next to me, as you did yesterday, and tell me what you thought about the dance. Politics apart, I fancy everything went like a circus, do not you?' Griselda was transporting two eggs, one of them opened and liquid, a plate bearing a slice of bread and butter, and a heavy bowl of cocoa. Before she had time effectively to reply Mrs Hatch continued: 'You're not very appropriately dressed. The clothes you were wearing yesterday would have been more suitable. You don't mind my speaking practically? Your Mother wouldn't be pleased with me if you were to go home with a streaming cold after our walk.'

Griselda looked at the windows. A curtain of water cataracted down the glass, completely isolating the room from the grey world outside.

'Are we walking in weather like this?'

Seated next to her hostess, Griselda saw that today Mrs Hatch was wearing a pair of waterproof trousers from Burberry's and knew that the game was up.

'You won't take any harm if you wrap up, and if you've never walked in the rain you should take this opportunity of making a start. It's enjoyable. But naturally you must not come if you would prefer not to.' Mrs Hatch said this perfectly kindly, and without any intent to shame; and Griselda responded accordingly. She never had walked in the rain except reluctantly, uncomfortably, and under the stress of need; but at Beams she had already liked a number of things which she had not thought to like or had never liked before.

'I'll come if I can borrow some suitable clothes. When do we start?'

'I usually start at half-past ten. But today we're burying Odile's dog first. I've just been settling the arrangements with Brundrit and Monk. I don't think we'll get away much before an hour after the proper time. Still we must think of Odile's feelings. We don't usually call our guests on Sunday. As I'm not prepared to stay at home and entertain them, I think it's only fair to let them sleep if they can. But today everyone's coming to the ceremony. Except, unfortunately, Austin Barnes, who has been really not at all himself after last night's incident. I have reluctantly come to the conclusion that Austin is no longer the man he was. It's a pity, because otherwise he'd be coming with us. Many's the hard tramp I've taken with Austin Barnes during the last thirty years. I cannot believe he'll be much further use to the country if he's really leaving me to go alone.' Mrs Hatch seemed genuinely upset by the Cabinet Minister's defection.

'I expect he's run down,' said Griselda sympathetically. 'Perhaps he's been in office too long.'

'I'm very fond of Austin,' replied Mrs Hatch after a moment's thought, and gulping a draught of cocoa. 'I've always been his inspiration, I believe; and through him I've inspired the course of events from time to time. Otherwise I prefer the company of women, in the main. They both feel more and have more common sense. So you gain both ways.'

Yet again Griselda felt herself blushing; this time darkly and hatefully.

'Though it's rarely enough I find myself having anything much in common with anybody. Another egg?'

'No thank you. I've had enough.' But suddenly Mrs Hatch's character had been enlightened to Griselda, far beyond anything Mrs Hatch had actually said; and Griselda, to her surprise, did not dislike what she saw. It had been the same with some others at Beams, she realized. The dreadfulness of people was possibly a product not only of their isolation, but also of their community and likeness to one another. Griselda, while pitying and even liking Mrs Hatch, felt curiously superior to her.

No one else appeared for breakfast.

'I'll lend you a waterproof. A proper one,' said Mrs Hatch, as she wiped her mouth. 'I'll send Mullet. The funeral's arranged for eleven. In the shrubbery down by the large pond. Among the fruit trees. You'd better meet me in the hall, and we'll go together.'

It was sad to miss a possible chance of seeing Louise. But in a short time Mullet appeared in Griselda's room with an enormous mackintosh and a pair of dark brown boots lacing to the knee.

'Mrs Hatch says will you try these for size.'

Griselda inserted her feet.

'Mrs Hatch keeps all sizes for her Sunday walkers. But she's good at guessing people's feet.'

'They fit perfectly.'

'Will I help you lace them?'

'I'll be lacing all day if you don't.'

The boots were wonderfully warm. They supported Griselda's calves in a manner which was new and unbelievably comfortable. She donned the vast mackintosh and drew the hood over her head.

Mrs Hatch awaited her in the hall, wearing a tunic and beret matching her trousers. Most of the other guests were also assembled, unbreakfasted and varyingly ill-prepared against the climate. George Goss, who apparently had a really dangerous hangover, wore a shaggy dingy ulster, the bottom edge of which varied greatly in its distance from the ground. Pamela wore an allegedly protective garment more calculated to seduce the eye than to resist the rainfall. Even Mr Leech was there, looking little worse than usual. There was a group of servants attired like refugees, and no more enlivened by the project before them than anybody else. Only the Duke and Duchess were missing.

'Shall I go up and offer a word of encouragement?' asked Edwin.

But as he spoke the bereaved couple appeared at the head of the staircase, contained in elegant waterproofs of Continental cut. The Duchess wore a small black velvet hat with a large black feather, a purple silk mackintosh and black Russian boots. A veil was drawn tightly across her face and knotted behind her head. Through it her features appeared completely white and her eyes very large. Altogether she looked most striking. Grislda recalled her very different aspect on the last occasion she had seen her. Clearly the Duchess responded with a whole heart to all life's different occasions, however contrarily they might succeed one another. The Duke carried a cherrywood box under his left arm, presumably containing the deceased.

'It will be a shorter walk in the rain for those of us who dislike getting wet, if we go through the ballroom,' said Mrs Hatch in a loud firm voice before the Duke and Duchess had reached the bottom of the staircase. Possibly she wished to save her guests from having to grope for further unconvincing commiserations. She began to marshall the cortège.

'Griselda and I will lead the way. Edwin and Pamela had better come next. Then will you, Mr Leech, follow with George? Then Gottfried and Odile. The rest of you can follow after. Would you like Monk to carry Fritzi?'

'Thank you, Melanie. He is light as feathers.'

'Very well. Then I think we had better go at once.'

They set off down the passage to the ballroom, their mackintoshes rustling in the silence, otherwise broken only by George Goss's heavy breathing. Griselda noticed that the Prime Minister was carrying a club-like walking stick. In the ballroom, which now looked depressing in the extreme, the Duchess, who was bearing up wonderfully, broke step and, crossing to the platform occupied the night before by the band, bore back a vast armful of carnations, not as fresh as they had been but still far from dead, which she proceeded to carry in the little procession like a prima donna, her head sunk among the petals. Mrs Hatch had opened one of the french windows, and the party entered the garden.

It was indeed a dispiriting day: one on which it was equally difficult to believe that things had ever been otherwise or that they would ever be otherwise again. The party advanced up the soaking wet lawn and entered the group of trees. Griselda was surprised that the distance was not greater before they reached a large hole, surrounded with adhesive black earth rapidly turning to mud, beside which stood her elderly gravedigger of the night before, leaning on his enormous spade.

'Is everything prepared, Hammersmith?' enquired Mrs Hatch.

'Ready it is, mum,' replied Hammersmith. 'Ready since midnight it's been. Ready and waitin' for yer.'

'Never mind about that now. Though it's always best to do things in good time, of course.' She addressed the others. 'There's going to be a short ceremony. Will you all please gather round the grave? You too, Hammersmith. Don't you go.'

Griselda, encased against the elements, glanced round her fellow guests. Pamela's teeth were chattering rather audibly. George Goss, who had augmented his horrible ulster with an antique cloth cap, resembled a dyspeptic bison. Mr Leech wore an expression of extreme resignation. Edwin looked as if his mind were on other things. Mrs Hatch, impervious to the rain and efficient as ever, looked trim and attractive by contrast with the rest. The aspect of the Duke and Duchess, as chief mourners, was such as to touch the heart of any statue. The aspect of Hammersmith, his vast muscles outlined by his soaking shirt, his red-brown eyes glaring at the coffin, was likely to unman any young woman less resolute than Griselda in her new boots.

'Proceed,' said Mrs Hatch. Griselda, whose Mother went regularly to church, gravely doubted the canonicity of the whole affair.

The Duke pulled his wide-brimmed homburg hat further over his eyes and made a short speech. On his wife's behalf he thanked them all for their attendance and even for their existence. When setting out for a weekend of joy with a lady beloved by all of them, their dear Melanie, they were unlikely to have foreseen an occasion to tragic as the present, and made so much worse by the weather. (At this point Mr Leech was seized with a spasm of sneezing, which continued to the end of the Duke's remarks. He sneezed inefficiently; giving on each occasion the effect of unsuccessfully attempted suppression leading to rising inner dementia.) Though only a dog the one they mourned was as dear to those who loved him as any prodigal son. He had been with them eleven years and now he was gone away. (Here Griselda heard the terrifying Hammersmith vigorously expectorate.) Where he had gone or whether dogs had souls like the rest of them, it was useless to speculate. In gratitude to them all for their sympàthy, however, in particular to their dear Melanie for her gift of so sentimental a resting place, he had prepared a poem, such being the custom of his country, which he would like to read to them. He had to apologize for the poem being in German, but his Muse, not very ready even in her native tongue, was dumb in another. He hoped that most of them would have enough German at least to follow the general theme; and that the rest would appreciate that he was speaking from the heart. Here was the poem.

The Duke produced a fair-sized wad of paper from the pocket of his waterproof, and, at a sign from Mrs Hatch, Monk raised an umbrella. Pamela, who disliked poetry, had seated herself upon a wheelbarrow, where she rocked backwards and forwards quietly moaning. George Goss simply walked off towards the house. Shortly they all heard him being sick among the bushes. The Duke took a step forward as from a line of Imperial Guards; Monk followed him with the umbrella; and the Duke began. Fortunately Mr Leech had stopped sneezing, though he was beginning to look very wet.

Before the poem was far advanced, indeed during the first five minutes, the Duchess was weeping fluently; and by the time the final antistrophe was due, she was in an appalling state of dampness, though Griselda had been offering what comfort she could. Edwin, who clearly appreciated every word and nuance of the poem, listened throughout alertly, like one assessing its merits in a competition. Mrs Hatch stood as to the National Anthem. The Duke read remarkably well, in full and expressive accents of passion and woe. Griselda wondered whether he too had been trained by Moissi. At the end there was an extremely long silence, though Pamela could be heard grunting miserably in the rear. The heavy rain was making the vapours rise from the newly strewn manure.

Now it was time for the committal. The Duke clicked his heels and passed the coffin to Edwin, who, his features distraught with fellow feeling, transferred it to Hammersmith. The hole was very much to big (it was impossible to resist the idea that Hammersmith had postulated some larger occupant); and had been filling for hours with surface water. Before Mrs Hatch could stop him, however, Hammersmith had hurled the coffin into the grave, splashing and muddying the mourners from their hats to their shoes; and had raised his left arm, bare from the bole-like-elbow, towards the sky in a cosmic Niebelungenliedlike gesture. Instantly there was a thunderous salute, as a maroon, released at the signal by the garden boy (hidden behind some laurels for the purpose), tore apart the hopeless clouds until it vanished into the empyrean. Hammersmith's face, neck, and shirt had been plastered with yellow subsoil from the grave, making him look more primeval than ever; but as Griselda averted her eyes, she saw that Mr Leech had fainted. He was not so used to loud bangs as Edwin the night before had implied.

They returned to the house: Edwin carrying Pamela in his arms: and Mrs Hatch and the Duke bearing Mr Leech (fortunately a lightweight) between them, as Mrs Hatch considered that Hammersmith had better fill in the vast grave before someone fell into it and damaged himself. The Duchess, distinctly more buoyant now that all was over, scattered the carnations in a wide circle round Fritzi's resting place; to which Hammersmith returned a grimly abrupt acknowledgement, his rufus eyes rolling, his ropey muscles extending and contracting all over him as he shovelled.

'Now that little Fritzi has been laid to rest, can we not once more be gay?' enquired the Duchess in her curious interglossal accent. It was nearly 11.30. Edwin had carried Pamela upstairs; and Mr Leech, his sensibilities revived by Monk, sat quietly in a corner drinking, at his own request, a tumbler of warm water laced with a dessertspoonful of brandy.

Mrs Hatch was seen to hesitate.

'I usually tramp until dusk,' she said, 'But today for your sake, Odile, I shall make an exception. I shall return for a late luncheon, if all of you are prepared to wait, and after luncheon we'll play games. If that is agreed, perhaps, Odile, you'd be so good as to order luncheon for 2.15. Mr Leech had better only have arrowroot. Come, Griselda; let us return to our elements.'

Though Mrs Hatch walked very fast, Griselda, used to long lonely walks almost since childhood (for conditions at home had tended both to drive her afield and to compel her to solitude), was perfectly able to keep pace with her. Mrs Hatch, moreover, had been right about walking in the rain. A proper costume made all the difference (just as Louise had said). Whatever else Griselda thought of her hostess, she would always owe to her the introduction to a new pleasure, which was more than was usually owed to anyone. As they walk through the lanes (some of them in process of development into the avenues of a new housing estate),

Mrs Hatch cross-examined Griselda about her life and Griselda schemed to find out more about Mrs Hatch. Neither was particularly successful, but each returned home with increased respect for the other, and a glow of joyous struggle. Griselda re-entered the house warm and dry, hungry and happy; also muddy to the tops of her boots, and healthy to the roots of her hair. She felt equal to anything: to Louise's love; or, contrariwise, even to an afternoon of organized playfulness.

On the doorstep they met George Goss, still wearing his horrid blanket and untidy bonnet, but green as a chameleon on a faded billiard-table.

'I say, Melanie, will there be a chemist in Hodley who's open on Sunday?'

Mrs Hatch, pushing out health and unbuttoning her tunic, took in the seedy figure of her distinguished guest.

'Nonsense, George, you don't want a chemist. Six or seven mugs of cold water will flush you much more cleanly. Besides how are you going to reach Hodley? If you walk it, you won't need any other remedy.'

George Goss shuddered all over. Then he said 'I was going in Leech's car.'

'I didn't know that Leech was leaving us?'

'Cabinet Meeting or something. As if I care. But his car's due any minute.' He spoke quasi-sotto-voce.

Lurking about the hall were four strange doughty-looking men in ready-made tweeds. Mr Leech, wearing an overcoat and hat of the type favoured by important public figures, was seated on a hard chair in their midst, his official despatch-case, his botanical vade-mecum, and a large Gladstone bag on the floor at his feet. As Mrs Hatch entered, he rose and came towards her, looking his most imposing.

'It is as Mr Goss says, Mrs Hatch. My hand is immediately and unexpectedly needed on the rudder of state. Now that we are subject to a Coalition, such sudden calls must, I daresay, be expected of us all.'

'Who are these men?' asked Mrs Hatch in a loud undertone.

'A foolish precaution deemed necessary by our new Home Secretary,' replied Mr Leech. 'One of Minnit's people, as you will recall. For my own part I should not only have preferred to take my chance, but should have insisted upon doing so. But it is necessary to tread softly in these early days, so I have subdued my natural inclinations.' None the less, Griselda thought, the Prime Minister appeared distinctly to have gathered confidence from some source or other.

'What about lunch before you go? Your arrowroot? After your misadventure, it would hardly be prudent to travel underfed.'

'Thank you, Brundrit was good enough to lay me out some brawn,' replied the Prime Minister a little stiffly, 'and I helped myself to a couple of Abernethy biscuits. I am too old a campaigner, you know, to require more.'

A large black car had driven up outside. It was visible through the open front door. A footman dismounted and stood in the doorway holding a camel-hair rug. Griselda noticed that he carried two pistols in holsters attached to his belt. The pistols were large and old-fashioned, and made him look like a pirate.

'I'm sorry you have to leave so suddenly,' said Mrs Hatch, 'but Griselda and I will see you off. As for you, George, you'd better go and lie down.'

'Lying down only makes me vomit,' said George. 'I'd have you know I've a headache.'

'Griselda knows about those things and may be able to help you,' said Mrs Hatch. 'All in good time. Do you think you have everything, Mr Leech?'

Griselda liked as little as ever the look on George Goss's face; and she turned to bid the Prime Minister adieu, Mr Leech had made for the door with an unusually determined step, almost amounting, indeed, to a stride. In many ways he seemed a changed man. His henchmen had taken up positions from which the entire scene could instantly be raked with gun-fire.

'Good-bye,' said Mr Leech, smiling gravely. 'And thank you. I know nowhere which offers such peace as the rose garden at Beams.'

'My roses are sensible of your devotion, Mr Leech.' At this point Griselda noticed the barrel of a musket projecting from the rear window of the Daimler.

'It is ever and again to the ample silent things of life that we return for renewal,' continued Mr Leech, his eye searching the watery clouds from under the brim of his important-looking hat. 'But too soon we are recalled by the reveille of duty.' A few big drops of rain fell from his hat on to the astrakhan of his lapels.

'Too soon, indeed,' replied Mrs Hatch. She began to

rebutton her tunic. There seemed no knowing how long this might continue.

Griselda realized that she had greatly grown since she had first set eyes on Mr Leech two days before.

'Good-bye,' said Mr Leech again, suddenly pulling himself together and smartly returning the chauffeur's salute. 'Good-bye, Miss de Reptonville.' Griselda remembered that success in public life is dependent upon remembering people's names.

'Good-bye, Mr Leech.'

The Prime Minister set aside the proffered camel-hair rug.

'Thank you, no. Not on this occasion.' The atmosphere was heavy with the crisis and the coalition as well as with the damp.

Mr Leech took his place beside the musket: the footman beside the driver. There was a moment's uncertain silence as the four bodyguards whispered among themselves, in the manner of Becket's murderers. Then one of them without a word opened the car door and, seating himself next to Mr Leech, manned the lethal object. He fiddled about with the mechanism like a wood-wind player tuning his instrument. The weapon still pointed directly at Griselda.

In the moment the car started Mrs Hatch cried out 'What shall I do about Austin Barnes?'

It was no good. Already the Prime Minister's eyelids were drooping into slumber. Mr Leech had been having a strenuous time of it.

'It's all very well, but what *am* I to do about Austin?'

Mrs Hatch seemed seriously to be seeking Griselda's advice.

'Everything's in order, Mrs Hatch,' said Edwin's voice in the doorway. 'I deeply regret to say that Austin Barnes has felt it his duty to offer the Prime Minister his resignation.' The moist air wafted the distinctive perfume of Pamela, heavy on Edwin's black suit, the very essence of fashionable mourning.

'Resigned?' It was a cry from Mrs Hatch's heart.

'Quite resigned.'

'I must go to him.'

'I think that would be best. The Prime Minister asked me to tell you after he had gone; and to apologize on his behalf for his inability to tell you himself. He was sure you would understand that the emotion involved was too much for him at the present time.'

Without a word, Mrs Hatch had re-entered the house.

'Permit me to escort you.' Edwin, who had not risked getting wet a second time in the same morning, also disappeared into the gloom within. The three surviving murderers had previously likewise vanished, their grim countenances set for food from Mrs Hatch's groaning granaries.

Griselda was left by herself waiting for luncheon in the rain she had learnt to love. Before going in, she put back her hood and raised her face towards the discouraging heavens. She was startled to see the head and shoulders of Louise projecting from an upstairs window. She was wearing a perfectly white mackintosh. There was no knowing how long she had been there. She threw Griselda a kiss with one hand and a letter with the other. Then she withdrew indoors, shutting the sash window with a marked slam.

Overwhelmed, Griselda looked at the letter. On a thick sheet of deckle-edged hand-made writing paper, it had been folded and sealed, in the fashion of the days before Sir Rowland Hill, with a big medallion of bright yellow wax. It was superscribed simply 'Griselda' in black ink and a large well-proportioned hand artistically simplified. Letting the heavy rain uncurl her hair, Griselda split the seal and unfolded the letter. In such a hand there was not room for many words upon a single side of a sheet of hand-made paper.

'Never forget, dear dove, that the sky into which you soar is full of falcons and that falcons fly higher than doves. As I listen, your heart is softening towards the falcons. Beware of the falcons! They not only kill: they disfigure. Their nests are matted with blood. The streets and fields are filled with bodies whose vitals the falcons have eaten. The falcons eat only the hearts, the brains, and the livers of their prey; whom, bored, they then return, like bottles, Empty. The Empties clutter our lives: they break easily, and becoming worthless become also dangerous.'

The letter ended with a single tender sentence which made Griselda very happy. Though dated it was unsigned. Raindrops, like tears, were beginning to spoil it. Griselda put it into a pocket of her borrowed mackintosh.

'We are waiting.'

Mrs Hatch had reappeared in the doorway. Some time must have passed, for she had changed into a skirt. Griselda, though extremely hungry after her walk, had forgotton about luncheon. There was no knowing how long Mrs Hatch had been standing there.

'I'm so sorry. You've taught me to enjoy rain. I've been enjoying it.'

She thought that Mrs Hatch's expression was equivocal and, for some reason, not very likeable.

'You need to take proper precautions.' Griselda raised her hand to her head and realized that her hair had become very wet. 'If you don't mind us starting to eat without you, I think you'd better go upstairs and dry yourself.'

Griselda entered the house. She opened the collar of her mackintosh. 'How is Mr Barnes?'

Mrs Hatch glanced at her sharply. 'I'm finished with Austin Barnes.' Something was obviously wrong with her: and presumably this was it.

Griselda wondered what to say.

'One of your oldest friends? Surely not?'

'Old and new, the world's much of a piece,' replied Mrs Hatch with intense bitterness. She turned from Griselda and entered the dining-room.

Upstairs, Griselda removed the heavy mackintosh and suspended it in the bathroom to drip and dry. After hours of it, she felt so underclad without it that she more clearly understood how little related to any consideration of utility is the quantity of clothes people wear. She towelled her short curly hair into a bewitching disarray. She put on a red pullover. She would have liked to remove her boots, but time pressed.

She descended to an extremely late luncheon. From inside George Goss's bedroom came an intermittent soft mooing as of a cow in her last labour before retirement from maternity. Griselda realized that her period of communion with the rainfall had among other things spared her from having to hold George Goss's sick head and necessary basin.

The party for luncheon was indeed depleted, in spirit more than in number. George Goss and Mr Leech were absent: and Pamela should have been, for she had contrived to contract a most unpleasant cold. Despite this malady and the inappropriate weather, she had refused in any way to wrap up, but sat sniffing and sneezing in a delicate eau-de-nil crepe-de-chine blouse, sleeveless and conspicuously open at the throat. It was noticeable that Mrs Hatch had apparently now washed her hands of all responsibility for Pamela's welfare and happiness. Even Edwin had seated himself as far as possible from the source of infection, where he was discoursing, as Griselda entered, upon the subject of the main item in the next St James's News-Letter.

'We all found ourselves in complete agreement,' said Edwin, 'that an attempt must be made – on a world scale, needless to say – to vitalize the inner life of the working man. Happily the means came at once to hand. That very same evening I spoke of the need to the wife of a certain Polish Prince, a woman having great wealth of her own – invested outside Poland, of course: who at once suggested that the answer was a film, but of an entirely new type, not a specifically religious film, you understand, but a film aiming in the same general direction though stated in contemporary terms, a film that would really penetrate through the top-dressing of propaganda and take root in the wholesome soil beneath.'

'So to speak, a non-religious religious film?' suggested the Duchess helpfully.

Mrs Hatch, Griselda noticed, was really looking very sour indeed: almost baleful.

'You might, I suppose, put it like that,' said Edwin rather doubtfully. 'At least in sophisticated society such as this. Anyway, the Princess (I am sorry I cannot tell you her name, but she particularly wishes to remain entirely nameless in this matter, which she conceives in the light of a high spiritual duty), the Princess is not only prepared to arrange finance for the whole project, but actually has access to an entirely suitable director for the film, a man who treats the cinema almost as if it were a true medium for art. The Princess has assisted in the birth of many of his past productions, and has often been very close to him in a number of different ways. She told me that the two of them together could do things that neither of them could do apart. It is true that the man's a Galician Jew, but the Princess says he has more of the real thing in him than any other Christian she's ever met. And, after all, it's her money,' concluded Edwin, descending to the world of fact.

The trouble was that no one seemed sufficiently interested, though the Duke and Duchess followed up politely.

'Who is he?' enquired Pamela, the resonating chambers of her (never very resonant) voice clotted with mucus.

'I beg you pardon?' enquired Edwin courteously.

'The director. What's his name? Or is that a whimsey little secret too?' Pamela was unused to not being answered first time.

'The director's name is not actually a secret, but I doubt whether any of you would know it.'

'Thought he was world famous,' persisted Pamela spitefully. Probably she had by now something against Edwin. She added with unwelcome acumen: 'How's he to reach the masses now if he hasn't done it already?'

'I don't think I actually described him as world-famous: only in certain informed circles.' It was the first time Griselda had ever seen Edwin reduced to the defensive. His entire narrative, moreover, seemed to her less impressive than some of its glittering predecessors.

'I see,' said Pamela, 'high hat. Tell your Princess she'd do better with Punch and Judy. More to remould society, I mean, if that's the idea, as you say it is.' Pamela seemed to doubt whether it was the idea. She tried to sniff, but her nose was so blocked that she failed to do so, which was much more distressing than even success would have been. The zymosis which choked her tubes seemed, none the less, somehow to have cleared her brain. She applied a minute hard ball of a handkerchief and began with the other hand to release drops from a bottle of bitters on to her pancake.

Griselda noticed that Mrs Hatch was barely even eating.

Real trouble broke out only when Brundrit brought in a large dish of medlars.

The trouble was that no one seemed to want medlars: no one except perhaps Mrs Hatch, and even she, like most people in such cases, seemed more concerned that the others should like medlars than happy that she liked them herself. She implied, with the faintest undertone of pugnacity, that these particular medlars had been preserved in exactly the recommended state of decomposition since the previous autumn, an undertaking involving much skill and difficulty, of which the present company were privileged to enjoy the benefit.

To begin with, the Duke and Duchess did not know what medlars were, and fogged themselves worse and worse with obscure Germanic polysyllables, cooing together like puzzled budgerigars. Then Edwin seemed afraid that the deliquescent fibres would damage his suit. And Griselda had experienced medlars in the past.

Pamela merely said 'They look rotten.'

The Duke, speaking German, made some reference to their smell.

'Not rotten at all,' said Mrs Hatch. 'The fruit is in the finest possible condition for eating. It is properly bletted.'

'What is bletted, Melanie?' asked the Duchess.

'Medlars cannot be eaten, Odile, until they mature. Then they are the most delicious of all fruit. Try one and see for yourself.'

The Duke and Duchess took one medlar each.

'Griselda?'

'No thank you.'

'Don't be narrow. Have you any first-hand experience of medlars?' This question clearly, in the grammarians' phrase, expected the answer No.

'Yes. I'm afraid I don't like them.'

'Then you're a silly girl. Pamela.'

'I'm only allowed to eat food which is perfectly fresh.'

'What about you, Edwin? You may use the table implements if you wish to preserve your appearance.'

'Please excuse me on this occasion, Mrs Hatch. I always lunch very lightly, you know. Usually only a single quail brought to my office from the Express Dairy or somewhere like that.' Edwin had begun to doubt whether the proposed film would regenerate the proletariat after all. This made even so perfectly balanced a man as Edwin a little standoffish. Perceiving the fact, Griselda wanted to restore his confidence, as he was so much more agreeable when confident.

But before she could think of anything to say, the Duke and Duchess had begun to misbehave. The re-arrangement of the table consequent upon the departure of Mr Leech, the absence of George Goss, and the reluctance of Edwin to risk contracting a nasty cold, had brought the Duke and Duchess against all custom to adjoining seats: and the difficulty they had experienced in identifying the strange foodstuff in the Duke's language, had amplified into intermittent and giggling exchanges of pleasantries in German. Suddenly the Duke said something very quickly to his wife under his breath; and the two of them burst into explosions of unsuitable mirth. They tilted back their chairs, roared at the ceiling, nudged one another, and gasped out confirmations of the joke which were strangled by new attacks of laughter beyond all control. It was plain what they thought of medlars, even when properly bletted.

Mrs Hatch said nothing at all, but piled up a heap of medlars on her plate, and began to devour them displaying much more appetite than earlier in the meal, and sucking rather noisily.

The Duke and Duchess went on laughing in an uncontrolled Germanic way. At first they were oblivious of their isolation; then suddenly they became over-sensitive to it and began long-windedly to apologize. The single medlars, still almost intact, were evidence of their good intentions.

'It was something of which Gottfried said they reminded him.' concluded the Duchess not very happily: especially as they then began both to laugh again.

'I was spending a night once inside the Great Pyramid,' began Edwin. He had overheard and understood the Duke's simile and was fearful of its disclosure. 'We had nothing to eat but dates. Not the artificially nurtured Tunis dates we buy in boxes, but the real native dates, small and packed into blocks and not very clean. The dogs, you know. Not to mention the heat and the native children. We had a little camel's milk too in a gourd. It would have been most unwise to introduce any

Western food, as we were entirely in the power of the group we had gone to meet.'

'Was it a pleasant meeting?' asked Griselda.

'Very profitable indeed. It enabled me precisely to foretell the date of the rebuilding of the Temple.'

'Which Temple?'

'The Temple of Jerusalem. As you probably know, I adhere to British-Israel. It is to my mind the only conceivable explanation of modern British history. We are mere tools.'

'Shall I serve coffee, madam?' asked Monk. Mrs Hatch who was still silently assimilating the putrescent-looking heap, merely nodded.

Griselda tried to talk intelligently about the Glastonbury Thorn and to discuss the question of whether or not the Prophet Jeremiah was buried on an island off the coast of Scotland, only to be reborn as General Booth; but it was difficult going. Edwin, naturally, was eager and convincing, politely countering possible objections and clarifying dark places; but the Duke and Duchess had sunk into a state of guilty abashment, quite unlike their usual mood, and sat drinking cup after cup of café au lait and wringing their hands under the tablecloth; while Mrs Hatch continued simply to sulk. She had been so agreeable on and before their walk that Griselda was unable fully to understand what was the matter with her, though Austin Barnes, shaker of nations and breaker of lives, almost certainly had something to do with it, she supposed.

Ultimately the house party fell to pieces like the ten

little nigger boys. Two were already missing. Then, as Edwin was explaining the mystical status of the Union Jack, Pamela abruptly remarked that her Father always insisted upon her going straight home when she was ill, and proceeded upstairs to pack, Mrs Hatch offering singularly little resistance. Five minutes later, by which time Edwin had arrived at the Biblical appointment of the site of Balmoral Castle, the Duchess, with exquisite anguish, observed that if there were to be no games in which all of them could join, she and Gottfried would like to retire for their usual afternoon rest, and departed easing the belt of her dress (she was a little flushed) and followed by her husband hard on her heels. Again Mrs Hatch stonily acquiesced, and sat glaring at the épergne. Suddenly Edwin stopped in the middle of sentence and, exclaiming 'The Aga Khan. I must, if you will forgive me,' hastened away. 'I wonder if the lines to that part of India are busy at this hour?' he enquired absently as he carefully closed the door.

Left alone with Griselda, Mrs Hatch was clearly about to say something of the utmost significance. Her mien was almost frightening with import. But Monk entered and asked if he could clear; and once more Mrs Hatch wearily acquiesced.

'Shall Stainer serve tea, ma'am? It's the usual time.'

'Do you want any tea, Griselda?'

'Yes, please,' said Griselda stoutly. 'If I could first re-move your boots.'

'Remove what you like,' said Mrs Hatch; then, ad-dressing Monk, added 'Tea for Miss de Reptonville. And

I suppose we may have visitors. Tea for five or six. Nothing for me.'

Griselda began to realize that few things are so important in any kind of shared life with the moods of the person it is shared with. Mrs Hatch was being quite unlike herself. Griselda recalled Louise's words about the difficulty of living with anyone, and that even Louise had shown signs of a moodiness which would doubtless wax on longer and less desperate acquaintanceship.

To judge by her past experience, she suspected that so many medlars had made matters worse by giving Mrs Hatch colic.

It took Griselda twenty minutes to remove the boots, and to oil and part her hair; and when she again descended it was to find that Mrs Hatch's single visitor that Sunday had arrived, a certain Mrs Cramp, the wife of a neighbouring landowner. It was still raining hard.

'Bitches,' cried out Mrs Cramp in a loud harsh voice like a police whistle, 'have two or three times the staying power of dogs. If not more.'

A fire had been lighted and the scene offered all the cosiness of an English country house at Sunday teatime; though none of the other guests seemed eager to partake. Griselda soon learnt that Pamela had already left without saying Goodbye to anyone, even to her hostess. In the end, however, George Goss clumped down the stairs.

'Think I've thrown up the worst by now, Melanie,' he announced. But he seemed too dispirited even to pester Griselda. He sat by himself crumbling a lump of the famous cake and casting round the furniture for the alcoholic provision normally made for him.

'Melanie,' he said at last. 'Could I have a drink?'

This time Mrs Hatch did not even answer; and George Goss continued to sit feebly opening and closing his fingers, like a frustrated crustacean.

Nor did Edwin fare better. When he reappeared from the telephone room (it had been converted from its previous function of downstairs lavatory), Griselda was startled to notice that his face was pale and his hair almost dishevelled round the ears. Manifestly he was using all his worldly knowledge and resource to conceal that anything was wrong. He accepted tea and cake; but every now and then Griselda heard him whispering to himself between mouthfuls. The words sounded like 'It can't be. It can't be.' The crisis came quite suddenly: Edwin sat up straight in his chair, and, returning his cup, from which he had been drinking, to his saucer, cried out: 'The Pope must intervene.' After that he seemed to recover rapidly, and to return to his normal, exceptionally well-adjusted frame of mind; but not before Mrs Hatch had said in the rudest possible way 'Edwin Polegate-Hampden, you bore me.' It was proof how hard to disturb was Edwin's fundamental equilibrium that he was able to smile and reply 'The ex-Empress used to say exactly the same.' Edwin then munched briskly and began to draft a long sequence of telegrams for Monk to spell out as best he could to a country telephone operator on a Sunday evening. Mrs Hatch even seemed almost to demur at Monk being given this employment.

Dinner was worse. The Duke and Duchess made a belated reappearance, the Duchess, evening dress being inconsistent with the Sabbath, in a short gown of olive-coloured satin, rather more shiny than would have best suited any other wearer but exactly right for her; and Edwin seemed entirely restored to cheerfulness by the knowledge that Monk was still faithfully at work on his behalf and on behalf of enduring humanity. But George Goss was still rather ill, and also empty, as the rattlings and roarings of his intestines bore witness whenever conviviality ebbed, which was frequently. For Mrs Hatch's mien had by now become such as almost to cancel all faintest prospect of the jovial. Griselda sincerely wondered what could be the matter with her.

It was unfortunate that none of the company, pleasant people though they all were, really appealed to Griselda as a sympathetic conversationalist. After all, it was her last evening as a guest at Beams. Did most house parties deflate in this way? she wondered. She tried to place in her mind the exact time when the gaiety had been at its height, the social balloon most stuffed with gas. She was unable to settle this time. She could only think of Louise, who seemed in no way whatever a part of her surroundings. This, however Griselda reflected, was probably wrong: one had to put up with George Goss belching and with hours of wasted living if one was to have any hope of minutes with such as Louise.

'The thing I can least abide in life,' announced Mrs Hatch, apropos of some behind-the-scenes domesticity, 'is deceit. Did you know, Stainer, that my grandfather in Greece once strangled with his own hands a servant who deceived him?'

'No, mum,' said Stainer, shaking all over, and beginning to snivel.

'It was only a small matter. It was the principle my grandfather cared about. And I feel precisely the same as my grandfather. Do you understand what I say?'

Stainer was now speechless.

'Answer me, please. Do you understand?'

'Yes, mum.' The words were hardly audible in the unpleasant hush that had fallen upon all present. Griselda reflected upon the fact that, unlike most domestic servants she had encountered, Stainer seemed to contemplate neither cheeking Mrs Hatch nor leaving her employ.

'Then you will never attempt to deceive me again?'

'No, mum.'

'Very well then. Serve the ortolans.'

Griselda thought not of ortolans, but of falcons: of a sky full of falcons and herself a dove amongst them. She was frightened.

Their spirits temporarily broken, the Duchess did not suggest games, nor Edwin bridge. Instead, Mrs Hatch, apologizing perfunctorily to her guests and referring them to their own devices, ordered Monk, by now as one shellshocked with telephoning, to bring her the big ledger, and settled down to an evening of entering up accounts, which she did with no small dexterity. The full deployment of her powers required concentration, however; and it was soon to be made clear to the luck-less company that the continuum was readily disturbed. Edwin who would probably have liked to attempt flirtation with Griselda, or something tending in the same direction with the Duchess, was reduced to drafting a study for *The Times Literary Supplement* to be entitled 'A Case for Holy Living.' The Ellensteins and Griselda felt remarkably bored, and began, in their different ways, to think of bed, although it was not yet half-past nine.

Suddenly George Goss roared out 'In Christ's name, Melanie, what's the matter with you?' Griselda realized that he was crazed from lack of liquor.

Mrs Hatch who was adding an entire long column, made a small tight gesture of exasperation, utterly murderous, but said or did nothing further. George Goss began to stagger away, questing for a drink, a lion at last.

The Duke and Duchess excused themselves. Mrs Hatch could not have seemed more indifferent. They ascended the staircase, a little shakily, Griselda thought. Nerviness riddled the entire community. Then Griselda decided to snap the link herself. After all, she had Sir Osbert Sitwell's 'Winters of Content' to read; and her bedroom was just the place for such a book.

'If you can spare me, Mrs Hatch, I think I'll go to bed too. Our walk must have tired me.' This last statement was untrue, but something of the kind seemed to be required.

Mrs Hatch was glaring at an invoice, seeking to pluck out the heart of its mystery. She said nothing.

'Well – Good night.'

Mrs Hatch still did not look up, but she said 'Good night.' Her tone baffled Griselda completely. It was certainly not noticeably pleasant. Griselda could not recall her Mother, or any of her Mother's circle, behaving like this in the capacity of hostess. But her Mother was limited, and her circle small. Nine-thirty struck in the hall as Griselda entered her room, leaving Mrs Hatch in malign solitude with her sums. It was raining harder than ever.

XII

The room was filled not with damp night, but with Louise's perfume.

Griselda softly cried out 'Louise!'

Then again she recalled that the perfume was Stephanie's also. But as apparently only Louise could see and converse with Stephanie, it was difficult to know what to do, except be frightened once more. More than ever, Griselda wanted Louise to be with her. But she had no idea where Louise was.

Griselda tentatively removed her wrist watch and laid it on the dressing table. A gust of wind, weighted with rain, so jarred the window that Griselda thought she would investigate. There was nothing to be done about that either: though the water was seeping into the room at many points between the well-made sashes and frames, and though it would clearly be a troubled night for any sleeper not enamoured of a storm. Fortunately, Griselda was not such a sleeper. She was simply a sleeper not enamoured of a ghost.

For when she returned to the dressing table, though her back had been turned upon it for only seconds, a strange object had appeared, and lay beside her familiar efficient wrist watch. It was a tiny knife: almost a dagger; conceivably a stiletto. The silvery blade, as if daily used and polished for generations, reflected a great bar of light across the ceiling. The ivory hilt was inlaid with purple amethyst, spiralling round it like the pattern on a Byzantine column. From butt to tip the knife was about five inches long. Griselda picked it up and tried the blade. The two edges were so sharp that it was difficult not to cut off at least a finger. They converged to a tip like the sting of a glittering insect.

Again there was a disturbance at the window. Such noises were likely to continue throughout the night, and Griselda took no notice, but went on staring at the knife. But the disturbance took on definition. It seemed to be rapping and crying. Someone appeared to be seeking entrance through Griselda's first floor window.

Supposing that it might be Stephanie, Griselda felt utterly appalled. But the noises continued; and, as when a bird enters one's bedroom, it was impossible indefinitely to ignore them. In the end, Griselda took the little knife, crossed the room, and once more drew back the curtain. Crouched on the sill outside was indisputably a figure. After a moment's terror, Griselda realized that it was Louise. She opened the window.

'What's that you've got?'

'I thought *you* might know. I found it on the dressing-table. It seemed to appear when my back was turned.'

Cascades of water were pouring through the open window, soaking everything. Louise's white mackintosh was the colour of clay; her long hair bedraggled like a corpse's.

She stood sniffing the charged air. 'I wonder if it's a

good sign or a bad one. Revenge or rescue. Pity it's so hard to know.'

Griselda shut the window, becoming seriously wet in the process. She redrew the curtains and stood in the centre of the room.

'I'm so very glad to see you, Louise. On my last night.'

'Did you think I wouldn't come?'

Griselda gently shook her head.

'Even if I had to swim the Hellespont like Leander visiting Hero.'

'Dear Leander.' Griselda put down the little knife. 'As you've been so long in the sea, you'd better take off your wet clothes.'

Louise began to remove her soaking mackintosh. She was wearing trousers like Mrs Hatch's.

'Are you locked out?'

'No. I've been waiting in the Pavilion for your light to appear. I didn't want us to waste time and the house is swarming, which makes communication difficult. Everyone seems to have gone to bed very early tonight.'

'Mrs Hatch is doing sums, and didn't want us. You're soaked. Undress. I'll lend you some clothes.'

Louise undressed. It took only a minute.

'Which clothes would you like? Which of my poor silly garments?'

Louise smiled. Then she crossed to the bed and put on Griselda's pyjamas, laid out by Mullet.

As Louise put on Griselda's pyjama's, a great wave of feeling swept through Griselda like a wall of flame. She was unable to doubt that this was passion. It left her muddled and stupid.

Louise sat down and dried her glasses on one of Griselda's handkerchiefs. Then she untied her hair and began to rub it. Seated in Griselda's pyjama's, and rubbing her long thick hair, she looked very beautiful.

'May I stay?' she asked, smiling like a representation of the Madonna, really the painter's mistress.

Griselda had herself begun to undress, but slowly. 'Of course,' she said. 'But there is one thing . . . dear Leander. Mrs Hatch said something at breakfast . . .'

'This is true love, my Hero,' replied Louise, rubbing her hair energetically. 'Love is only possible where there is like feeling. Sometimes that can be found in a body which is unlike: more usually it cannot. Love without like feeling is something best left to little Fritzi. Do I make things reasonably clear to you?'

'Perfectly clear, darling. Not that it was really necessary.'

'Then I may stay?'

Griselda shivered. 'If you don't mind the haunted room.' It was growing seriously cold; and she began to hasten the day's last rites.

'Really and truly I don't mind anything now.'

The clock in the hall below struck ten. Louise was scenting herself with Griselda's scent, which made her smell very strange.

XIII

The clock in the hall below struck six.

Griselda, happier than she had ever been or would ever be again, heard it strike. Shortly afterwards there ensued, and quickly terminated, a train of events which she never in her life wholly understood; never, so to speak, got to the bottom of. Actual enquiry or close investigation were, in the nature of things, forever debarred to her. Later on in life she concluded that this applied to most mysteries she really cared about. This particular train of events took place, moreover, largely in silence, at least as far as concerned human utterance; and the crucial events largely in darkness also, as the bedroom curtains were still drawn, it was not yet fully daylight, and no one turned on the electric light until the crucial events were over.

There were steps outside, the bedroom door opened, and someone entered with a firm step in the uncertain light. Louise who was still asleep, was dragged from bed on to the floor, then hauled along the floor towards the door; all by the person with the firm step. On the way to the door, Louise, however, sufficiently realized the position to tear herself loose. There was a scuffle in the vicinity of the dressing table and a sharp groaning cry. Griselda guessed that one of the combatants had got

hold of the dangerous little knife. At the cry a second in-
truder entered the room: and the two of them succeeded
in dragging Louise away, still struggling valiantly but
in utter silence. Griselda could hear the contest continuing down the passage outside. There was a lapse
of time before courage enough came to enable her to
leave the warm bed for the cold world, especially as,
having brought only a single pair of pyjamas to Beams,
she was naked. She put on her dressing-gown and went,
trembling, to the open door. Outside all was now unexpectedly and frighteningly quiet But suddenly the figure
of Mrs Hatch, in trousers and her usual heavy grey
sweater, loomed up and came towards her.

'Get yourself dressed and packed immediately,' said
Mrs Hatch in a voice of matter-of-fact command. 'You
will leave the house within half an hour: before anyone
else is up. Maghull is aready waiting with the car to take
you to the station. When you have joined the train, he
will drive to your Mother with a letter I have written
her. She will have had time to read the letter carefully
and, if necessary, repeatedly, before you arrive. I am
sorry I cannot offer you breakfast, but the kitchen staff
will not be down before you go. Hurry: or you will have
to leave as you are.'

She walked away.

It never occurred to Griselda not to do what Mrs
Hatch had ordered. She shut the door, turned on the
light, and groped into her garments. Shaking all over,
she packed. She packed Louise's letter. She noticed
Louise's glasses, still on the bedside table. She wondered

what had become of the little knife, and even perfunctorily searched for it. It was missing. Griselda recollected that she did not even known upon whom it had inflicted hurt. Whether the knife was meant to revenge or to rescue, remained unkown.

When, carrying her suitcase, she descended the familiar staircase to the hall, she saw that the front door stood open, the car waited outside, and that discoloured daylight was creeping into and around the house like mist. There was no sign of Mrs Hatch, or of anyone else other than Maghull on his box; but upon the hall table the large ledger lay open, the final balance, reached at no one could tell what small hour, ruled off and repeatedly underlined in gay scarlet ink. Entering the lavish vehicle, Griselda noticed that Maghull's left hand was largely concealed by a newly tied bandage.

In the car Griselda wondered whether it would help Louise if she were to go to the Police. But she was not even sure whether her love for Louise might not be taken as an offence against the law. Griselda, in fact, felt at the moment too scared and ill to do anything effective. She began to weep, her tears spreading across the soft blue upholstery. She had to be assisted by Maghull into the railway compartment. He had the grip of a fanatic. No one asked to inspect the return half of her ticket.

It was only in the train that she clearly realized, in a series of horrifying shocks of perception, that neither she nor Louise had any means whatever of making contact with the other. Later it occurred to her that much trouble might have been saved, indeed two hearts from breaking and two lives from ruin, had either she or Louise thought to lock the bedroom door.

Part Two

XIV

But it was useless to continue weeping after the train had passed Clapham Junction. Not only was the compartment now filled with early wage-earners, looking pugnacious and embittered at their unjust destinies (one of them, a middle-aged woman, shapeless and sagging with repeated mismanaged maternity, stood for much of the journey upon the toe of one of Griselda's shoes); but it had become clear to Griselda that a broken heart does not annihilate routine necessities, but merely makes them considerably more difficult to contend with.

Griselda's Mother being the woman she was, it was now out of the question to return home, especially considering the trouble which had attended Griselda's last year at school. This circumstance gave Griselda a marked feeling of relief. It was no comfort at all for having lost Louise that she was also rid of her Mother; but her new freedom from her Mother comforted her for much else. As the train passed Queen's Road station, Griselda disentangled her left arm, opened the purse in her handbag, and was surprised to count three pounds, fourteen shillings, and sevenpence. Her Mother had made provision for her to tip: and she had not tipped. She had not even tipped Maghull. On the other hand, the clothes in her suitcase were appallingly inadequate as equipment for life: that is to say for what her Mother's brother, Uncle Bear (his first name was Pelham, but he had never lived down a hit he once made in a school play), for what Uncle Bear termed '*real* life.' On the other hand again, it was spring, and summer stretched ahead, warm and endless.

By the time the train had passed Vauxhall and had settled down for the wait common to all trains entering Waterloo, a brief spell enabling the traveller the better to meet the massed claims of the terminus. Griselda had resolved firstly to seek out the Great Exhibition Hotel and secondly to seek out Lord Roller. The Great Exhibition Hotel had been strongly recommended to her by a schoolfriend who had the habit of spending odd nights in Town. Lord Roller had offered employment.

At the other side of the compartment, four labourers, their clothes smeared with yesterday's earth, were playing a simple form of nap, easing the run of the cards with monosyllabic obscenities. The train jerked into motion: as it racketed across the barricade of points, every second, it seemed, about to be derailed, the regular passengers rose to their feet and pressed towards the doors, hypnotized by routine into an appearance of striving to meet life halfway. Before the train had stopped, they were leaping on to the platform and running towards the sliding iron gates. The ticket collector had difficulty in controlling them. Until one looked again at their faces, it was for all the world as if they had an incentive in their existences.

Griselda, to whom the morning rush hour was a new

experience, remained seated for a moment, fighting back the instinct to run with the herd. Then she drew down her suitcase from the rack and stepped from the train to find the platform deserted, and the ticket collector, a few seconds ago flustered and perspiring under the stampede, now irate and resentful of her dilatoriness.

'Come along there. You'll be late for work.'

Having delivered up her ticket, Griselda sent her Mother a telegram from the station telegraph office.

'Taking job in London please don't worry get better quickly much love Griselda.'

It seemed to be in the tradition of messages sent on these occasions, though it was Griselda's first of the kind.

She knew her Underground, and proceeded to South Kensington, changing at Charing Cross. Each train was again abominably crowded; and the only excuse for a crowd, collective conviviality, conspicuously absent. At every station men and women fought in the doors and on the platforms. Between stations they joyessly read newspapers. The whole grim business was utterly orderly.

The Great Exhibition Hotel proved larger than Griselda had expected, and distinctly more pretentious. She booked a room for a week, thereby (after some firm bargaining) incurring a liability of three pounds ten shillings, supposing she passed seven days without eating. A porter in his shirtsleeves took her in a tiny, slow lift to the fifth floor and to 79^A.

'They knocked 79 in half,' he explained, hanging about for recognition. Griselda gave him sixpence: which he regarded with a look which meant that women were all the same. The process of adaptation had proved fatal to the proportions; but the room was not exactly dirty, but offered a good view in the direction of Earl's, possibly even Baron's Court, the busy Inner Circle railway being in the foreground. The furniture was bright yellow but capacious. The bed bore a far-flung counterpane, hand-wrought in patterns of sheep-coloured wool, entirely different on the two faces. It was unbelievably heavy, the labour, obviously of years; superfluous labour Griselda thought. Beneath it was a flat and slithery eiderdown, covered in livid patchwork; and no fewer than four good blankets, tightly wrapped in on each side. Griselda deduced that many elderly ladies spent the evening of their days looking out towards the ghosts of old Earl's Court and its Great Wheel from the casements of the Great Exhibition Hotel: possibly, as they gazed, they matted coverlets heavy as lead sheeting, sewed gaudy scrap to gaudy scrap.

As in a royal palace, the water closet was of the gracious valve type. Small trays sprinkled with small breakfasts, were beginning to fidget towards the bedrooms as Griselda descended. In the Lounge sprawled several residents of a different type: one of them even whistled through his front teeth as Griselda passed. It was hard to believe that these residents needed bedrooms of their own: they seemed to live in the Lounge talking shop: and when they needed a bedroom, to have recourse, inevitably, to someone else's.

Griselda had noticed a Tariff in the Hotel which stated 'Breakfast 3/6. With Meat 5/6. Preserves Extra'; and set out to look for a teashop. She found one open, and breakfasted excellently for one shilling and seven-pence plus twopence gratuity (forbidden but extracted). She then found that she lacked twopence with which to telephone Lord Roller, and had to return to the cash desk a suppliant. A further sixpence having been reluc-tantly converted into four pennies and four halfpennies (it was clear from her manner that the harridan in the little box lost hopelessly on the transaction), Griselda realized that she did not know the name of Lord Roller's firm. Nor was Lord Roller himself in the Telephone Directory, even at a private residence.

At a loss, Griselda peered through the glass of the telephone cabinet. The morning rush was over; the crowds had vanished into air. There were much refuse, two dogs, an ineffective cleaner, and a belated young man with a bowler hat and umbrella, obviously bound for the City.

'Excuse me,' cried Griselda, breaking out from her place of confinement. 'Could you very kindly tell me where I might find Lord Roller?'

The young man immediately stood quite still, staring round him, and blushing almost purple. 'I – don't – know,' he said after a long pause, forcing out the words through lips shuddering with embarrassment. 'Sorry.' He lifted his hat, looked at his wrist watch, and hastened on towards his world of familiar things.

The cleaner was also standing immobile, regarding. Suddenly she spoke: 'You try Arkwright and Silverstein. That's where you'll find 'is lordship, dear. Arkwright and Silverstein. London Stone double two double two. You try and you'll find 'im.'

'Thank you very much,' said Griselda.

'Don't forget to remember me to 'is lordship.' She gave a gurgling laugh and began to clatter furiously with her bucket. This made telephoning difficult, but Griselda did not care to complain.

Lord Roller had not yet arrived, but his secretary, on learning that Griselda had met him at the All Party Dance, made an appointment for her at ten forty-five.

'Ask for Miss Guthers,' said the secretary.

The Inner Circle, which bore Griselda back to Charing Cross and then on to the Mansion House, was now almost deserted. Apart from a small intrusion of foreign tourists at Victoria, the clanking train had become a very fair place for hearkening to the inner voice. Griselda's inner voice remarked to her that she was wrongly dressed for seeking a job.

This contention received support when Griselda encountered Miss Guthers. Miss Guthers was dressed expensively and fashionably, though she did not look expensive or fashionable owing to years of overwork and the effort to control cheeky and lazy subordinates upon always just too little authority for the purpose. She regarded Griselda kindly, and seated her in a minute mahogany waiting-room like a large coffin, lined entirely with bound volumes of *The Merchant Banker*. A small table bore a single newspaper, a copy of *The Times*. Griselda opened it and read the principle headline: 'Aftermath Of The Roller Report'. She looked at the first leading article: 'The Roller Report: What Next?' She turned to the Court News: 'Reception for Lord Roller' (provided two nights previously, she read, by Edwin's dazzling friend, Lady Wolverhampton). The paper contained only one photograph: a special study by a staff photographer of the typical English village of Lydiard Bust, with an entirely new crop of oats filling up the foreground, and much of the background also. Griselda began to read Mr Morgan's glittering comments on last night's play.

'Lord Roller will see you now.' Miss Guthers almost conveyed concern that the interview should go well. There is no one it is easier to like than a first class woman private secretary; and Griselda liked Miss Guthers.

Lord Roller, however, wore an expression of extreme gravity. He rose as Griselda entered, and personally offered her a mahogany chair.

'I must tell you quite frankly, Miss de Reptonville,' he said, 'that I did not expect to see you quite so soon. That, none the less, would have been entirely in order, and I should have been pleased to assist you in your project of leaving the Secretariat of Sociology. But under the circumstances which now obtain, you will, I am sure, understand that any help from me is out of the question. Please do not hesitate to smoke.' He extended an open cigarette case: it was made of gold and was one of a consignment sent out the previous year as

Christmas presents by the Ministry of Mines.

'Thank you, Lord Roller,' replied Griselda, 'but I don't smoke.'

'An excellent thing. I wish my position allowed me to follow your example.' He sat back watching her: his fine head reflected in the many photographs above the fireplace of past Permanent Secretaries to the Treasury, all of them signed, and many with warm words of greeting added.

'I have not actually got a job in the Secretariat of Sociology. I've merely been offered one. You very kindly advised me against taking it and said that you might be able to offer me something – something better, I think – yourself.'

'I recall our conversation perfectly, I assure you. Miss de Reptonville. A good memory is unfortunately required by the nature of my work. I say "unfortunately", because it is seldom that I have anything to remember which is so agreeable as was our little talk.'

'That is charming of you, but I understood you to say just now that you were unable to help me? I gathered that you must have found me a pest, after all.'

'Not in the least, Miss de Reptonville. I found you a most engaging young woman. I still find you a most engaging young woman.' Lord Roller rotated his swivel chair and took a large cigar from a silver box on a table behind him. 'Nor must you suppose, not for one moment, that I am passing any kind of judgment whatever. Not in the very least: I know much too little of the world to attempt any such thing.' He took a match from a little ivory box on his desk, struck it, and drew heavily but gracefully on his cigar.

'But the offer of a job is closed?'

'It would be quite inconsistent with the obligations I have accepted. I know you will appreciate that. I do not have to say that the matter is entirely impersonal. I am subject to various duties, which take many decisions out of my hands. Very narrow lines of conduct are laid down. For better or worse. I frequently think for worse. But now let us say nothing more about these particular matters. I am sure you will agree. Let us discuss something else. I have no other engagement, I am delighted to say, for the next ten minutes.' Lord Roller consulted his watch, a fine inherited repeater, and added: 'Indeed, eleven minutes.'

Griselda hesitated. Could her love for Louise be already such common knowledge? Had Lord Roller gone over to the side of her Mother? Was there a cabalistic communion, based presumably upon telepathy, between such all eminent personages as Mrs Hatch and Lord Roller? Miss Guthers had seemed ignorant of anything amiss. Or was it because of knowledge that she had been so pleasant and agreeable? In any case a good private secretary was supposed to differentiate in her reception of the Recording Angel and of the man to read the gas meter, in degree only, and not in kind. Griselda began seriously to worry about her inexperience of Uncle Bear's 'real life'. But then her love for Louise seemed much more 'real' than her obligation to Lord Roller. Repelling another onset of tears, Griselda reflected that unless she had a reasonable job by the end of the week, she would go to jail for debt, which would put society still more against her.

'Lord Roller,' she said bravely, 'I need a job. Suddenly I need a job badly. I have no right to bother you, but since we still have eleven minutes, or perhaps ten by now, I wonder if you can suggest anything? Or must it be the Secretariat?' Griselda thought of living in a loft with Louise. Tears, tears. Almost she wished that she smoked. Lord Roller had already made the room like a luxuriously aromatic engine house. The reek of his mammoth cigar deadened the nerves of even non-smokers.

'It will not be easy,' he said. His tone implied that his magnanimity in offering to say no more about Griselda's offence (if that was what he was offering to say no more about), was meeting with insufficient acknowledgement. But even now it was uncertain whether his present remark alluded to more than the depressed state of trade, so alarmingly revealed in the Report; was more than an accepted and standard observation to job-hunters. 'You may have to enter the Secretariat after all.' It was as if Griselda had to enter a convent for a course of spiritual rectification; even that being, all things considered, a lucky escape.

'I should so much rather not.'

'Naturally. But it is not in every case possible to choose. Often our present is decided for us by our past. I do not wish there to be any misunderstanding, however: any doubt that I am anxious to do everything possible.

Though I should so much prefer to talk about the daffodils I noticed growing in the Green Park this morning, or the newest novel which I lack time to read, and can only read about.' He smiled: then expelled a cloud of smoke so dense and unexpected as to make Griselda cough.

'I *am* so sorry. Let me ring for a glass of water. And we might have the window a little open perhaps, just for a moment.'

'Thank you. I'm perfectly all right.' It was almost the sensation of crying again.

But Lord Roller had already rung. Miss Guthers appeared instantly.

'Could you possibly fetch a glass of water, Hazel? I have nearly choked Miss de Reptonville.'

'Certainly. Lord Roller.'

Again in an instant, Miss Guthers was back with a tumbler filled to the brim with water. Despite the speed of the transaction, not a drop was spilt: an achievement which Griselda found difficult to sustain.

'Could you open a window too?'

'The noise is rather bad today, Lord Roller. Now that it's almost summer, it's difficult to have the windows open. All the roads are coming up and the traffic's being diverted. You can hear the hooting.'

'None the less, please open the window, Hazel. Miss de Reptonville requires air. The Ministry of Transport has no business to repair the roads anyway, with the country in the state it is. Write a letter to Leech pointing that out and I'll sign it. See that it catches the midday post or it'll never arrive with the posts as they are now. You might even send it to Number Ten by messenger.'

'The messenger service isn't at all what it used to be, you know. Perhaps I'd better telephone Downing Street and ask *them* to send a messenger to collect.'

'Please don't trouble,' interjected Griselda.

'I beg your pardon?'

'The window. Please don't trouble, I'm perfectly all right.'

'That's splendid.' Miss Guthers smiled encouragingly. 'What about some more water?'

'No, thank you. I still have more than half a glass. I wonder if we could possibly finish what we were saying, Lord Roller?'

'Of course we can. All right, Hazel. Just let me know when Sir George arrives.'

'Yes, Lord Roller. Shall I take your glass?'

'Thank you so much for the water.' It was probably wise to keep on the right side of Miss Guthers, especially as Griselda's last remark might have been interpreted as a dismissal and as presumption.

'Well, Miss de Reptonville, you want suitable employment.' Lord Roller took a sheet of paper from a satinwood stationery stand which stood on the table with his cigars. He began to write. 'An opportunity has occurred to me. It might prove to be the very thing.' He scratched away. 'You don't mind working out of London?'

'I should prefer London, but, obviously. I'm in no

position to choose. How far away will this be?'

'Not far, you'll be pleased to hear. Not far at all. Just the other side of Seven Kings.' He signed the document: a swift, driving, single name; then folded it and put it in an envelope. 'No. On second thoughts, you'd better read it.' He withdrew it from the envelope and passed it folded to Griselda.

The paper bore two or three sentences in a hand, dashing and sloping eagerly to the right, but not one word of which could Griselda read.

She stared at the indecipherable words while Lord Roller stood behind his desk watching her and waiting.

'I'm terribly sorry. I'm bad at handwriting. I can't read all of it.'

'Doesn't matter in the least, Miss de Reptonville. Hardly worth showing you. Conventionality, simply; but I hope it does the trick. My fist's got worse and worse, I'm afraid, with increasing years of service. Give me the thing back and I'll pack it up again.' Griselda gave it back. 'Just find your way to this address and they'll take care of you.' He was writing on the envelope. 'I'll do it in capitals.' He smiled again at Griselda.

'I feel I'm rather a fool, Lord Roller.'

'Hardly worth employing, I'm sure.' He said this with the kindliest of irony. 'There.' He returned the letter.

Miss Gathers was back in the room.

'Sir George, Lord Roller.'

'Show him in, Hazel. And bring a lot of whisky. Better open a new bottle.'

'Yes, Lord Roller.'

'Good-bye, Miss de Reptonville. I do hope I've been of some small help. Your position is difficult.' He extended his hand. 'But whatever you do ... don't worry.' It was the last word on the subject.

'Thank you for giving me so much of your time.'

'I should so much have preferred to talk of the daffodils in the Park.'

'Perhaps on another occasion.'

He glanced at her.

'I hope so.'

Miss Guthers had rather to rush Griselda's departure from the office, as Sir George could be distinctly overheard stamping like a thoroughbred in a loose box.

XV

Mr Shooter, to whom Lord Roller's letter was addressed, hardly even attempted charm; nor did The Bedrock Accessories Supply Company, her prospective place of employment, impress Griselda much more favourably. Even when with the assistance of Messrs Arkwright and Silverstein's outside porter, she had located Seven Kings, it seemed to take several hours to reach the place by train from Liverpool Street, so that on arrival she at least expected spring buds on the trees and skipping lambs. But Seven Kings seemed little different from the less attractive parts of London. It was now lunchtime but Griselda did not dare to eat; nor did there seem facilities, even had she dared.

Mr Shooter worked in an untidy office entirely walled with a special kind of glass. Outside, a press of some sort was noisily making accessories. Every thirty seconds it stamped something out; so loudly that conversation above the concussions was difficult, and hardly easier between them. Grinding and rolling mills made up a background evocative of the nation's industrial effort. Mr Shooter possibly found the general atmosphere of toil, stimulating; but as he was entirely bald, and rather yellow, it was not easy to say. The plywood door of his office bore the legend '*Personnel* Manager. Do NOT

Disturb' in ugly modern lettering. Above his electric heater was a large framed reproduction of de Laszlo's portrait of Lord Roller in the robes of a Baron.

Griselda was shown in by a sniffing child, fresh from some Essex hamlet.

'Maudie,' screamed Mr Shooter, as the infant was about to depart, 'I want some real tea, not this stinking slops. Get busy, will you, and don't forget next time.'

Maudie shuffled away.

'Take the tray with you.'

Maudie returned for the tray. As she bore it towards the door, she winked at Griselda. It was impossible for Griselda to wink back, even if she felt so inclined. The office door rasped along the floor every time it was opened or shut.

'Well?'

Griselda handed Mr Shooter the letter. Mr Shooter really did not seem an easy man to talk to.

'May I sit down?'

'If you think it worth while. Bring that chair over from the window. You can put the box of samples on the floor under the dictaphone.'

'Thank you.' The box of samples was difficult to lift and tended to burst open.

'Sorry. Can't read this. What's it say?' Mr Shooter tossed the letter back in the direction of Griselda, but it fell off his desk on to the floor. 'Sorry. You read it.'

'I can't read it.' Griselda had succeeded in towing up the rickety little chair. 'I'm sorry.'

'It's from the great white chief isn't it?'

'From Lord Roller, yes. Is this *his* factory? I didn't know.'

'One of his factories. He's got twelve in Canada alone. This one's only a sideline.'

'What do you make?' enquired Griselda politely. 'I'm afraid I'm very ignorant'

'Nothing but accessories,' replied Mr Shooter. The fact seemed to pain him; but it was as if the pain were something he had learned to bear. 'Let's stick to you. What's it all about?'

'I understand from Lord Roller that you might be able to offer me a job. If you think I'm worth it, that is.' Griselda was far from sure that, even desperate as she was, she wanted to devote herself to making merely accessories.

'You got that from the chief personally?' Mr Shooter stared hard at Griselda. His eyes were like guns mounted behind slits in the yellow pillbox of his face.

'Certainly,' said Griselda with hauteur.

'Well, there's one thing.'

'What is it?'

'Welfare.' Mr Shooter's eyes were keeping Griselda covered more ruthlessly than ever.

'I might be able to help with that.' Griselda saw herself dressed as a hospital sister and wondered whether she could call upon the required amount of saintliness. At once she doubted whether she could.

'Our last four welfare officers have had to leave us rather suddenly. Oh, personal reasons in each case. Quite sufficient. But now the job's going once more.'

He stared again at Lord Roller's letter, which Griselda had replaced upon his desk.

'Could you tell me a little more about it?'

'Knowledge of people, that's the main thing. Knowledge of the common people. The welfare officer must be guide, philosopher, and friend to every worker in the place. She must be able to get inside their minds. If she can do that, special qualifications are less important. There's a bit of simple nursing, of course, and first aid, naturally. Have you a first aid certificate?'

'Actually, yes.'

'You have?' Mr Shooter seemed surprised and impressed. He took a writing pad from the drawer of his desk and made a note.

'Then there's librarianship. Do you read?'

'It's my favourite thing.'

'We don't want a bookworm, you know,' replied Mr Shooter, glowering. 'Only the lighter stuff. Religious guidance is another side of the work; for those who want it. Mostly the young girls. You do that in co-operation with Mr Cheddar, the priest-in-charge. What else is there? Oh yes, help with games of all sorts, and advice upon the food in the canteen. Mrs Rufioli superintends the actual cooking, gives the kitchen girls hell and all that; but the welfare officer has to see to it that the canteen expenditure doesn't exceed the firm's financial provision. I suppose you can keep simple accounts?'

The figure of Mrs Hatch and her terrible ledger recurred in Griselda's imagination. 'I think I can,' she said faintly.

'The main thing is that the welfare officer must be on her toes morning, noon, and night. If she keeps on her toes all the time – and I mean *all* the time – the job's not difficult to hold down.'

Griselda looked at her toes. Whatever Louise might imply, she thought her shoes were rather attractive. She wondered at what point the applicant introduced the matter of remuneration. Mr Shooter, his oration finished, had produced a rectangle of madeira cake on a plate from another drawer in his desk, and now sat crumbling it into debris, and stuffing untidy briquettes of the debris into his small round mouth. It seemed to Griselda an inefficient way of eating madeira cake. Meanwhile, Mr Shooter said nothing further.

'How much,' enquired Griselda tentatively—

But Mr Shooter cut her short. 'The usual Rawnsley Committee rates,' he said with his mouth full. There was little difference in hue, Griselda observed, between the cake and Mr Shooter's complexion.

'And hours?'

'I think we're adopting the Giddens Council recommendations, but the whole subject's still in the melting-pot. You've nothing to worry about, though. This is a modern factory, based on efficient time and motion study.' The banging press outside underlined his words. 'Besides which, we go all out for welfare.'

The door rasped and Maudie reappeared with her pale green plastic tray. The teapot was smeary; the cup, saucer, and milk jug discrepant. The sugar basin, however, was of the sanitary variety. Maudie had evidently resolved to seek re-entry to Mr Shooter's favour by augmenting her allure: she had shaded her eyelids, cast off her cardigan, and assumed a mode of speech modelled upon that of Miss Myrna Loy.

'Your tea, Mr Shooter,' said Maudie, still sniffing. 'Nice and strong.'

Mr Shooter looked up at her. 'Thanks, Maudie,' he said, in almost cowboy tones. 'Sorry I was short with you.'

'That's quite OK, Mr Shooter. We all know how hard you work.' It was difficult to believe that Maudie would long continue an accessory. In two years time, when she would be fifteen or so, she would be conquering new and wider fields. Griselda suspected that Maudie was precisely the type which brought welfare workers into existence and rendered their existence unavailing.

'Now I must go into rather a lot of details,' said Mr Shooter, imbibing strong tea, to Griselda. 'Some of them are pretty personal, but there's another lady present to see fair play.' Maudie had seated herself on a stack of unopened parcels. They appeared to contain Government circulars upon questions of personnel management.

Griselda rose to her feet, 'Please do not trouble,' she said. 'I don't think the position is quite what I am looking for.' She felt entirely regal as she swept from the room; the regality being modified only temporarily by Maudie emitting a long squelching sound through her incorrectly painted lips.

XVI

After purchasing and eating four penny buns and drinking a mugful of Bovril, Griselda decided to seek a job by a different method. She took an omnibus from Liverpool Street to Piccadilly Circus, and rambled through the back streets north of Piccadilly and west of Regent Street, looking in the shops, and seeking also a place where she could possibly want to work. It was what her school had described as the Direct Method. On this occasion, the Direct Method proved immediately efficacious.

The aspect of a certain small bookshop appealed to her greatly. The window was stocked neither with Books of the Month nor with sombre ancients; but with a well chosen selection of books published during the preceding fifty years or thereabouts. Unfortunately for the enlightened management, the shop appeared to be empty. Above the window was the name 'Tamburlane.'

Griselda entered. A tall, well-made man, with a red face and white fluffy hair, emerged briskly from an inner room.

'I'm afraid we are out of Housman today,' he said in a gentle cultivated voice.

'I already have him, thank you.'

'Indeed? I must apologize for my precipitancy. I

supposed that like my other customers today, you might have been guided here by that thing in *The Times.*'

'I'm afraid I missed that particular thing in *The Times.*'

'Just as well, really. At least in my opinion. Not that I've anything against the old man himself. But *The Times* does rather dote, don't you think? On A.E.H. and J.M.B.?' His articulation of the word 'dote' was pleasantly idiosyncratic.

'Yes,' said Griselda. 'Now you mention it, I really believe that *The Times* does.'

'Insufficient catholicity. Their enormous parsonical readership is at the back of it. It's useless attaching blame to the Editor. Quite a broad-minded well-read chap in his private life. I'm told. I wonder if you'd care for a small glass of port? I always indulge myself after luncheon and it's all too seldom I have a friend to indulge with me.'

'There's nothing I'd like better.'

'Delightful. You have spontaneity, the one real virtue. But I must not let myself stray into compliments. Please sit down.' He indicated a Chines Chippendale chair. Griselda saw that there were a number of them in the inner room.

'Are you Mr Tamburlane?'

'Yes and no. But yes for present purposes. Certainly yes. And you?'

'Griselda de Reptonville,'

He was filling two beautiful little glasses, from a

beautiful little decanter, with assuredly most beautiful port.

'That is the most delightful name I have ever heard. In what is vulgarly known as "real life", of course. I do hope I shall enrol you among my permanent customers.'

Griselda swallowed half the contents of the glass at one unsuitable gulp.

'I really rather hope to be enrolled among your employees.'

He was sipping like a rare and fastidious fowl.

'Well, nothing could be easier than that. Nothing at all. I take it you love books?'

'Perhaps I love them more than I know about them.'

'Indeed I certainly hope so or you would stand little chance here. In view of what you say, you're engaged. Do you wish to start work now?'

'Would tomorrow suit you?'

'Excellently well. Naturally you will not be expected to lower the shutters. Ten o'clock I therefore suggest?'

He recharged the two glasses. The wine looked rich as Faust's blood.

'I think I should tell you of my qualifications. For working in a bookshop I have one or two.'

'They are apparent to me. You have beauty and spontaneity, and you love books. Those things are rare and becoming daily rarer. They suffice. Indeed they suffice.'

'I shall try very hard indeed,' said Griselda.

'Never forget the words of the great Prince Talleyrand: "Surtout, point de zèle." That advice will carry you far in life. Though I am perfectly sure that you will be carried far in any case.'

'I have made a sadly slow start.'

'"He tires betimes, who spurs too fast betimes." I never can overcome my lust for Shakespeare. Can you?'

'I haven't tried. Should I try?'

'Peasant stuff much of it really; but none the less a genius. Indisputably a genius. I was speaking only figuratively. You mustn't take anything I say too literally.'

Griselda looked up from her port.

'Oh, don't take alarm. My words are not serious, but my deeds move mountains. Or so I sometimes like to flatter myself.'

A man entered the shop and began to explore the shelves.

'Perhaps I should go,' said Griselda. 'Thank you very much indeed for the port. And for the job.'

'It has been the greatest possible joy to me. Such a lovely head, such lustrous eyes: always about the shop. Blessedness, indeed: beata Beatrix, and all that. And don't misunderstand me in any particular. My homage is entirely aesthetic; wholly impersonal, so to speak. My eros veers almost entirely towards Adonis.'

The customer looked up at these words, uttered in a voice like a ring of treble bells; and suddenly left the shop.

Griselda noticed the repeated claim of men to be regarding her impersonally. Their motives for this claim seemed as varied as their implication that the process ennobled them was consistent.

'I entirely understand,' said Griselda, 'Good-bye until tomorrow morning.'

'Take something to read,' cried Mr Tamburlane. 'Take this.' It was *Rupert of Hentzau*. 'I presume you've read Prisoner?'

'I'm afraid that's one I've missed.'

'Then take *The Prisoner* too.'

'You are most thoughtful. I'll return them very quickly.'

'Indeed not. You'll read them for solace in years to come, most blessed damozel.'

It was only later while eating an éclair in Fullers that Griselda realized that this time the matter of wages had not been mentioned at all.

XVII

But it settled itself quite suitably. As soon as Griselda diffidently raised the subject upon her arrival the next morning, Mr Tamburlane cried out: 'Please, please, please. No more holding back, I beg. Though alas, I cannot be prodigal. You will soon see for yourself the state of business, and I make it my policy to try to confine outgoings to a sum not exceeding takings. Would four pounds per week keep your slim gilt soul, if I may quote my old friend, within your rosy fingered body?'

'I believe that's about the market rate,' replied Griselda, perhaps a little disappointed, however unreasonably. 'Thank you very much.' It would be necessary to depart from the Great Exhibition Hotel as soon as possible.

'The shop shuts at six o'clock, and at one on Saturdays. You will find that much of the business, such as it is, takes place each day during the general matutinal interregnum.'

In many respects the job was an ideal one. The work was of the lightest and unfailingly interesting; and Mr Tamburlane, apparently the only other person connected with the running of the business, became upon further acquaintance more and more likeable and sympathetic. The few customers were mainly artists, aristocrats, idlers, and scholars; persons bashed by life into extreme inoffensiveness, varied in certain cases by mild and appealing eccentricity. There was also a small number of exceedingly beautiful women customers, who lighted up the shop as with nimbuses. The main drawback, perceived by Griselda from the outset, was that the job entirely lacked what she believed to be termed 'prospects'. Until one knew him, it was difficult to understand what need Mr Tamburlane had of an assistant. After one knew him, it was plain that his need could not truly be translated into financial terms.

Griselda also experienced much difficulty in finding a dwelling place. Having little idea how to set about this search, she attempted several unsuitable neighbourhoods, and a greater number of much more unsuitable landladies. She knew that she needed advice, but hesitated to apply for it to Mr Tamburlane. By the end of her first week in the shop, she was still lodged at the Great Exhibition Hotel, and facing insolvency for lack of a few pounds.

In other ways, however, her acquaintanceship with her employer throve exceedingly. He proved a man precisely of his word: he complimented her ceaselessly and often imaginatively upon her appearance, her ideas, and even her work; but showed no sign at all of ever intending to go further. It seemed to Griselda an admirable attitude for an employer.

The real trouble, of course, was the loss of Louise. The extent and hopelessness of this loss, and also its unnecessariness, saturated Griselda's thoughts and feelings only by degrees. By Friday, however, she felt so despairing, and her acquaintanceship with Mr Tamburlane had developed so warmly, that she resolved to confide in him, at least in part. It was necessary to confide in someone or die; and she could think of no other possible person among all her few friends and relatives, most of whom were, moreover, geographically unavailable. She was not sure that she would want to live in quarters found by Mr Tamburlane; but in the matter of Louise, and Louise's disappearance, there might well be less suitable confidants. So early in the morning there was little risk of interruption by customers.

'Indeed I can help,' cried Mr Tamburlane, at the conclusion of the mournful tale. 'You poor thing. And how fortunate today is Friday.'

'I am glad that something about it is fortunate,' said Griselda.

'Friday is the very day of the week for such a sad narration. Friday is the day Miss Otter calls.'

'Who is Miss Otter?'

'I shall tell you. There is a certain weekly newspaper. It circulates only privately – to subscribers, you undersand; only to subscribers. Not many people know about it, but it serves a variety of special and important purposes. There is no need for me to be more specific. I am sure I have said enough for you to take me?' Griselda thought of the St James's News-Letter; wondered if Mr Tamburlane were talking of something similar; and nodded. The drift of Mr Tamburlane's words seemed utterly beside the point, and had Griselda spoken, she would have started to weep.

'The paper is generally known among its subscribers as *The Otter*. It has, in fact, an entirely different, rather dull name, which is printed at the top of every copy; but *The Otter* it has been for years, simply as a tribute to Miss Otter's personality, Miss Otter is the Editor, so to speak; certainly the entrepreneur. She visits me each week and we decide the contents of the next issue. I am proud to say that from time to time it has been owing to me that there has been a further issue. The sum involved is really very tiny. But as the unacknowledged offspring of a rich nobleman – rich even in these days – I happily have some very small resources of my own, with which I endeavour to add to the douceur of life.'

'Unacknowledged, Mr Tamburlane?'

'For good and obvious reasons, I'm afraid, Miss de Reptonville. Please don't think I'm the rightful heir deprived; or even a younger son deprived. Nothing at all like that, I entirely uphold the strictest interpretation of the rules of blood and succession. Without them the nobility would very soon become unfit to govern.'

'I thought they'd ceased to govern anyway,' said Griselda, interested in spite of herself.

'Temporarily they have indeed. But you do not suppose that the present political bacchanal will last many years, I take it? As a wise and beautiful young woman, you cannot be deceived about that?'

'You will remember that I attended the All Party Dance, Mr Tamburlane.'

'I am answered as by an oracle. But to return to *The Otter*. It is fortunate indeed that you decided to confide in me. For *The Otter* exists largely in order to help with just such problems as yours, Miss de Reptonville. But, as I live, here comes Miss Otter in person.' He dashed out of the little inner room where this conversation had taken place.

Griselda looked at the new arrival with much curiosity. Miss Otter was a bent little woman, dressed, not very well, entirely in black. She had a quantity of white hair, and a brown wrinkled face, with a huge nose and enigmatic eyes. She wore no hat, but a wide black velvet band across her white hair.

Mr Tamburlane introduced Griselda. Miss Otter accepted the introduction after the affable style of an important personage, took Griselda by the hand, and remarked: 'I perceive you are in much distress of mind. I am grieved. Please accept my sympathy.' The last request was delivered somewhat in the tone of a dethroned Queen.

Griselda could only say: 'Thank you very much.'

'You are indeed right, Miss Otter,' said Mr Tamburlane, 'as always. Miss de Reptonville lives under a heavy burden. But fortunately you and I may be privileged to assist in lightening those slender shoulders.'

'It will not be our first such case,' said Miss Otter, smiling graciously.

'Nor yet our our one hundred and first, if it were possible to keep a reckoning. Now, Miss de Reptonville, I leave the shop entirely in your management. Miss Otter and I have affairs to discuss. If any problems arise, you must call upon your own good judgement to solve them. For Miss Otter and I must on no account be disturbed. Help yourself to sherry and biscuits if you require to relieve responsibility with refreshment. Miss Otter and I shall not emerge until teatime. When I am sure we shall all be very ready for crumpets and anchovy toast.' He waved Miss Otter into the inner room and entering behind her, shut the door. Griselda noticed that Miss Otter carried a portfolio of papers and had a slight limp.

As usual there were few customers, though a young man who wanted a book on the botany of the Andes, became quite offensive when Griselda, after much searching, was unable to find him one. A tired woman brought her son, aged about ten, to select his own birthday present. She seemed prepared to spend up to fifteen shillings, and urged the claims of a book of scientific wonders illustrated with many polychromatic plates, and acres of isonometry. The boy insisted on a copy of the Everyman Mabinogion. Despite the economy, his Mother seemed angry and disappointed An elderly man prefaced his requirements by presenting Griselda with his card: Professor O. O. Gasteneetsia, FRS. The Professor then showed Griselda a minute cutting from a penny daily. It advised a book entitled 'What About A Rumba?' Griselda offered to order it for him. But he kept saying 'Tonight. I come again tonight' until drawn from the shop by a newsboy shouting about a crisis of some kind.

Griselda wondered whether she should procure

crumpets and anchovies, but hesitated to leave the shop. The neighbourhood, moreover, seemed unpropitious, at least for crumpets. At about 5.15, however, when she had drunk all the sherry and eaten all the biscuits, and still felt exceedingly famished, a pleasing smell began to fill the shop. At 5.25, the inner door opened and Mr Tamburlane called to her: 'Enter, Miss de Reptonville. The fatted calf is dead. Alas! that Miss Otter has to leave us.'

The room was full of blue smoke, the beautiful eighteenth century table spread with hot crumpets and buttered toast, a Wedgwood Chinese teapot, with cups and plates to match, an opened jar of anchovies, and a litter of papers in process of reassembly by Miss Otter. Among the papers, Griselda noticed, seemed to be a number of very grimy and unpractised looking letters; others were inexplicable drawings in pompeian red on fresh white cartridge paper.

'All this clutter!' ejaculated Miss Otter, smilingly. 'No, please don't help me. I am an untidy old woman. You sit down and eat your tea.'

Griselda had never previously met with tea in the shop, or indeed, any other meal. It was true, however, that each day she left Mr Tamburlane to provide for himself while she took lunch in a teashop. Today she was ready to tuck in.

'Good-bye, Mr Tamburlane,' said Miss Otter, strapping her portfolio, 'I'll find my own way to the door. Good-bye, Miss de Reptonville. If you'll take an old woman's advice, you'll turn down the next proposal you receive. Come what may, you should turn it down. No matter how keen on you the other party seems to be. Feelings change, you know, with the passage of the years. Nor is that the only reason.' She was on her way through the shop. 'Don't forget what I say. Miss de Reptonville.' The outer door shut.

'Don't you worry.' said Mr Tamburlane to Griselda, repeating Lord Roller's counsel. 'I talked to Miss Otter very fully about your tragic misfortune. I think that together we shall have the great happiness of recapturing the lamb that has strayed. It is fortunate indeed that I was by when your need arose. Have a Bath Oliver?' He extended an exquisite Wedgwood biscuit box.

'Thank you. I'd like another piece of anchovy toast first.'

'I imagine, Miss de Reptonville, that my words of cheer fill you with scepticism?'

'I'm afraid I'm not very hopeful that I shall find my friend. But it is very kind of you to concern yourself.'

'You probably think that I am a crank and that Miss Otter is mad?' He was eating crumpet after crumpet.

'Certainly not.'

'And that our weekly paper, if it exists at all, has less than no power in the land?'

'Not at all.' Griselda began to wish she had never confided in Mr Tamburlane.

'Yes, Miss de Reptonville, you certainly think all these things; How surprised you will be! That is all I care to say at the moment. How surprised you will be! How pleasantly and delicately surprised!'

'Would you let me see a copy of your paper?'

'Subcribers only, you will recall. I fear your sceptical attitude unfits you as yet to enter that charmed cricle.' He had begun to drink cups of tea in as quick succession as he had eaten crumpets.

'I see.'

'Child of loveliness, yours but to reap where Miss Otter and I have sown.'

He began to talk about books; and very shortly afterwards Griselda was engaged upon a dreary quest for lodgings in and around Ladbroke Grove.

XVIII

In the end, a decision being urgently necessary, she settled upon a small rectangular residence in a block of flats built for young, and presumably underpaid, office workers of her own sex, by a semi-charitable organization, the New Vista Apartments Trust. Situated just off the western side of that great dividing thorough-fare, the Edgware Road, Greenwood Tree House purported to improve upon such commercial lodgings as could be obtained for a like rental. Under the rules, tenants had to move out upon reaching the age of thirty; and were expected, though not compelled, to interest themselves in the work of the YWCA or in some cognate organization approved by the Management Committee. The block was not an unreservedly first-class piece of construction, owing to shortage of funds; but it had been designed (for less than the rightful fee) by an eminent cathedral architect, and therefore reflected the very best in contemporary design.

In addition to her depression about Louise, Griselda now began to suffer from positive loneliness. Although Mr Tamburlane's mysterious paper was stated to be issued weekly, he soon made it clear that nothing was likely to come of the quest for Louise for several months. Combined with the obscurity about how the paper in any way forwarded the quest, and Mr Tamburlane's incommunicativeness upon matters of detail, this announcement confirmed Griselda's view that the whole episode was a dismal exercise in whimsicality, conducted at her expense, or possibly a patch of moonshine from the minds of two near-lunatics. Miss Otter visited Mr Tamburlane regularly each Friday, but rarely remained closeted with him for so long as on that first occasion. Upon entering and leaving, she continued to favour Griselda with cryptic and prophetic observations: 'Next time a title comes your way, Miss de Reptonville, I think you would be most unwise to lose your chance'; or simply 'More friends are what you need most at the moment, my dear.'

In three months of inner misery, Griselda made only a single friend, apart from Mr Tamburlane, who continued as punctiliously complimentary as on the day she met him. The new friend was Peggy Potter, her neighbour in Greenwood Tree House. Peggy was a broad, well-built girl with a large bust; a little taller than Griselda, and with a quantity of more or less fair hair hanging to her shoulders. She wore woollen dresses, of which Griselda felt that Lousie would have strongly disapproved, and had a reserved air derived, as Griselda soon discovered, from a conviction that she had little in common with her fellow inmates. This circumstance, combined with the fact that, before coming to London she had passed her entire existence in Bodmin, where she had graduated at University College, made her as a friend for Griselda something of a cul-de-sac. Ultimately Griselda realized that inner misery was a positive handicap when seeking to extend a social circle.

It was the pipes in the passage which brought Peggy and Griselda together. Each apartment was equipped with an electric radiator dependant upon a shilling meter; but outside in the passages were occasional steam coils, installed to guard the cocoanut matting and other decorations from injury by damp. The flow of electricity was so costly that the tenants formed the habit of drying their stockings and underclothes on these pipes, which were kept hardly more than lukewarm. The practice was specifically forbidden in the Rules: but as the Rules in most cases failed to provide for sanctions (the Management Committee felt that small fines, for example, were anachronistic and reminiscent of the evil days before the Truck Act) this particular Rule was obeyed only by those who wore no stockings. The practice was to steal out after eleven o'clock and drape the coils: realistically, the difficulty was the insufficient number of the installations. Griselda and Peggy became friends upon Peggy suggesting that they sidetrack the general run of inmates by sharing the use and the cost of a single electric heater. This arrangement involved them in constant use of one another's rooms.

They began to drink tea together, and Griselda lent Penny a packet of 'Lux.' In less than a week, Peggy suggested that Griselda accompany her to hear some music. It proved to be a recital of songs by Duparc, given by a rather elderly Belgian woman, retired some years previously from the provincial operatic stage of her country.

The Wigmore Hall was almost empty, and Griselda was slightly scared by the unaccountable permanent decorations behind the platform; nor were the seats which Peggy and Griselda occupied either very cosy or very close to the centre of interest: none the less Griselda enjoyed the evening because she was so glad to have a friend to share her enjoyment. During the interval, which was rather long, she gave expression to this feeling by offering to stand Peggy a cup of coffee: but the Wigmore Hall proved not to offer refreshments. Outside, at the end of the recital, a group of excitingly dressed women with collection boxes and very little English beset the small audience for contributions some continental charity. Griselda gathered that the charity had been founded to commemorate the recitalist's wonderful work for the Allies during the World War.

One thing followed another, and soon Griselda was accompanying Peggy to other entertainments: a production by students at the Rudolf Steiner Hall of a seldom performed Elizabethan tragedy; and a recital at Friends House of works by lesser members of the Bach family, the performers being partly professional and partly amateur. One Sunday afternoon they ambled round the Tate Gallery, where Peggy was much addicted to Mr Graham Robertson's Blakes.

'Have you read that book of his? His reminiscences?'

'I found him an exhibitionist. He's not my period, of course.'

'Shall we go and see the surrealists some time? At the Zwemmer? I'd like to.'

'Once is enough for surrealism; just like Madame Tussaud. You go, Griselda, and you'll see what I mean.'

'But the critics say that the surrealists are the modern equivalent of Blake, and you say you like Blake?'

'Blake had belief. The surrealists have no belief. Surely that is fundamental?'

'Have you belief, Peggy?'

'Not yet. But I am prepared to have.'

They passed on to some water colours in the basement, with which Peggy was clearly well acquainted, as she discoursed upon them most convincingly and exhaustively, though water colour landscapes were not Griselda's favourite kind of picture.

Peggy seemed to live in a general condition of contingency: her prevailing attitude was the provisional. Thus although a permanent civil servant, and apparently well advanced in the service for her years (though remarkably ill paid, Griselda thought, considering her Honours Degress and years of youth devoted to passing difficult examinations), yet Peggy's attitude to her job was merely, as she put it, 'marking time'. Where she aimed to go when her march was resumed, was, however, indefinite. Equally her sojourn at Greenwood Tree House was described by her as a 'passage through'; while even her health she referred to upon Griselda once enquiring about it, as 'under observation.' She accumulated almost no possessions, and seemed content to have Griselda as her only friend. There were times when Griselda wondered whether Peggy was not in a state verging upon suspended animation.

One evening towards the end of June, they were seated in Hyde Park. Peggy was reading *The Listener*; Griselda a book from Mr Tamburlane's stock. Peggy suddenly spoke.

'I'm taking some leave in August.' It was the first time Griselda had heard the military term applied to civil life. 'I'm going to Italy. Not the big towns and tourist centres, of course; just some of the smaller places in the south. Right off the beaten track. I try to visit a new country each year. I suppose you wouldn't come with me?'

'I can't afford a holiday yet. Nor am I entitled to one, I think,' It was difficult to imagine Mr Tamburlane raising an objection; but, oddly enough, it was equally difficult to imagine the job being still there, or even the shop upon return from a holiday. 'I'm terribly sorry. Of course I'd have loved to come.' Griselda's regret was tempered inwardly by a distinct reservation in favour of the big towns and tourist centres: particularly, she felt, in Italy.

'I could find the money for both of us, if that's what it is. You could repay me later. Or not at all, if you couldn't.'

'That's terribly generous. Thank you, Peggy.' Griselda touched her hand, which Peggy slightly withdrew. 'But as things are with me, I don't see how I could *ever* repay you.'

'You needn't. I said that. Only if and when you can.'

'I couldn't agree to that.' Griselda knew that she could agree quite easily had she wanted to visit tiny poverty-stricken Italian villages with Peggy. 'But thank you again. It is a very kind idea.'

'Not particularly, I want you to come with me, Griselda. Do think it over. Believe me I'm quite good at digging out just the places no one else ever gets to.'

'There are many better people than I am for that sort of holiday.' But Griselda thought with guilt of her fondness for long walks, of how difficult she was to tire, her prima facie suitability for the undertaking. 'What about the people you've gone with before?'

'I've usually gone alone. But I'd like *you* to come.'

Griselda glanced at her: at her big bust, her rather dull hair, her indifferent clothes, her face already drawing on its iron mask of frustration, only to be removed by death.

'I'd like to come, Peggy. But I mustn't. I really mustn't. Please don't tempt me.'

'I thought we could have a good time.'

It occurred to Griselda as possible that Peggy, despite appearances, really cared for her: not in the least as Louise cared for her, and she cared for Louise, but in some other way, not necessarily the less authentic because probably approved by society or because completely unaccompanied by any display of feeling. Griselda was incapable of feeling very much without showing that she felt something; without tendering her affection. It seemed a simpler way than Peggy's.

'Next year, perhaps. Where do you plan to go next year?'

'Finland. I don't think you'd care for that.'

Peggy resumed *The Listener*. In the end they went to the Marble Arch Pavilion together, as if nothing had happened.

Later, while washing stockings in Peggy's room, Griselda said: 'Would you like to borrow *Old Calabria* before you go? Doesn't it deal with just the part you're visiting? It's a book Mr Tamburlane always has in stock, and I could easily lend it to you for a week or two.'

'Thank you. Griselda, but I think I'd rather form my own impressions. I don't know that I'd care to see things through Norman Douglas's eyes.'

Griselda began to squeeze out a wet stocking. 'Peggy,' she said. 'What do you want most in the world?'

Peggy looked faintly hostile, as in the Park.

'I don't think the question has much significance for me.' she replied. 'I don't think I see life in quite those terms.' Then she added, obviously trying to please: 'What do you want most in the world?'

But, contrary to Peggy's notion, Griselda had neither expected nor desired that the question should be thus lobbed back at her. She was merely trying to enter into a corner of Peggy's mind; fractionally to explore an outlook which she believed to be as habitual among her neighbours as it was alien to herself. 'I want to know about *you*.'

'Really I'm remarkably content as I am.'

'I'm not content as I am.'

'I know you're not. And of course I know why you're not.'

'Why am I not?'

'Griselda, we're not schoolgirls. We don't have to go into all that at this hour of the night.'

Her attitude was so impossibly aloof, that Griselda became momentarily filled with a younger than schoolgirlish urge to shock. 'What I want from life is ecstasy.'

'What will you do when you've got it?' Peggy had taken off her dress and stood in her knickers and brassière. 'I mean *after* you've got it?'

'I shall reconsider the whole subject,' said Griselda.

Peggy smiled slightly, relieved that the conversation was apparently being dropped. By way of farewell gesture she said: 'If you really want to know, Griselda, I'm not the marrying kind.'

'*I'm* not. I rather thought *you* were.'

'No, I'm not.'

'I see.' Not that she did. 'Anyway you don't want to borrow *Old Calabria*.'

'Afterwards, perhaps. If I may?'

'Of course. If I'm still at the shop.' Griselda gathered together four wet stockings, like bits of ghosts which had been out in the rain. 'Good night, Peggy.'

Peggy's preparations for bed had advanced no further. She jerked into speech. 'Tell me something, Griselda.'

'Yes.'

'Is my bust too large?'

'Of course it isn't. It's much better than having too small a bust like me.'

'Then it *is* too large?'

Peggy's face was white. She was very near tears.

'It's larger than most people's. I wish mine was. It's a good thing.'

Peggy was visibly making a great effort. 'I sometimes feel self-conscious about it. Not often.'

Griselda kissed Peggy gently on each breast. Suddenly she felt a hundred years older than Peggy; and oddly enough, glad to be so. 'Attractiveness is mainly a matter of thoughts.'

Peggy had removed her last garments and was putting on her nightdress. 'It's easy for someone as attractive as you to say that. Most men never get as far as a woman's mind.'

Griselda recalled Louise's words about fellow feeling. 'I expect not,' she said sadly.

'I've decided to do without them. You can if you try. At least I can. It's not even very difficult.' Peggy began to brush her teeth.

'I need *someone* to love me.'

'I'm glad to say I don't. It's extraordinary how well I do on my own.'

'I can see there are advantages.'

'Not that I'm bigoted about it. It's just what suits me.'

'I think you're very wise to do what suits you. But I still think *you* have a particularly attractive figure. Shall I turn out the light for you?'

'You're kind to me, Griselda.' She was climbing into the divan bed.

'You're kind to *me*. Shall I open the window?'

'Please. Quite wide.'

'The sky is full of stars.'

'More rain, I'm afraid. July is often a wet month, though not so wet as August.'

'Surely it would mean rain if there were *no* stars?'

'It depends. Often it means rain either way.'

'What a pity! Good night. Peggy dear.'

'Good night. Griselda.'

Griselda returned to her own room, and, switching on the electric heater, began to dry the two pairs of stockings, to eat chocolate wafers, and to conclude her interesting book.

During the small hours she was awakened by screams and groans from the next room, and deduced that Peggy must be having a nightmare. She reflected that, as a friend, she should intervene; but before thought had turned to action, she was once more dreamlessly sleeping.

XIX

Griselda preferred a light luncheon at Fullers, comparatively dear at the price, to a cheaper and more substantial meal at Lyons or the Express Dairy. Some time after Peggy had invited her to Italy, she was making for Fullers' shop in Regent Street when she encountered Geoffrey Kynaston. After several days of rain, it had suddenly become humidly hot, and Kynaston was wearing a white shirt, open at the neck, and grey flannel trousers, neither garment being noticeably new, clean, or appealing.

'Hullo, you,' he said in the most casual manner.

'Hullo.'

'Still alive and kicking after the bust-up?'

'As you see.'

'Got some new clothes too. A great improvement, if I may say so.'

Indeed it could not be said that Griselda was saving any money at all. She was not even attempting to do so.

'Thank you.'

'I didn't grasp that you were that way?'

'What way?'

'That way.'

'I'm not. Or not entirely.'

'I see. Thank you for clearing my mind. I'm not that

way at all. I think I told you.'

'You did.'

'In the light of your explanation, I'm glad to see you. More glad, I mean, than had it been, as I supposed, otherwise.'

'I'm glad.'

'Perhaps we could start something up?'

'What?'

'Light refreshments first, I suppose. To judge by your air of purpose. Can you pay for two?'

'With difficulty.'

'If you can do it all, you're better placed than I am. Let's go.' There was a second's pause, and he added: 'You don't mind do you? I did feed you at Hodley.'

'It's quite all right,' said Griselda. 'Come on.' They advanced up the hot busy pavement

'You don't work, if I remember? I suppose you have an allowance?'

'No.'

'Not a *job* after all?'

'Why not?'

'How grimly disillusioning.'

'I'm sorry. How's dancing?'

'Packed up. What did you suppose?'

'It never occurred to me.'

'It was on its last legs when you arrived. You could see the state of business for yourself.'

'I'm sorry. What about poetry?'

'Same as before.'

'That was better than nothing.'

'Very little.'

They reached and entered Fullers. Kynaston's costume was not precisely what the management was used to at that particular branch.

'What'll you have?' enquired Griselda, putting forward the menu.

'Just a large fruit salad,' said Kynaston, without looking at it 'And a cup of Ovaltine or something like that.' Seated opposite him. Griselda observed that he seemed really emaciated.

'Wouldn't you care for something more solid?'

'Not in this heat.'

There was a pause.

'How's Doris?'

'Down with TB. Never mind about her. I want to know about you. Or are you still uncommunicative? Of course, I see now that you had your reasons. Not that you need have had. I'm utterly sympathetic in principle. I hope you gather that?'

'Could we talk about something else?'

'I like masterful women – in fact, I direly need one myself to organize things for me.'

'I remember.'

'And, of course, that kind of woman often—'

'Please could we talk about something else?'

'I thought that perhaps you would be grateful for an utterly sympathetic listener?'

The arrival of the waitress spared Griselda an answer.

'There's no Ovaltine.'

Griselda supposed that he would order Nescafé; but

he said 'A sundae will do. When I've finished the fruit.'

'Which sort of Sundae?'

'Any sort.' Later he was brought a sundae costing 3/6. It was the biggest and best

'Let's come to realities.'

'Haven't we?' asked Griselda.

'I mean our joint future.'

'I'm provided for. I've got a job in a bookshop.'

'You can't be getting much?'

'No. But I like the job.'

'Which shop?'

'It's called Tamburlane.'

'Rather beyond the means of most people who can read. But reputable.'

'You know it?'

'By reputation. Tamburlane was the son of pauper parents and raised in the East End. He always wanted to own a bookshop: a morbid respect for learning based on frustration. In the end he made a bit of money out of prospecting in Alaska and got his way. There! I feel well-informed.'

'Better than I am.'

'You pick up things like that from the sort of people I've mixed with. Where are you living?'

'Off the Edgware Road.'

'Do you like it?'

'Not very much.'

'Monica Paget-Barlow says there's a flat in Juvenal Court. It's not altogether an ideal home, but I expect it's better than what you've got. Possibly the two of us could afford it? That is if I could settle on something which brought in money steadily.'

'I'm perfectly content where I am.'

'You mean you've not yet had time to get round to the idea of living with me?'

'Not yet.'

'You don't feel equal to organizing me?'

'Not even myself.'

'I'm sorry, Griselda. I'm not really heartless.'

At a neighbouring table, a child was sick on the floor. It was impossible to believe that so small a vessel could have held so much.

'I'm unhappy.'

'Of course.'

'I'm glad to have met you. I need a friend.'

'I've always been fond of you, Griselda. You know that.' He spoke as if his was a hopeless passion of many years standing.

'Where are you living now?'

'Friends house me for odd nights.'

'Are you looking for a job?'

'The jobs available are mostly rather hell.'

'I know.'

'I'm trying to work up my plastic poses.'

'Do they help?'

'It's an extension of Laban's teaching. But entirely original.'

Across the room a waitress overturned a tray laden with portions of roast veal. She was a pretty girl and several men began to assist her with the re-assembly. But their efforts were competitive and helped very little.

'Now that I've met you I think I'll close with General Pampero.'

'Who's he?'

'The Liberator of Orinoco. He spent most of his life in exile: naturally in London. The Orinocan Government have just bought the house he lived in. They want someone to curate. Very few Orinocans are allowed out of the country. I know a girl who works in the Embassy. She claimed I was a D.Litt. and got me the offer.'

'Where's the house?'

'Somewhere the other side of Mecklenburgh Square. Quite a healthy neighbourhood.'

'Why haven't you moved in already?'

'I'm afraid of acquiring roots.'

'You had roots in Hodley.'

Kynaston stopped eating and looked into Griselda's eyes.

'Griselda, I suppose you wouldn't marry me?'

'I'm in love with someone else.'

'In love?'

'Certainly.'

He continued to gaze at her.

'*I'm* in love with you.'

'I doubt it.'

'Of course I'm in love with you,' he said with faint irritation. 'You're unique.'

Griselda said nothing.

'Let's stick to realities. Is there any *future* to this other business?'

Griselda still said nothing.

'I mean we've both made pretty good messes of our lives so far. I think we should cut our losses.'

'I'm in love with someone else, Geoffrey.'

'I have an intensely devoted nature. I could make you happy.'

'Are you happy yourself?'

'*You* could make me.'

'I expect most married couples have exactly those expectations of each other.'

'They're perfectly reasonable expectations. People aren't designed to be happy in isolation like sentries in boxes.'

He seemed startlingly in earnest.

'What about Doris?'

'I'm very fond of little Doris but I don't want to marry her. Besides, as I told you, she's got TB.'

'Does she want to marry you?'

'She can't marry anyone. She's very ill. I can only see her once a week.'

'You do still see her?'

'Of course, I do. I'm very fond of her. I'm not a monster.'

'I'd like to see her some time.'

'I don't think you've much in common. But you can if you want to.'

'I suppose we haven't really.'

'I am glad you can see it. It'll save a lot of nervous tension and train fares. Will you come and look at this flat in Juvenal Court?'

'Won't you live where you work?'

'The Orinocans have sublet most of the house. The General's relics hardly fill two rooms. There'll be an Orinocan Enquiry Bureau in a third room. That's me too. An Orinocan trading concern have got the rest. But I can't afford Juvenal Court without you. It's quite amusing. Friends of mine live in the other flats. Come and see it this evening. The flat won't stay empty for ever. I'll call for you.'

'Geoffrey,' said Griselda. 'I must make it plain to you that the chance of my marrying you is entirely and absolutely nil.'

XX

But when the shop shut, Kynaston was lurking outside.

'After all, I've nowhere else to go,' he said.

He even assisted Mr Tamburlane to put up the shutters: so that Griselda had to introduce him. Though he was reasonably good-looking by modern male standards, his clothes appeared as inappropriate as in Fullers.

Mr Tamburlane seemed unperturbed. After they had stood about on the pavement outside the shop mumbling disconnected generalities, he said: 'I wonder if the two of you would care to join me in a small repast? I usually go to Underwoods. They know my ways.' It was the first such invitation Griselda had received from him.

Kynaston immediately accepted for himself and Griselda. They proceeded on foot to a restaurant near the Charing Cross Road. Mr Tamburlane, although the hysteria of the evening rush hour was at its height, and tired workers were flickering and zigzagging across the pavement like interweaving lightning, walked slowly and contemplatively, his eyes directed upwards to a group of swallows swirling after flies, his expression that favoured in coloured representations of the Blessed St Francis.

'Sister, my sister, O soft light swallow,' quoted Mr Tamburlane, gazing upwards in a warm and gentle rapture, as the trio clove a passage through the toilers frenzied for the consolations of home.

'Sister, my sister, O soft light swallow,
　　Though all things feast in the spring's guest-
　　　　chamber.
　　　　How hast thou heart to be glad thereof yet?
For where thou fliest I shall not follow,
　　Till life forget and death remember.
　　Till thou remember and I forget.'

'There is no felicity,' he continued, as they stood outside Swan and Edgars, waiting to cross the road, 'exceeding that which can ensure upon utter disregard of the consanguineous prohibitions.'

Underwoods claimed to combine the tradition of the English chop-house with that of the cosmopolitan restaurant-de-luxe. The tables were set in dark mahogany boxes, but there were attractive red-shaded lights, and the benches had been ameliorated with padded upholstery. The tablecloths were very white, the cutlery very glittering, and the menu cards large as barristers' briefs. There were dimly illuminated portaits of Daniel Mendoza and the Boy Roscius. There was a greeny-grey skull in a glass case bearing a silver plaque inscribed with the names 'William Corder' in pleasantly extravagant Gothic script. Griselda thought it might well prove the most agreeable restaurant she had so far visited.

Mr Tamburlane seemed to be exceedingly well

known, both to the staff and to many of the other customers. Preceded by the head waiter, whom he had greeted with a quiet 'Good evening, Andrews,' he advanced between the lines of boxes, frequently acknowledging greetings. Griselda, following him, attracted almost as much interest; and Kynaston came last, looking more unsuitably dressed than ever. There were an unusual number of men in the restaurant; and few of the women but looked exceedingly striking. Under-waiters with long white aprons darted about like trolls.

Mr Tamburlane was shown to a table near the back of the room. 'I hope you will have no objection,' he enquired of his guests, 'to caviare, turtle soup, sole, a fillet steak, and a bird? I am becoming increasingly set in my ways.'

Griselda noticed that Kynaston seemed entirely able to eat a normal meal provided that it was offered and organized by someone else.

As they ate, and drank the excellent and appropriate wines which their host ordered out of his head and without recourse to the Wine List, Mr Tamburlane talked more and more expansively, breaking off every now and then to impart to an under-waiter a request for French Mustard or another baton. He called the under-waiters by their Christian names: Leslie, Frank, and Noel. By the deference shown him in return Mr Tamburlane might have been his namesake, the Scourge of God. It even seemed to Griselda a little exaggerated, like a caricature of good service.

'It gives me particular pleasure,' said Mr Tamburlane, 'to meet another acolyte of the golden and gracious Miss de Repteonville, for another acolyte I readily perceive that you are. Miss de Reptonville has rapidly set up her own particular and especial altar in my soul. I am sure she has in yours also?'

'I proposed marriage to her today. During lunch.'

'Then' cried Mr Tamburlane, transfigured, 'this little dinner is an agape, a love-feast, without my knowing it. How limited your news makes me feel, how squat and lacking in vision! We should have drunk from the fountain in the temple of Lanternland, and the livers of young white peacocks should have been our sustenance. For, if I may for one single moment be personal, your youthful candour and clear brow give assurance of our goddess's response.'

'Not quite,' said Kynaston. 'It's still an open question.'

'You did not cry out and leap to his waiting arms,' said Mr Tamburlane in amazement to Griselda.

'We were lunching in Fullers at the time, Mr Tamburlane.'

'Do it now, Miss de Reptonville. They know me here and I can declare a plenary indulgence for all possible consequences. Take him and let us inaugurate a rite which shall last till Venus succumbs before the onrush of Apollo. On a later day, I shall myself take the bridegroom aside and, old man that I am, show him secrets of joy most germane to your bliss, Miss de Reptonville, most unknown to his heart.' Mr Tamburlane's fluffy white hair was moist with rapture, good wine, and the

217

heat of the restaurant, his beaming face, the image of the Japanese ensign.

'I'm afraid I turned the offer down,' said Griselda. 'I'm very sorry to spoil things.'

'But why, dear Anaxarete, make yourself stone?'

'You know very well, Mr Tamburlane, that I have no inclination to marry anyone.'

'But you could fall into no error more fundamental! If you wish to continue – if you hope to rediscover—' But suddenly, with a sound like the discharge of a cork, the excited Mr Tamburlane, ignorant of the extent of Kynaston's knowledge, discontinued his observations. 'Fear nothing,' he said to Kynaston, his eyes still very bright, 'nor let your night's rest be troubled unless with anticipation of raptures. I shall myself speak apart to our erring one during business hours tomorrow.'

'It will make no difference,' said Griselda, smiling sweetly. 'I'm resolved to marry no one.'

'Noel,' exclaimed Mr Tamburlane, 'we're ready for the steak.'

It was exquisite; as was the ensuing bird, which Mr Tamburlane carved personally, with a long thin knife, like a rapier, incredibly sharp, and a fork fiercer than Morton's. Afterwards came flaming pancakes, and rich Turkish coffee in cups bearing the insignia of the establishment, and two Benedictines each. Mr Tamburlane completed the occasion by appending to the bill his curving, speckled, backward-sloping signature; and giving a pound in largesse. He then suddenly excused himself to Griselda and Kynaston, and rapidly disappeared through a little door beneath a reproduction of Winterhalter's portrait of the Duke of Sussex.

'Enjoy your dinner, miss?' enquired Noel.

'Very much indeed, thank you.'

'Nice gentleman, Mr Tamburlane.'

'He comes here a lot?'

'Usually with his Indian friends.'

'I don't know about them,' said Griselda, her curiosity surmounting her manners.

'All in coloured robes and covered in diamonds and rubies.' He placed his hands on the end of the table and sank his voice.

'I'm afraid we don't live up to that.'

'No, miss,' said the waiter, glancing at Kynaston's torn and dirty cricket shirt. 'Of course, Mr Tamburlane gets all his money from India.'

'How?' asked Kynaston.

'Business with the rajahs and such like. They've all got as much money as a dog has fleas.' He lowered his voice still further. 'They say it's them who keep his account with us in order.'

But Mr Tamburlane was standing behind him.

'Beg pardon, sir. I was just asking the young lady whether she enjoyed her dinner.'

'Of course, she enjoyed her dinner, Noel. This is the happiest day of her life.'

Used to such situations in the course of his work, the waiter took Mr Tamburlane's meaning immediately.

'My respectful congratulations to you, sir. And to you, madam.'

'Thank you, Noel,' said Kynaston calmly. 'I've done nothing to deserve my good fortune.'

'And what becomes of us now?' enquired Mr Tamburlane, seating himself on the corner of the upholstered bench. 'The night is still a virgin. All right, Noel. You can go.'

'Thank you, sir. Good night sir. Good night madam. Good night sir.'

'Tell me, young bridegroom,' resumed Mr Tamburlane, when the adieux to Noel were concluded, 'what was your intention tonight in bearing off Miss de Reptonville? You must, I suppose, have had some intention. Or perhaps not; perhaps you thought merely to let the gale of love blow whither it listed? If so may I blow with it for a spell? May I savour, if only by proxy, la premier souvenir d'amour?'

'We were going to look at a flat.'

'The hymeneal shrine! Nothing could more perfectly suit me. Let us go there at once. Frank,' cried Mr Tamburlane. 'please ask the doorman to summon us a taxi. No, wait. Ours should be a ritual progress. Make it a hansom. There is always one stationed at the bottom of Piccadilly.'

'There is one thing which is being overlooked,' said Griselda when the flurry had subsided.

'Name it,' said Mr Tamburlane. 'It shall be my privilege to provide it. Shall night-scented flowers be strewn before us as we pass through Leicester Square? I presume that is the direction?'

'Juvenal Court,' replied Kynaston. 'Just off Tottenham Court Road.'

'Shall the fountains in Seven Dials run wine? Shall two white oxen be roasted whole in St Giles's Circus?'

It occurred to Griselda that Mr Tamburlane was a little drunk. Possibly his meals when his Indian friends were actually present, were less far-reaching.

'The point we are overlooking,' said Griselda, 'is that I have no intention of marrying.'

'Let us leave events to take their course,' replied Mr Tamburlane. 'Indeed I have absolute faith that they will do so.'

The doorman entered the restaurant and came to Mr Tamburlane's table.

'Hansom, sir.'

Mr Tamburlane rose.

'Swift as the thoughts of love. We are grateful to our Hermes.' Griselda's worst forebodings were confirmed when Mr Tamburlane produced his wallet and found it empty. The pound he had given to the waiter must have been all it contained. He sought for change in his trousers pocket and produced sevenpence. This sum seemed far from satisfying the doorman, who, for one whom presumably he had regarded as a very special customer, must have run all the way to Piccadilly Circus.

'Blimey,' said Hermes. 'That all you've got?'

'The privilege of serving Eros must make up the balance.'

'What's a ruddy statue got to do with it?'

'Come,' cried Mr Tamburlane, 'let us mount the car of love.'

'Bloody swindler,' said Hermes. 'Look at that!' He extended his hand bearing the seven coppers to Frank seeking sympathy.

'More fool you,' said Frank. He added something which Griselda failed to hear, being now on her way out of the restaurant. She noticed, as she followed Mr Tamburlane, who firmly took the lead, that his many acquaintances among the customers gave an impression of knowing him only by sight. They smiled and bowed as he passed, but said nothing. The doorman could still be heard execrating Mr Tamburlane in the background. But Andrews, the head waiter, was as deferential as ever.

'Hope to see you again soon, sir.'

'Tomorrow and tomorrow and tomorrow,' replied Mr Tamburlane.

'Would you care to book a table now, sir? Like yesterday?'

'All our yesterdays,' said Mr Tamburlane; and, suddenly remembering the customary usage, stood aside for Griselda to precede him into the warm summer air. There could be little doubt that he was the worse for drink.

There was the appalling question of who could pay for the hansom; including, Griselda supposed, an extra passenger. Only one answer being possible, Griselda attempted to recall the total sum in her handbag. Did hansom cabs charge at the same rates as taxis, she wondered; and would there soon be a scene like the one with the doorman?

'Mount,' said Mr Tamburlane to Griselda.

The door of the cab hung back against the side, and Griselda put her foot on the little step and entered. She had never been in a hansom cab before. The vehicle, although astonishingly open to the air, somehow managed to retain a strong, utterly unknown smell.

'Mount,' said Mr Tamburlane to Kynaston.

Kynaston ascended and seated himself. He looked somewhat dishevelled with wine, though less so than Mr Tamburlane.

Mr Tamburlane's foot was on the step when the driver shouted down out of the sky 'Two's the legal limit.' He flourished his whip.

'Stuff,' replied Mr Tamburlane.

'I'll lose my licence.'

'I'll buy you another one,' said Mr Tamburlane.

'Mind you do,' said the driver. Mr Tamburlane had looked like a tip of unprecedented size, and the driver was used to eccentrics who could pay for their indulgences. He flicked Mr Tamburlane on the left ear.

Kynaston had moved close to Griselda, making a small amount of room for Mr Tamburlane in the far corner. But Mr Tamburlane ignored this provision and fell heavily into place between the two of them, sending Kynaston sliding away along the slippery leather.

'Permit me,' he said, putting an arm round each of them. 'For warmth.'

Indeed it was surprisingly draughty for such a warm evening.

'Will you be cold?' said Griselda to Kynaston along

the back of Mr Tamburlane's neck. She had completed her mental arithmetic and a last desperate hope entered her mind. 'Perhaps we'd better go by tube?'

As she spoke she felt through Mr Tamburlane's body his other arm tightening on Kynaston.

'Thank you, Griselda,' said Kynaston gulping. 'I'll be warm enough. I loathe wrapping up.' But his tones were soft. They expressed pathetic gratitude for what he took to be Griselda's first piece of solicitude for him, her first essay at managing his diffused and migrant life.

'Vile were if indeed,' said Mr Tamburlane, muscling in still further, 'for the Lachender Held young Siegfried to mask his manhood with draperies.'

There was a moment's silence while Mr Tamburlane consolidated his grip, and Griselda looked up at the stars.

'Well?'

The cabman had lifted the little hatch in the roof.

'Advance,' said Mr Tamburlane.

'Once round the Park?' asked the cabman. 'Or along the Victoria Embankment?'

'Juvenal Court,' said Kynaston. 'Just off Tottenham Court Road.'

'It's not usual,' said the cabman. 'I don't cater for regular fares. Can't afford it. There's taxis for that. I've got my living to earn.'

'We'll see that you don't lose by it,' said Mr Tamburlane, his voice full of banknotes.

'Take care that I don't.'

'Young love is on the wing tonight,' said Mr Tamburlane.

'Honeymoon couple? OK.'

He shut the trap and they drove off. At the moment of departure the doorman appeared: 'Watch out,' he shrieked. 'They'll welsh you.'

'Lie down and cool off,' rejoined the cabman ungratefully.

It was pleasant, though squashed. Griselda remembered Lord Beaconsfield's phrase 'The gondola of London.' To journey from one gilded hall to another by hansom cab alone with the person one truly loved must indeed have been heaven. As soon as the present journey started, however, Griselda realised the origin of the unusual smell. It came from the horse. The vehicle. moreover, lacked a jingling bell: that essential appurtenance for romance.

They clattered along swiftly. Pedestrians, habituated to vehicles equipped with audible warnings, were several times all but slaughtered, to the accompaniment of dreadful language from the cabman. Walking-out couples, glad of something to do, and parties up from the country, stood on the pavements sentimentally staring. Police constables were irritable or facetious. An elementary school child threw a fire-cracker, which fortunately failed to discharge. At Cambridge Circus an elderly woman shouted several times to the driver 'It's unsafe. It's unsafe. It's unsafe'; at which the driver lifted the trap in the roof and bawled down 'She's dead right', then went into roars of Mephistophilean laughter.

Griselda wondered whether the fiery and erratic behaviour of the horse reflected some kind of incorrect
feeding.

Juvenal Court appeared to be three adjoining mid-
nineteenth century houses run together and converted
into a rabbit warren. There were lights at every single
window including one or two very small ones. A girl's
head was projecting from one of the upper windows.

'Barney,' she cried, 'come to me.' Presumably she was
addressing an intimate on a lower floor.

Instantly a man looked out. 'I'm tired,' he shouted
back in a cultivated accent. The street light showed that
he had much smooth black hair and a large nose. The
girl moaned and withdrew. Griselda had seen that she
was wildly beautiful.

Kynaston had squeezed himself from Mr Tamburlane's grasp and began to stand about ineffectively on
the pavement. He seemed worried.

Mr Tamburlane, though his eyes were open, indeed
unusually wide open, continued supine.

'Well?' enquired the driver.

Griselda opened her purse. 'How much?'

'I leave that to the party concerned, miss.' The driver
implied that the question was in curiously bad taste.

Griselda submitted two halfcrowns. Instantly and
wordlessly the driver hurled them on the granite setts of
the gutter.

'It's all I can spare.'

'Who's asking *you*?'

Kynaston had ascended the steps to the surviving

front door and stood lurking in the shadows. The other two front doors had been superseded by kitchenettes.

'Come on, Mr Tamburlane. We're there.' Griselda dragged at his arm, but it merely came away as if it had dropped off his shoulder. Mr Tamburlane continued to stare at the horse's tail out of unnaturally large white eyes.

The driver lifted his hatch. He adressed one word to his fare.

'Out.'

Mr Tamburlane hardly moved, but the horse swished his tail and whinnied. Kynaston was fidgeting. He seemed distinctly upset.

'Please, Mr Tamburlane,' cried Griselda weakly, but still, she thought, firmly.

Mr Tamburlane turned a little away from her, groaned slightly, and addressed himself to the space formerly occupied by Kynaston. His voice was low and throbbing. *'Γυγη, γυναιξὶ κόσμον ἡ σιγή φέρει,'* said Mr Tamburlane.

Griselda turned her back on him and called to Kynaston. 'Can you come and help?'

'What do you suggest?' said Kynaston from the doorstep. He seemed almost shifty.

Griselda looked up at the cabman; who again lifted his little flap and in accents of deep distaste uttered another single word.

'Scram.'

The effect was surprising. The horse reared a little, neighed noisily, and clattered away down the street. The

227

tumult of his shoes on the granite setts was considerable. As the vehicle disappeared from sight it seemed for some reason to be swaying from one wheel to the other. The driver looked to have lost his reins and, at undoubted peril, to be erect on his perch expostulating. Soon, however, all was quiet once more and Kynaston was holding back the heavy front door, covered with letter-box flaps each with several names, for Griselda to enter.

'Thank God that's over,' said Kynaston.

'I don't want Mr Tamburlane to be hurt,' said Griselda.

'I expect a policeman will pull them up soon. The police are always doing things like that. Anything rather than have him back. It's most unfortunate how strongly I attract that type of man. Young or old, it always happens. I regularly appeal to the wrong type in both sexes. I wish I attracted you, Griselda.' He stopped groping for the switch and began to grope for Griselda.

'Let me advise you to recover the cash.' A door had opened on to the dark hall and Barney was looking out. Kynaston saw the switch and turned on the light.

'Thank you very much,' said Griselda. 'I will.' She had forgotten her two important half-crowns.

She returned to the gutter but the coins were not to be seen.

'Can't you find them?' It was Kynaston, once more at the top of the steps.

'Come and help to look for them.'

He remained in the shadow. 'I'm better at losing than finding.'

'Let *me* look.' It was Barney. He wore a check shirt and brown trousers. He descended to his hands and knees, and crawled along, striking matches.

'Please don't trouble.'

'How much was it?'

'Five shillings.'

'No trouble.'

Kynaston was clearly bored. He still seemed uneasy.

'It's very good of you.'

'Five shillings is five shillings.' Barney groped along like a small brown bear taught to let off a train of tiny fireworks.

'Please stop now. It really doesn't matter.'

Barney resumed the human posture. 'The scum of the earth live round here. They wouldn't miss a chance like that.' The street seemed deserted. 'Would you allow me to reduce the loss? I imagine Geoffrey's in his usual condition.' He put his hand in his trousers pocket and offered Griselda half-a-crown.

'Certainly not. I mean thank you very much; but No thank you. It really doesn't matter at all,' Griselda added extenuatingly.

'Please yourself.'

'I do mean thank you all the same.'

'So long as you know what you mean.'

Kynaston was looking embarrassed. He changed the subject.

'Is Dykes in?'

'I suppose so. Why?'

'We want to look at the empty flat.'

'Empty what?'

'Empty room.'

'We?'

'I'm going to marry Griselda. Griselda de Repton-ville. Barney Lazarus.'

Griselda had heard of him. Paintings by Barney Lazarus were sometimes mentioned by the Art Critics of *The Times*. She hard understood that he painted mostly Mothers.

'How do you do?' said Barney. They shook hands on the pavement. 'I cannot possibly congratulate you.'

'It's the man you congratulate,' said Kynaston.

'That remains to be seen,' said Barney, looking Griselda up and down. 'I've known Geoffrey for years,' he remarked to her, 'and I would rather marry King Kong.'

'I don't know King Kong,' remarked Griselda, smiling sweetly.

XXI

Dykes, who lived entirely in what had once been the larder of the house (the other rooms in the basement being let to tenants), proved to be wholly drunk. Roused by Kynaston, he stumbled up the battered stair singing snatches of old songs. His memory being ruined by the bottle, however, he was unable to recall which room was to let. Furthermore, having forgotten all he had ever learnt at school (if not more), he was incapable of distinguishing between the numbers on the different doors. The three of them bounced and crashed from amorous routines to solidary drudgeries until Kynaston asserted 'I am sure Monica said Number Thirteen.'

He and Griselda climbed another flight; but Dykes said his heart would carry him no higher. 'We may not need a key,' said Kynaston. 'I daresay it's lost.'

Across the landing before them, a dark brown door was inscribed 13. Kynaston turned the elaborate brass handle and entered without obstacle (the key being on the inside); then sagged back, standing upon Griselda's toe.

'Good God, Lotus,' he said faintly and peevishly, 'this is really too much.'

The room was medium sized, middlingly furnished in a style unexpectedly like Greenwood Tree House, painted in the same dark brown as the door, and with hideous paper leaving the walls and ceiling. Standing on the dust coloured carpet was the girl who had shouted from the upper window. At closer quarters, she was still wildly beautiful, with well kept golden-red hair, bright green eyes, a prominent somewhat Iberian nose, a large but well-shaped mouth, and a perfect skin. She wore crêpe-de-chine pyjamas, intended for parties. She was rather plump, though well-proportioned; and appeared to be expensively corsetted. Griselda found her age unusually difficult to guess.

She glared at Kynaston for a moment; then at Griselda.

'If you must be unfaithful to me, Geoffrey,' she said in a voice as beautiful as her face, 'then you need not insult me as well by always seducing an ingénue. There are other mondaine women in London.'

Kynaston stood his ground remarkably well. 'Lotus, I'm going to marry Griselda. Griselda de Reptonville. Mrs Lamb.'

'Are you insane, Geoffrey?'

'You can't look after me, Lotus. I thought you could, but I was wrong. I really believe Griselda can. And without bullying me, as you do. As well as being sensible, she is sweet and sympathetic. Besides you yourself refuse to marry me—'

'I am above such a thought!' she interrupted. Suddenly she extended her hand to Griselda. 'Ignore my remark. It was intended only to hurt Geoffrey not you. As you love Geoffrey, you must forgive me for that also.'

'I don't love Geoffrey.' replied Griselda, smiling and shaking Lotus's hand.

'Perfect. That's the only possible basis for marriage.'

'I'm not going to marry.'

'Monica told me you'd gone away,' said Kynaston interrupting.

'I've come back. I'm living with Barney now.'

'I suppose that also is intended to hurt me.'

'Certainly. And it's quite true.'

'You've been quick enough.'

'And you? Or is this merely another Doris Ditton?' Turning to Griselda she added: 'Please don't think I mean anything personal.'

'I'm going to marry Griselda.'

'She says not.'

'She'll be sorry for me in the end.'

Lotus sat on the edge of the divan. 'You know, Geoffrey,' she said, 'I'll take you back. This instant, if you like.'

'I can't understand what you see in me, Lotus. I'm not your kind of man at all.'

'What are you going to live on without me?'

'I've got a job. Anyway you've never supported me.'

'Paid your debts. It's much the same. What sort of a job have you got?' She seemed genuinely to wonder; and remarked to Griselda: 'Geoffrey's incapable of work of any kind.' It was a simple statement of fact.

'I think we'd better face reality,' replied Geoffrey.

'I inspired all his poetry too,' continued Lotus to Griselda.

Suddenly she fell sideways on the divan and began to sob. She sobbed beautifully. Kynaston looked distracted.

'Good night,' said Griselda.

'For God's sake,' cried Kynaston clutching both her elbows and holding on.

'It's late. I really should go.'

'I beg you,' cried Kynaston. 'You can see how utterly wrong for me she is and always has been.'

'She's very beautiful,' said Griselda falling into the new convention of speaking as if the person spoken about were not present.

'You're beautiful too, Griselda.'

'Not in the same class.'

Lotus looked up. 'You are. You are. You know you are.' Huge separate tears streamed down her lovely skin. 'I love you Griselda. I need you. Please don't leave me now.' He was still desperately gripping one of her elbows.

Lotus dropped off the bed and knelt on the floor crying her heart out. 'When you've married him, will you let me see him? Ever?'

But the door had opened and Barney entered. He spoke very quietly.

'I thought I heard Lotus crying. Silence, Kynaston, while I break every bone in your body.' Barney was a painter of the traditional school. Griselda had never before seen anyone in so dreadful a rage.

His first blow laid Kynaston on the floor, where Barney began systematically to maul him.

Deeming explanation useless, Griselda began to drag

at Barney's shoulders from behind. This was equally un-availing.

'Could you please help?' she said to the tear-stained Lotus. Even Lotus's pyjamas were becoming dark and saturated. Her beautiful tears were particularly wet.

Lotus rose from the floor and with a single kick from one of her attractive shoes, mastered the situation. Barney stopped half-murdering Kynaston, and looked up at her, all rage evaporated.

'I thought–'

'You thought wrong. Get out.' She kicked him again, unexpectedly and maliciously.

'I wanted—'

'Go to bed, Barney. You said you were tired.'

Once more his expression changed. 'You'd made me desperate. I'm not a pekinese.'

'You foul the air.'

Barney flushed; rose to his feet; and took Lotus in his arms. Quite calmly, as it appeared, she bit deeply into his left cheek. Barney's blood on her big well-shaped mouth made her look like a beautiful vampire.

Barney felt in his trousers pocket for a handkerchief, but he was unprovided. Remembering the half-crown, Griselda extended her own handkerchief. He began to dab at his streaming cheek. Griselda's handkerchief was much too small.

'Are you going back to Kynaston?'

'I'm not going back to you.'

'I see.' He turned to Griselda. 'And you? Where do you come in?'

It was difficult to know what to say. Lotus saved Griselda the trouble.

'Stop asking questions and leave the room, Barney.' She took a short step towards him. It was like the school bully and her victim, Griselda thought.

'I'll kill myself.'

'The best thing you can do.'

His bloodstained face was now completely white.

'You don't believe me?'

'I don't care.'

Hanging from the washbasin was a dirty towel, the property of a former tenant. It might have hung there for months. Lotus snatched it and flicked it with a loud report in Barney's face.

'Lotus.' His voice was a voice from the tomb. 'Lotus, I love you. I love you terribly, Lotus.'

Before she had succeeded in driving him from the room, she must have been hurting him quite considerably.

When Barney was outside, Lotus locked the door and stuck the key into the top of her black corselette, which her exertions had exposed to view.

Griselda was alarmed. But Lotus only looked dreamily at her for several seconds, her large eyes full of lustre, her exquisite hands making small groping movements; then with a low cry fell upon the prostrate Kynaston, all beautiful compassion. Again she looked at Griselda.

'Do you know any first-aid?'

'A little.' Griselda reflected. 'Very little.'

'Can you tell if he's alive?'

'I think I can.'

Griselda held the mirror from her bag against the side of Kynaston's mouth pressed against the dust coloured carpet. A slightly yellow mist immediately clouded it.

'He's alive.'

Lotus sqatted back.

'I don't mind if you marry him so long as you let me go on seeing him. It's only his body I want really. I don't at all care about your having everything else.'

'I quite understand. Hadn't we better try to bring him round?'

'So long as you understand. It'll be no different from any other marriage. Except, of course, that Geoffrey will never be able to keep you. Still I want him to be happy and might be able to help with that: always through you, of course. Geoffrey can't tell the difference between fourpence and ninepence.'

'That's very kind of you.'

'It's not only kindness. There's a close connection between a man's happiness and his vitality, you know. In many ways, men are exactly like animals. Perhaps you don't believe that?'

'Shall we chafe his extremities?'

'Why?'

'It's what we were taught.'

'Then you'd better do it.'

Griselda hesitated.

'Have you any brandy?' She thought that this might, among other things, get the door unlocked and Lotus out of the room.

'Of course.'

'Do you think you could bring it?'

'I suppose so.' Lotus rose to her feet, stretching the cramp from her leg muscles. 'What a curse men are.' She was looking for the key. 'Wait.' She had unlocked the door and was going upstairs. Indeed she had left the door open.

To her own surprise Griselda remained with the body.

When Lotus returned, she once more locked the door. 'We don't want a crowd,' she remarked. She bore a half-full bottle of excellent liqueur brandy; distinctly superior to what might be expected of Juvenal Court.

'Shall we force it down him?'

'I suppose so. I've never done it.'

'I've never done it either. I always let other people deal with emergencies.'

Tenderly Lotus rolled Kynaston on to his back.

'Give me that tooth-glass. I don't see why we shouldn't have some first. The whole thing's Geoffrey's own fault.'

'It needs washing. There are two dead flies in it.'

'All right. Wash it. But be quick.'

Griselda emptied the flies to the floor and cleaned the glass to the best of her ability.

'I'll dry it.' Somewhat to Griselda's distaste, Lotus dried the glass on the grimy towel. 'Now then.' She half-filled the glass with brandy. 'Me first, if you don't mind.' At once the glass was again empty. 'Now you.' Griselda's allowance was considerably smaller.

'Thank you.' It was certainly wonderful stuff.

'How do you force drink between tightly clenched jaws?'

'Geoffrey's mouth is open.'

'Oh yes. Still I don't want to waste it.'

'Let me try.' Griselda was beginning to worry lest Kynaston have concussion, whatever that might be.

'Careful.'

Griselda poured about half a tablespoonful of brandy into the glass and released it drop by drop down Kynaston's throat.

'Careful.'

When the glass was nearly empty, Kynaston seemed to have a violent spasm. He curled up instantaneously, like a caterpillar which has taken alarm. His mouth closed sharply and a curious rattle came from somewhere inside him. It frightened Griselda so much that she swallowed what remained in the glass.

'Of course.' she said, 'he's been having very little to eat.'

Lotus stared at her dreamily; again half-filling the glass.

'Don't forget your promise,' she said, drinking.

'What promise?'

'You may not think you'll marry Geoffrey. But he'll marry you. You won't be able to resist him: and he'll make marriage his price.' She had unbuttoned Kynaston's shirt and was running her free hand over the upper part of his body. 'Or part of his price.'

'Shall we call a doctor?'

'How innocent you are, Griselda!'

239

Suddenly Lotus had cast the tumbler into a corner of the room, where it shattered with rather too much noise and into rather too many pieces; had thrown herself upon the half-naked Kynaston: and was frenziedly kissing his mouth. Instantly Kynaston sat up.

'Beloved,' he said, clasping Lotus in his arms. Then, seeing Griselda, he gave a groan of shock and disgust, and was on his feet, buttoning his shirt.

Lotus lay on the floor. She appeared to be looking round for another glass. As with the locked door, she seemed to find difficulty, Griselda thought, in sustaining her romantic emphases.

'Come away at once,' said Kynaston, apparently none the worse. 'We shall have to live elsewhere.' The knock-out seemed to have awakened in him a slightly hysterical dignity.

'No need at all,' replied Lotus from the floor. 'Griselda and I are on the best of terms. We are going to be great friends.'

'I didn't know,' said Kynaston. 'Griselda needs some friends.'

'We've made a bargain.'

'What bargain?'

Lotus smiled her lovely smile. 'Geoffrey,' she said, 'do organize a picnic for next Sunday.'

'All right, Lotus.'

'We'll all come. It'll be like old times.'

'So long as no one crosses me about the arrangements.'

'Who would?'

He smiled back at her.

'Griselda hasn't seen you at your wonderful best until she's been on one of your wonderful wonderful picnics.'

Now Griselda smiled also.

Kynaston was at the door.

'It's locked.'

All three were still smiling.

'Where's the key?'

Lotus knelt, sitting back upon her ankles, and, her hands clasped behind her, extended her plump black-corsetted bosom towards him.

'Reach for it.'

The key being extracted, and the door opened, they left Lotus, the search for another glass abandoned, imbibing direct from the bottle.

'Marry-in-haste,' she said between gulps.

'I never shall,' said Griselda still smiling.

XXII

Through his door on the ground floor, Barney could be clearly heard grinding his teeth and his colours.

As Griselda and Kynaston passed into the summer night, the clock on the local Crematorium struck midnight, an intimation repeated a few minutes later by the doubtless more accurate clock at the Palace of Westminster.

'I should have told you about Lotus.'

'She's no affair of mine.'

'I never expected to see her again. It's Monica Paget-Barlow's fault. She misled me.'

'I see.'

'All the same she's rather splendid.'

'Miss Paget-Barlow?'

'But I'm quite finished with her none the less. She lacks your glorious independence.'

'I've lost the thread.'

'You'll come on the picnic?'

'No. Thank you.'

'Don't be jealous. It's absurd of you. Really it is.'

'I'm not jealous. I have another engagement.'

'What?'

Without particularly thinking. Griselda answered the

truth. 'I'm spending the day with my friend Peggy Potter.'

'Where are you going?'

Regrettably, Peggy, with her passion for the provisional, always, when possible, refused to agree upon a plan in advance.

'Does that matter?'

'Bring her with you. There'll be a crowd. She'll pass unnoticed.'

'No, thank you. She'd hate that.'

They were walking southwards down Tottenham Court Road, as Griselda did not care to risk the passage of the back streets at midnight. Outside Goodge Street Station, Kynaston stopped, again took hold of Griselda's elbows, and said: 'Griselda, I love you with all my heart.' He seemed to mean it. But as he spoke a lift arrived, and they were pushed about by a load of tired revellen and resentful night workers.

Absurd though the declaration was, Griselda had too soft a heart to feel unmoved. 'Where will you go tonight?' She asked sympathetically.

'I've made arrangements . . . Please marry me.'

'No, Geoffrey. It's impossible . . . You'll be all right?'

'I'll be far from all right if you won't marry me. Besides I've got a slight headache.'

'When do you take up your job?'

'On Liberation Day. Next Wednesday. It's a job for a D.Litt. There's very little money in it.'

'Poor Geoffrey! I really must go. I shall miss the last tube.' Griselda had previously intended to walk.

'You won't need an address for me as I shall look in the shop every day.'

'No please, Geoffrey, I'm sure there'll be trouble with Mr Tamburlane.'

'Yes. I suppose there may.'

'I wonder if Mr Tamburlane's still alive? Poor Mr Tamburlane.'

'Promise to come on the picnic and we'll leave it at that for the moment. I've got a lot of things to do anyway before I'm tied by the leg on Liberation Day. Promise, Griselda.'

'Certainly not.'

'Ten o'clock next Sunday at Juvenal Court. Bring your own lunch. Tell your friend to bring enough for the two of you.'

'Good night, Geoffrey.'

'May I kiss you?'

'No.'

He kissed her. Although it was Goodge Street Station and another lift had come up, Griselda realized that Kynaston really had feelings. It was most surprising.

Despite her efforts, he felt her respond.

'Griselda darling . . .'

But Griselda had been swept away by a flood of sad ineluctable memories and a posse of half-drunken suburbans on their way to Hendon, Edgware, and Trinity Road, Tooting Bec.

The tide of grief because Louise had been lost was so overwhelming, and the prospect of Sunday spent alone with Peggy so depressing (fond of Peggy though she was), that when she arrived back at Greenwood Tree House, Griselda, though it was late by Peggy's standards, knocked at her friend's door. With so many weightier cares to keep her from sleep, Griselda knew that she would lie awake all night unless she settled the matter of the picnic before the retired.

'What is it?'

'It is I. Griselda. Please let me in.' Peggy always locked her door.

There was a curious sound of shuffling and putting away, which continued for an unexplained time. Then the key was turned and Peggy stood in the doorway.

'Come in Griselda,' she said quite pleasantly.

'You needn't have bothered to put on your dressing-gown.'

Peggy said nothing.

'Do get into bed again. I can quite easily talk to you in bed.'

'I'd rather not. Sit down.'

They sat formally in the room's two chairs. Peggy must have been putting away her clothes and under-clothes, as none were visible.

'Had you anything in mind for Sunday?'

'Need we settle so long beforehand? After all, it's not work. Can't we leave it till the time comes?'

'We've both been asked on a picnic.'

'Both?'

'I've been asked and asked to bring you.'

'I see. Will the people like me? Seeing that they don't

know me or I them. I should hate to spoil your day.'

'Of course you won't spoil my day, Peggy. I hardly know the people myself. I shall be glad to have you for company.'

'Are they a married couple?'

'There's to be quite a number of people, I believe. You'll be able to pass unnoticed, if you wish.'

'Not if they're my sort of person, I hope. And obviously not if they're *not* my sort of person,' said Peggy, patiently smiling. '*Are* they my sort of person? You won't mind my asking.'

'Not exactly,' replied Griselda thoughtfully. 'But I'm sure you'll like them. I do,' she added without particular regard for truth.

'Could I let you know later?'

'No. I want to know now. Or I shan't sleep.'

'All right, I'll come. Thank you for asking me.'

'Thank you for coming.'

'I suppose it must be important to you. There's someone expected? Somone in particular?'

'Nothing like that. Just a group of old friends. Very pleasant people,' replied Griselda, seeing mental pictures of Lotus flagellating Barney with the towel and Barney trying to beat out Kynaston's brains.

XXIII

When Griselda arrived at the shop next morning, Mr Tamburlane was taking down the shutters as usual.

'Since I had to hurry away last night, let me at once whisper in your hymeneal ear, Miss de Reptonville,' he exclaimed as she approached.

'Are you quite safe, Mr Tamburlane?'

'I glow. I bask. I kindle.'

'Then that's all right.' Griselda entered the dusky shop with its smell of scholarship.

'Advance the nuptials. Miss de Reptonville. It's the best thing you can possibly do. Afterwards you can throw the traces right over and – your tastes being what they are, of course – Society will do nothing but smile upon you.'

'Please don't concern yourself.'

'In my anachronistic way I feel called to advise you; both as your employer and also quasi-paternally.'

'It shows thought, Mr Tamburlane.'

'But perchance the plough has entered the furrow without aid from me?'

At that point a young man came into the shop and saved the situation by calling, in an affected voice, for the Complete Incubology of St Teresa of Avila, which had to be got up from the basement.

None the less, all day Mr Tamburlane made himself quire a nuisance with his sympathetic but entire misunderstanding of Griselda's situation. Nor did the heat help.

Saturday was really hot.

'Need we go tomorrow?' enquired Peggy, as she lay beside Griselda in the Park, her head on an old copy of 'Headway'.

'It may not be so hot.'

'Then it will be raining. It's August.'

'Look at that duck.'

'That's a widgeon.'

'We don't have to go if you don't want to.'

'I don't want to spoil it for you.'

'I agreed to spend Sunday with *you*, Peggy. It's for you to say about the picnic.'

'It's only the heat. I'd love to come otherwise.'

'Surely it'll be hotter in Italy?'

Sunday was hotter.

Griselda had passed the night naked on top of her bed and had slept perfectly; but she feared that Peggy might not have slept at all.

'Are you awake, Peggy?'

'I'm making sandwiches. Come in.'

Griselda entered. Peggy was fully dressed in a pale blue cotton frock covered with small sprigs of pale pink flowers; and was being exceedingly useful. Griselda was delighted by her energy and practicality. Kynaston's cynical suggestion was coming to pass. Peggy was preparing lunch for the two of them.

'I'll go away again and get some clothes on.'

'Do you like mustard with tinned salmon?'

'Please. It adds a flavour.'

Immediately Griselda thought that this might be interpreted as offensive. So she added. 'They're beautiful sandwiches. So even.'

'Got the knack at College,' replied Peggy. 'I made sandwich lunches for my group every day.'

'Didn't the others ever take a turn?'

'Catch them,' said Peggy with much meaning but no explanation.

Griselda put on a dark flame coloured silk shirt and her black linen skirt.

At five minutes to ten they were at Juvenal Court. Peggy had insisted on bringing her rucksack. It seemed to Griselda to go somewhat queerly with her cotton frock, but certainly came in useful as a repository for the little packets of food.

Seated on the steps were Barney, dressed precisely as before, and a young man in a tennis shirt, with fair hair and an open innocent face. Behind them on the step above, was a girl in a khaki shirt and grey flannel trousers. She had sharp but lively features, including a longish nose and almondish eyes; dark skin and black hair, drawn tightly back and tied with a length of wide khaki ribbon. She sat with her legs rather wide apart; but not sprawling: on the contrary, giving an impression of alertness and vigour.

Barney rose, followed by the innocent looking young man. The mark of Lotus's teeth was plain on Barney's cheek.

'How nice of you to be so punctual.' It was as if nothing had happened: almost as if nothing had happened ever. Barney's tone was the pink of polite nothingness.

'We've walked,' remarked Peggy. 'From the other side of the Edgware Road.' Griselda did not really understand Peggy. Possibly she profited from being brought out.

'How sensible of you to bring your rucksack.'

'I like to keep my hands free.'

'Naturally.' Barney turned to Griselda. 'Do introduce your friend.'

'Peggy Potter. Barney Lazarus.'

'The painter?'

'Himself. How do you do?'

'I know your work.'

Barney was admiring Peggy's large bust.

'Better than knowing me.'

'Stop fishing for compliments, Barney. She's only just set eyes on you.' The girl on the step above was speaking. 'I'm Lena Drelincourt.'

'How do you do?' said Griselda. 'I'm Griselda de Reptonville.'

'Not patient Griselda?' cried the innocent looking young man in a public school voice and high glee.

'This is Freddy Fisher,' said Barney, embarrassed because he had failed to introduce Griselda.

'I write,' explained Lena Drelincourt.

'I work in a bookshop. Perhaps we stock you.'

'I shouldn't think so.'

'There are several more of us to come,' said Barney, making conversation. 'Guillaume and Florence. Your friend Geoffrey Kynaston. And, of course, Monica Paget-Barlow. And Lotus.'

'And Lotus,' said Lena Drelincourt, underlining.

'More women than men, I'm glad to say,' resumed Barney.

'Twice as many,' said Lena, 'not counting Freddy, which you can't. It's an incitement to unnatural vice.'

Freddy Fisher blushed all over his head and neck.

'So many of the younger generation of men like to stay in bed over the week-end,' explained Barney.

'Where's Geoffrey?' asked Lena. 'If he doesn't appear soon, I'm going to take charge.'

'Why are the arrangements always left to Geoffrey?' asked Freddy Fisher.

'Because he makes a scene otherwise,' answered Lena.

'He's not a child.'

'No. He's a baby. He only feels grown up when other people do what he says.'

A tired looking girl, obviously much younger than she seemed, with a small round head and a small round face, nondescript hair and nondescript clothes, came out of the house. Barney introduced her as Monica Paget-Barlow. She smiled quickly, said nothing, seated herself on the top step and began to knit.

She was immediately followed by Guillaume and Florence. Guillaume was an elderly-looking man

251

(though he also was probably younger than he looked), with long sparse grey hair and an air of unsuccessfully applied learning. His other name was announced as Cook. He was exceedingly untidy.

Florence was a slender dark woman of about thirty with short brown hair and a Grecian nose. She gave an impression of quietness and docility, which, like her appearance, was far from unattractive. She wore a tight shirt of dark-blue jersey-silk, which emphasised her slenderness and lack of figure, and dark blue trousers. Consciously or otherwise, the costume was well chosen to present her to advantage. She was introduced as Florence Cook, but probably was not. Griselda liked her at sight, and wondered what she found in Guillaume, supposing that she found anything.

'We could hardly have a better day,' said Guillaume in accents of deep anxiety. Before long Griselda perceived that it was his habitual tone. He spoke seldom and slowly and, though his words were commonplace, he appeared to worry very much over choosing them. Now he continued to stare at the sky, already almost colourless with heat.

'Have you all got your lunches?' enquired Barney.

Everyone had. Monica Paget-Barlow's was contained in a round bundle, somewhat resembling a pantomime Christmas Pudding.

'I could put some of the packets in my rucksack,' suggested Peggy, who, though Griselda had sat on the step, still stood on the pavement.

'Splendid,' said Lena. 'Many thanks.' She extended her packet.

'I don't think you should do that,' said Freddy Fisher to Peggy. 'Or let me carry the rucksack.'

'I'm used to walking with a rucksack.'

Florence was restraining Guillaume from offering their joint packet.

'There's Geoffrey,' cried Freddy Fisher.

They watched him approach. He was entirely unencumbered. His dancer's gait was exhilarating.

'Hullo Griselda. Hullo everybody. Anyone got any lunch to spare?'

No one spoke.

'I expect there'll be things left over when the time comes. Where's Lotus?'

'Lotus!' shouted Lena Drelincourt without moving and at the top of her very clear voice.

There was an expectant pause. But nothing happened.

'Go and get her,' said Lena.

Without either intending it, Barney and Kynaston looked at one another for half a second.

'Shall I go?' asked Freddy Fisher helpfully.

'You go,' said Barney and Kynaston, each to the other; and Freddy Fisher went.

The expectancy became a strain.

'Where are we going?' enquired Florence.

'Epping Forest. Walk to the Dominion, Number Seven bus to Liverpool Street, train to Chingford,' replied Kynaston. 'There are Day Tickets.'

'Tell us about the Forest,' said Florence.

'There are parrots.'

'Anything else?' enquired Lena.

'Epstein at work,' said Barney.

'I know his work,' said Peggy.

Suddenly Lotus appeared, followed by Freddy. It was as when the Conductor goes to fetch the Prima Donna. Everyone, moreover, stood up.

Lotus wore a black shirt buttoned to the neck, and a white linen coat and skirt, expensive, fashionable, and likely to remain clean for one day only, or for less. Alone among the women she wore silk stockings, and her shoes had the air of being specially made for her. By daylight, Griselda thought her lovelier than ever. Standing in the doorway with the dark passage behind her, she surveyed the party with her bright green eyes, looking through Barney, and over Peggy, until she saw Kynaston slightly concealed behind Guillaume.

'Geoffrey,' she said, 'let us lead the way together.'

She looked like 'Harper's Bazaar', but she walked like Boadicea. In fact, she could probably outwalk all of them, except Griselda, and (if the walk were far enough off the map) Peggy Potter.

On the Number Seven bus, Lotus sat with Kynaston in an empty front seat; Peggy with Barney; Monica with Guillaume; Griselda with Florence; and Lena by herself, peeling a large pear with a larger clasp knife, which had been dangling from her belt. There was no seat for Freddy, who volunteered to stand inside; where, the others being all outside, he paid all the fares. Monica and Guillaume travelled in silence. At the bus stop Monica had brought her knitting from the discoloured circular reticule in which it travelled, and had resumed work, hardly ceasing even in order to climb the stairs of the vehicle. She was producing a small tightly knitted object, the colour of a brown-green lizard, more brown than green. Guillaume seemed lost in sad thoughts.

'He suffers a great deal,' said Florence to Griselda, regarding with apparent fondness the blotchy back of his scalp. Her voice was sweet and quiet.

'Why?' asked Griselda.

Lena stopped peeling for a moment and cocked a faun-like ear.

'He is a disappointed man.'

Lena resumed peeling.

'Why?'

'He is disappointed in the world. He is disappointed in himself.'

'Can nothing be done?'

'I do what I can. But I sometimes think he's disappointed in me.'

'That's absurd. I mean I'm sure he isn't.'

'I am too small a thing really to enter into him.'

'How long have you been together?'

Lena had finished peeling and begun eating, cutting the soft ripe flesh into precise sectors.

'Twelve years. Since I was nineteen. He has been my life.'

'I know how you feel.'

Lena glanced at Griselda sharply. Florence gazed at

her for a moment, then said: 'These picnics! Why do we go on them?'

'I don't really know,' said Griselda. 'It's my first.'

'I wonder how many of us really enjoy them ... I mean *really*. You know what I mean by enjoyment?' She looked solemn, and a little timorous.

'Yes,' said Griselda. 'I know what you mean by enjoyment.'

In the front seat, Lotus, early in the day though it was, laid her beautiful golden-red head gently on Kynaston's shoulder; who squirmed slightly, then appeared to resign himself. The bus had only reached Holborn Viaduct. Barney and Peggy were talking about tactile values. Lena shut her big shining knife with a loud snap, and reattached the weapon to her person.

On the train they were unable to find a compartment to themselves and they had to pack in with a couple travelling from one side of London to the other, in order to spend the day with a married daughter. Even without Freddy, who was queueing for tickets, it was very congested on such a hot day. Monica's knitting needles became entangled from time to time in the male stranger's watch-chain.

'Yuman personality,' said the male stranger to the female stranger. 'It's sacred. You can't get past that.'

'We're all as we're made,' said the female stranger.

'No system of Government will change yuman personality.'

'Either way it's the same.'

'Yuman personality is sacred.'

'It bloody well isn't,' interjected Barney. 'You try being a nigger in the deep south.'

'Kindly refrain from using foul language in the presence of my wife,' said the male stranger.

'Behave yourself, Barney,' said Lotus. 'Or you can go home.'

'No offence,' said the male stranger. 'Not really.'

'*I* am offended,' said Lotus.

'I should think so too,' said the female stranger. 'Dirty Yid!'

Barney, so easy and self-possessed before Lotus had joined them, flushed slightly, but said nothing. Peggy threw Griselda a glance of unsatisfactory anticipations fulfilled.

Freddy only managed to race up the torrid platform and hurl himself amongst them just as the train started. There seemed nowhere for him to sit but the floor; with which, however, he professed himself quite content.

The embarrassment, discomfort, and tension were little relieved by Lena producing a thin pocket book from one of the breast pockets of her shirt and commencing to make some small drawings.

'Anti-semitism is so *unnecessary*, don't you think?' said Florence quietly to Griselda, as the train puffed up the incline to Bethnal Green. 'I know it's one of the things *he* feels particularly. Though he doesn't say so, I know it.'

'Is he a Jew?'

'Oh no. He feels with all who suffer. The people everywhere.'

'Look at that,' said the male stranger, savagely indicating Bethnal Green. 'Shocking.' He glowered accusation at the misjudged Barney.

'What does Lotus live on?' asked Griselda in an undertone.

'She's an heiress.'

'Then what's she doing in Juvenal Court? I'm sure you know what I mean.

'She likes living with artists. Also she's in love with Geoffrey and he's not in love with her. It's her way of ever seeing him.'

'Are you sure Geoffrey's not in love with her?' It was difficult to believe that any man could resist Lotus's beauty, passion, imperiousness, and riches. Moreover, she was holding Geoffrey's hand at that very moment.

'Quite sure. You can tell because he refuses to let her keep him. That's a sure sign with Geoffrey. Though he's weak of course, he refuses to be kept by anyone he's not in love with.'

'Have you known Geoffrey for long?'

'He lived in Juvenal Court for two years; when he was teaching the recorder you know.'

'Do you like him?'

'Everyone likes Geoffrey. He's weak, but sweet.'

'Like that nauseating tea,' said Lena quietly.

'Florence,' said Guillaume across the compartment. 'Look at the sunlight on the windows of that gasworks.'

'Yes, darling. Beautiful.'

'If only it could be made as sunny and glittering within.' He seemed more troubled than ever.

'People like you and me don't know how the factory

workers live,' observed the male stranger, disentagling Monica's wool from the lower part of his braces.

'What the hell's the good of going somewhere as lovely as Epping Forest,' soliloquized Lena in her clear voice, 'without a man to ravish one?'

After that the strangers fell silent until the next station, at which they alighted.

At Chingford, under Kynaston's direction, they struck up the road to the Royal Forest Hotel, then descended to Connaught Water. Kynaston and Lotus still walked ahead, their easy efficient movements a pleasure to watch. Had she not known them, Griselda might have taken them for gods descended to Essex earth. The rest of them advanced en masse, two of the number knowing the others hardly at all, the rest knowing them perhaps too well. Peggy was conserving her energy, as if a range of mountains would have to be crossed before nightfall. Lena slouched with her hands in her pockets; but her slouch was somehow electric.

'Do you see how the water catches the reflection of the willows?' said Guillaume to Florence.

'Yes, darling. Beautiful.'

Outside the Hotel were motor coach parties drinking. When they set eyes on Lotus, they whistled and catcalled because she was so beautiful: but Lotus strode past, like a Queen on her way to execution, not increasing her pace or diminishing her poise.

'Anyone know what that is?' asked Peggy, taking no notice and pointing to Queen Elizabeth's Hunting Lodge.

'It's one of the places where the upper classes get together to kill things,' said Guillaume.

'Damn good sport,' said Freddy Fisher. 'Done any beagling?' he enquired of Griselda.

'No, never,' replied Griselda.

'I beagled almost every day for a month last autumn. You can if you've got a fast car.'

'What do you do with the rest of your time?'

'Learn to paint. Animals and birds, you know. I've got to for a living, more's the pity. Dad's lost his last halfpenny. Horses, you know.'

'But you've still got a fast car?'

'Not any more.'

'Oh dear.'

'You're terribly pretty, Griselda. I should have liked to ask you home. Mum would have taken to you no end.'

'Perhaps I shall meet her sometime,' said Griselda politely.

'She's dead. Drugs. Dad was to blame.'

'I am sorry. But I don't know that you should be so sure it was your Father's fault.'

'Of course it was Dad's fault. He had to stop it all coming out at the inquest.'

'Still it's often hard to be sure.'

'Of course I'm sure. It's spoilt my whole life.'

'Can we stop for a moment?' asked Monica. 'There's a drawing-pin in my shoe.'

When Connaught Water came in sight, covered with boats, Florence's sensitive face lighted up. 'Oh I should like to go out in a boat.'

Guillaume's brow became rigid with apprehension. 'Hardly with so many other people, Florence. I am sure the boats must be dirty.'

Florence smiled gently and said 'It just passed through my mind, darling.' Married or not, Florence was suffering from that cancer of the will which Griselda had observed so often to accompany matrimony. She and Lena exchanged glances.

At the lake they left the road and entered the trees. Within five minutes the clatter had become inaudible. They passed several times from thicket to clearing, the change in temperature being each time overwhelming, and soon were among the hornbeams.

'Everyone,' cried Lotus over her shoulder, 'must look for a parrot.'

Kynaston caught Griselda's eye and looked deeply unhappy.

His distress of mind possibly accounted for the fact that within ten minutes from leaving the road, they were lost. Kynaston did not for some time admit this, but urged them on, with unnecessary expressions of confidence, along a rutty but diminishing track; they could make a right angle in any direction, but could not continue in their course.

'I wonder which of these would be the quicker?' soliloquized Kynaston. Clearly there should have been a path through the brambles which lay straight ahead.

'Don't be silly,' said Lena. 'they go in opposite directions. You'd better choose.'

'I wish we had a map among us.'

'We rely on you.'

Kynaston looked wildly from left to right and back again while they waited for him to decide.

Guillaume broke the long silence. 'Both ways look equally beautiful,' he said helpfully.

'Does it matter?' cried Lotus. 'Do we really have to get anywhere?'

Peggy's expression changed from aloofness to horror.

'To travel is better than to arrive,' said Guillaume.

'To travel *hopefully*,' corrected Lena. 'What hope have we?'

'Surely we should enjoy ourselves?' said Florence. 'On such a lovely day?'

Monica had begun to knit. Freddy was brooding about his Father's wickedness. Barney had been filling his heart with tears ever since the train.

'The thing is, Griselda,' said Kynaston desperately, 'that I'm better at organizing picnics than walks.'

'I remember,' said Griselda, taking pity on him.

'Remember what?' enquired Lotus.

'I've been on a picnic with Geoffrey before. I enjoyed it.'

'Shall we go back to the lake?' suggested Florence being constructive.

'It's true that you're never actually lost so long as you can find the way back,' observed Kynaston, hoping, like many greater men to preserve his leadership by retreat.

'Surely we shouldn't admit defeat?' said Guillaume. He wished to keep Florence from the boats.

'Besides,' enquired Lena, 'can you find the way back?'

'Naturally, I can find the way *back*.' The implication that he would rather they went forward contrasted so much with the attitude of his previous remark that it was obvious to Griselda that he could not find the way back, and had suddenly realized the fact. She wondered what he would do, thus totally trapped.

'For heaven's sake, let's go *somewhere*,' cried Peggy. Her outburst made Monica drop a stitch.

'Shall we toss for it?' suggested Florence, still patiently seeking to advance the general well-being. It struck Griselda that Florence would make a wonderful mother, though possibly her hips were too small for easy childbirth.

'Geoffrey!' said Lotus. 'Tell us what to do and we'll do it. You *can* be so self-confident.'

'This is the moment,' said Lena.

Suddenly Kynaston resumed the leaderhsip. 'Let's have lunch. It's just the place.'

Kynaston got very little. Peggy had at first said to Griselda that she had not walked far enough to acquire any appetite at all; but managed none the less to eat most of her share. Lotus, seated on a small mat, ate nothing but a little hothouse fruit (although it was summer) and some walnuts. Guillaume was on a diet which involved him in eating several times the normal amount of the few things he was permitted to eat at all. Barney almost surreptitiously unrapped some unusual but not unappetising comestibles approved by his community. He insinuated himself alongside a tree which Peggy was occupying, somewhat in the background; and, glancing from time to time at Peggy's bust, began to cheer up.

At the end of the meal, the situation had once more to be faced.

After various desultory and generally unrealistic suggestions from the others, Lotus said 'Why move from here? Are we not quite comfortable as we are?' She sank her left hand into Kynaston's hair as he lay on the ground beside her.

'Perfectly comfortable,' said Guillaume, yawning as his diet disagreed with him.

Monica began to knit at a different angle. Perhaps she was turning the heel. But the rapidly increasing product of her labours seemed without any such precise points of reference.

'There's the difficulty that we don't know the way back,' pointed out Florence.

'We'll be all right when the time comes.' This was Barney.

'I,' said Lena, 'want a walk. Anyone join me?'

'I'll join you,' said Griselda, rising. 'What about you, Peggy?'

'It's too hot.' To her surprise, Griselda, now that she was on her feet, could see that Peggy's ankles were tightly clasped in the crook of one of Barney's arms.

'Anyone else?' enquired Griselda. She had not expected to have to walk alone with Lena.

'I'd love to some other time,' said Freddy regretfully. By this he meant that he would love to accompany Griselda, but he was frightened of Lena, whom he thought unsexed and a bluestocking.

'Florence?'

Florence looked lovingly at Guillaume, who was begining to fall asleep. 'I don't think so, Griselda.' There was something charmingly tender about her; something unusual and precious which Griselda felt was going to waste.

'Come on, Florence. I'd like you to.'

Florence smiled and shook her head. Then she laid a handkerchief over Guillaume's brow, and settled down to watch over him.

Lena meanwhile was slouching up and down impatiently. Griselda walked across to her through the recumbent group.

'Which way?'

'Not again!'

'This way then.' Griselda indicated the turn to the left.

'Thank God you know your own mind.'

They set off along the track. Griselda's last recollection of the group was the look of agony in Kynaston's eyes as she vanished from his sight and a lock of Lotus's splendid red-gold hair touched his cheek.

XXIV

'Pity Florence wouldn't come.'

'She's better where she is.'

'Isn't Guillaume rather selfish?'

'That's why Florence loves him.'

They walked some way in silence. It was almost too hot to talk. Also Griselda divined that Lena, although a little alarming, was one of the favoured people with whom silence is possible even on short acquaintance. Soon the track turned into a sunken glade.

'What are your books called?'

'*Inhumation* is the one I like.'

'I should like to read it.'

'It's not based on experience.'

'I'm sure that doesn't matter.'

'It matters to me. *Inhumation* is based on frustration. I've never succeeded with men; although I've tried very hard from time to time. I'm too cerebral for the dear dolts. Not clinging and dependent. Florence is what they like. Or you.'

'I'm not clinging and dependent.'

'Aren't you? Sorry. I don't really know you, of course.'

Again they walked for some time in silence. The glade was full of dragonflies, with their quaint air of impossibility.

'The only proposal I ever received,' remarked Griselda after a while, 'was on the grounds that I was *not* clinging and dependent. Proposal of marriage, that is to say.'

'Geoffrey Kynaston is unlike the ordinary male. I should accept him. You'll be lost otherwise if you're the type you say you are. I'd take him myself if he'd have me.'

Griselda had wondered why Lena had been so rude to Kynaston.

'How did you know?'

'Barney.'

'Is Barney a good painter?'

'He's not a Rubens or George Goss. He can only paint Mothers. He has a fixation.'

'I knew he painted Mothers.'

'Udders, you know.'

Griselda nodded.

After another silence, Lena said 'Is love important to you, Griselda?'

'Yes, Lena,' replied Griselda. 'Love is very important to me.'

'We're in a minority.'

'I suppose so.'

'I meant what I said in the train. I should like a man now.'

'It's the main thing about beautiful places.'

Suddenly they turned a corner and came to a high wrought-iron gate. It was surmounted by a painted though discoloured coat of arms, consisting simply of a mailed fist. It was apparent that the truck had been constructed as a subsidiary drive to a house; and that the glade was an artificial excavation designed to keep the drive on a level.

'We can't go back,' said Lena. 'We shall rejoin the others, and I'm not ready for that yet.'

'The gate's open,' said Griselda.

Lena pushed it. It ground on its hinges, but opened wide at a touch. They passed through, and Griselda closed the gate behind them.

The drive stretched on among beeches which, though presumably in private ownership, were indistinguishable from the publicly owned beeches in the forest outside.

'Do you know who lives round here?' asked Griselda.

'I'm afraid not. I'm a stranger in these parts.' Lena's tone had lost its previous habitual colouring of sarcasm. She had become entirely friendly. Griselda surmised that this might be a privilege, and that Lena might be a good friend to have.

'I suggest,' continued Lena, 'that we find our way out the other side of the Park, cast round in a circle, and rejoin the others from the opposite direction.'

'Perhaps they will have gone?'

'Perhaps they will.'

A few minutes later, Griselda said 'I suppose we may be stopped?'

'You must use your charm, Griselda. It's there if you'll bring it out.'

'What will you do?'

'I shall climb a tree.'

'Are you good at that?'

'Watch.'

She darted away from tree to tree.

'We must have a clean tree. I don't want to dirty my trousers. Wish I hadn't lent my blue ones to Florence.' Even though she was quite close, the Forest had begun to echo her clear voice.

Suddenly she was ascending: with unbelievable speed and agility; like a small grey and buff monkey. In a minute or two she was out of sight among the dense green summer foliage.

'Be careful,' called Griselda up the tree trunk.

'I'll be careful,' cried Lena from the greenery; and the Forest shouted: 'Careful, careful, careful.'

'Look out below.' Something was descending. It was a shoe. It was followed by another shoe. Then, a few yards away, at the perimeter of the tree, fell a pair of socks and Lena's shirt and trousers. Griselda looked up and saw Lena brown and naked at the very end of a thick branch. She was sitting on the branch with her legs drawn up; leaning back upon the left arm and hand, which rested on the bark behind her.

'How brown you are!'

'The sun was my stepfather.' Now she was standing on the branch, her hands above her head and clinging to wisps of leafy twig hanging from the branch above. 'I'm going to the top. Then down again. Wait for me, Griselda. I'll be very quick.'

Griselda waved up to her and she had disappeared

again among the leaves.

After a pause a fairly large whole branch crashed down from high above. It lay on the ground like the handiwork of a hooligan.

'Lena! Are you all right?'

There was no answer, but before Griselda felt alarm, Lena could be heard descending.

'Did you get to the top?'

Lena paused about twenty feet from the ground. In the hot streaks of sunshine she looked startlingly in keeping.

'We're nearer the house than we thought.'

Griselda laughed. 'Then you'd better dress quickly!'

'It's not that.' Lena's manner had changed a second time. Now she seemed almost subdued. 'There's something going on. There are tall trees near the house, but at the very top I could see over them. I think someone's dead.'

'What did you see?'

'I'll dress and we'll go on. Then you can see for your-self.'

She stood on the ground shaking bits of the tree from her brown body. In a minute and a half she was dressed, and combing her hair.

'What do you call those things you see in churches?'

'Cockroaches,' said Griselda.

'Wooden things. To do with funerals.'

'Coffins,' said Griselda.

'You're wise to wear your hair short.'

'Yours is too beautiful.'

'I know. That's why I keep it. It's my sole physical asset.'

'Not quite,' said Griselda smiling.

'Much good has it done me.' She was retying the khaki ribbon. 'Now come and look.' She slouched ahead, her hands once more in her pockets.

After two or three hundred yards, the track became paved with kidney stones, sunk far into the earth with neglect. After another two or three hundred yards, it gave upon a well-kept lawn, round which it curved to the door of a big late seventeenth-century house, in dark red brick, with large windows at long intervals, and heavy pre-Georgian details. The front door (from which the main drive stretched away in the opposite direction) was concealed by a bulky columned porte-cochère; high above which, rising on its own against the sky above the front wall of the house, was a massive relief representation in stone of the emblem which Griselda and Lena had noticed on the gate, the simple mailed fist. About the lawn were enormous isolated cedars of Lebanon.

Before they left the shelter of the Forest, Lena caught Griselda by the arm. 'Look! That's a thing to see from the top of a tree.'

In the sunshine before the porte-cochère, a strange figure sat upon the stones of the drive working. It appeared to be a dwarf. It had very long arms (like a cuttle-fish, Griselda thought), very long black hair (somewhat like horsehair), and a completely yellow face. Its ears were pointed, with strands of stiff black hair rising from the top of them. It wore black clothes. Very industriously, despite the great heat, the figure was polishing a large black piece of wood.

'You were right,' said Griselda, speaking unnecessarily softly; 'that's a hatchment.'

'Would that be the undertaker?'

'No. Undertakers must have charm.'

'Dare we go past?'

'I think so. Unless you'd prefer to go back.'

'Aren't we trespassing?'

'This is the twentieth century.'

'Should we take advantage of that?'

'I'll apologize and ask the quickest way out.'

They advanced from the safety of the trees. Instantly, against the ponderous grandeur of the house, they felt themselves misplaced and insignificant, wrongly dressed and intrusive.

The dwarf went on polishing until they were almost upon him, whereupon, without haste or appearance of surprise, he rose, bowed ceremonially, and extended his long left arm rewards the door of the house.

'I'm afraid we've lost our way,' said Griselda. 'Will it be all right if we go on down the drive?'

The dwarf who had completely black eyes, bowed again, and continued to point to the front door.

'Let's see for ourselves,' said Lena after a second's silence. She tried to pass the dwarf on the other side, with a view to making for the drive.

The dwarf, still with his arm extended, stepped to the right and barred her way. Now by gestures with the right arm he seemed to reinforce the invitation already made with the left. Griselda saw that the big double front door wood wide open.

'Shall we go back?' said Lena.

The dwarf took a further step. He now stood facing the door and with the lawn behind him. Both his immense arms were fully extended, so that he looked like a queer tree. The hatchment lay face downward on the stones.

'What is there inside?' asked Griselda.

The dwarf bowed once more, this time stretching back his arms and upturning his hands. His hands were unusually large and white; and wiry black hair grew in the palms.

'Let's go,' said Lena.

She looked about to run for it, but the dwarf, his arms still extended, leapt right off the ground like a goalkeeper, and descended in her course.

Griselda, anxious to prevent an unpleasant and undignified dodging contest, which, moreover, she feared the dwarf would, in at least one case, win, said 'I think we'd better investigate. They may need help.' Most of the blinds in the house were drawn.

'If you say so.'

They entered the house, the dwarf one pace behind them.

When they were through the front door, he returned to his polishing in the sun.

The drawn blinds made the hall very dark, despite the strong light outside. At once, however, the two girls saw that a figure stood motionless at the bottom of the stairs which rose before them. It was an elderly woman, very tall, very upright, very grey, and wearing a grey dress reaching to the ground.

'So you've come. This way.'

She began to lead the way upstairs, then stopped.

'Only one of you.' She peered at them. 'You.' She indicated Griselda. 'You,' she said to Lena, 'can go – or wait. Just as you choose. It won't take more than five or ten minutes now.'

'There's some mistake,' said Griselda. 'We—'

'Hardly,' interrupted the woman, smiling a slight, hard, weary smile through the gloom. 'But you won't have to stay long. Your friend can wait if she chooses. Come upstairs, please.'

'Why me?'

'I'm not sure your friend would serve. Please sit down,' she said to Lena. 'And wait.'

'Why won't I serve?' enquired Lena.

'There is a condition which must be complied with. You'll be perfectly safe,' she added somewhat contemptuously, 'Both of you. Now,' she said to Griselda, 'follow me.'

Griselda followed her up the wide staircase and into a gallery on the first floor, which seemed to run the length of the house and was filled with tapestries, there being apparently no other furniture of any kind except a carpet, though it was difficult to be sure in the dim light. Beyond the gallery were several large dark rooms filled with dust-sheets. Then there was a high double door.

The woman opened one of the doors very softly, disclosing artificial light within; and with an authoritative gesture from the wrist, indicated that Griselda should pass by and enter. The light in the room within enabled Griselda for the first time clearly to see her face. She looked imperious but sad; like one leading a dedicated life.

The room Griselda now entered was hung with black, which kept out all daylight. It was illumined by several hundred candles assembled on a frame such as Griselda had seen set before images in Catholic cathedrals; but larger, and formed of fantastically twisting golden limbs. The light fell upon a single enormous picture standing out against the black hangings: in an elaborate rococo frame, it depicted an Emperor or conqueror at his hour of triumph, borne by a white horse up a hill into a city, apotheosed alike by the paeans of his followers weighed down with loot, and by the plaints of the mangled, dying, and dispossessed. Opposite the picture was an immense four-poster bed, hung like a catafalque with black velvet curtains which descended from a golden mailed fist mounted in the centre of the canopy high up under the extravagantly painted ceiling. The carpet was of deep black silk. In the air was faint music.

The writhing candelabrum stood near one of the posts at the foot of the bed. While leaving all but the bed and the picture shadowy, it lighted up the room's occupant. Griselda at once recognized him. That look of a censorious Buddha, those clear yellow eyes, were, indeed, not to be forgotten. The man in the bed was Sir Travis

Raunds. He looked older than ever, and horribly ill, but he was turning the pages of a black folio volume containing coats of arms exquisitely illuminated on vellum.

As Griselda entered, the sick man looked up from his escutcheons.

'Ah, my dear,' he said in a high musical voice, 'in a world as near its end almost as I am, you at least do not fall short. You are as lovely as any of the dear women who performed your office for my ancestors. Kneel: there, where there is light.' He pointed to a patch of carpet, and Griselda knelt before his bed in the candlelight. Though the black curtains kept out the sun, the candles made the room very hot.

'Thank you. Now give me your hand.' He made a slight, weak gesture. 'You are perfectly safe. It will only be for a minute. Though time was—' But his remarks were tiring him, and he broke off with a Buddha-like smile.

Griselda extended her left hand. He took it in long thin white fingers, like those of a high-born skeleton, and lightly drew her towards him. She found that a stool stood beside the bed and seated herself upon it.

'How are you, Sir Travis?' she asked gently.

'Listen, my dear. Listen to your answer.'

Griselda listened. The music was as of a very large orchestra very far off: too far off for any particular melody or instruments to be recognized.

'What is it?'

The dying man seemed to hear more than she did. '"'Tis the god Hercules, whom Antony loved, now leaves him.'" He was listening intently.

'Sir Travis,' said Griselda, 'tell me about life.'

'Lord Beaconsfield told me that men are governed either by tradition or by force. I have since found it to be true.'

'But,' said Griselda, a little disappointed, 'that's a rule for governing other people. What about yourself?' She noticed that the distant music was ebbing.

'You do not need to govern yourself, my dear, if you succeed in governing other people.'

Suddenly Griselda thought of something: something that it was past belief she had not thought of before.

'Sir Travis,' she said, eagerly; too eagerly for a sick-room.

He did not answer.

'Sir Travis!' She almost shook his hand and arm.

But Sir Travis's mind was elsewhere. 'Tell Venetia,' he said smiling wickedly, 'that I'm leaving her for ever.' And his high musical voice died away.

'Sir Travis!'

'One more thing only,' said a voice from the shadows. 'And then you will be free to go.'

A young man in a dark suit stood before Griselda on the other side of the huge bed. He was small and looked French. He seemed to hold some small object clasped in each of his hands.

'I thought we were alone.' Griselda looked over her shoulder. There was no sign of the tall woman, but the door through which she had entered, had disappeared behind the black hangings.

The young man smiled slightly; then stretching out his hands across the bed, opened the palms. In each lay a large gold piece, which glittered in the candlelight.

'You know what to do?' His alien mien was confirmed by a slight accent.

'Is he dead? How do you know?'

'I know.'

Looking at the man in the bed, Griselda knew too.

'Poor Sir Travis!'

'Of course. It is very sad.'

Griselda lifted the hand which had just held hers and laid it on the bed. She had never before touched a corpse. She almost expected the hand to be cold: it was much more shocking that it proved as warm as in life.

'You know what to do?' The young man still held out the gold pieces.

'I think so,' said Griselda. 'But why me?'

'It is all that remains. Then you can go.'

Griselda took the pieces from his hand.

'They're five-pound pieces! And quite new!'

'Sir Travis made a special arrangement with the Mint.'

'For this?' Griselda's voice sank in awe.

'For what else? Gold coins are no longer taken in shops. Only pieces of paper.'

'They're beautiful.'

But the young man indicated the slightest touch of impatience.

Very carefully and tenderly, Griselda laid the gold pieces on the dead man's eyelids.

'Thank you, mademoiselle,' said the young man, indicating the slightest touch of relief. 'Now if you will follow me.'

Coming round the bed, he drew a section of the black hangings, and Griselda followed him back to the dim hall.

At the top of the stairs, the tall woman awaited them in the shadows.

'Is all in order, Vaisseau?'

'But naturally.' His tone was as proud as hers.

'And she can go?'

'Immediately.'

Lena stood below. 'Is everything all right, Griselda?'

Griselda squeezed her hand. 'There's nothing to keep us, Lena. Let us go.'

The tall woman and the young man silently, and almost invisibly, watched them go back into the hot sun.

Outside was a strange disturbance. The hatchment had gone and the dwarf, it seemed, with it; but looking round for the origin of an unaccountable noise which filled the summer air, the two women saw him crouched on the paving stones in a corner behind the porch. He was not weeping, since there were no tears; he was crying like an animal, but like no known animal, for, as they now perceived, he had hitherto been dumb.

They looked up from the distressing sight and saw that high above them, beneath the immense mailed fist, hung the hatchment, polished and varnished and renewed, until in the afternoon sunshine it shone the very pennant of death triumphant.

XXV

Griselda was unable to imagine why she had never thought to look up Hugo Raunds's address in 'Who's Who', or even in the Telephone Directory, and write to him for possible news of Louise's whereabouts.

Distracted by the omission, and full of resolve to repair it as soon, as possible, she imparted to Lena, who seemed pleasingly without over-pressing curiosity, a somewhat slender account of her recent experiences.

'But is it a madhouse?'

'I *think* it's just a very old family.'

They were walking down the drive towards the main entrance to the park. As the big elaborately wrought gates came into view, it appeared also that a small crowd was assembled outside. The first idea that they were faithful tenants come to enquire about the course of their protector's illness, or to mourn his passing, was dispelled by the way they stood packed together in the heat, by the fact that the lodge-keeper seemed to be remonstrating with them from behind the bars, and, most of all, by the noise they were making. In the end, Griselda saw that some of them carried placards, hideously lettered with slogans: 'Aid To Abyssinia, Guatemala, Democratic Spain, And Chiang-Kai-Shek'; 'Workers! The Intelligentsia Stands Behind You'; and, most immediate in its application, 'Sir Travis Raunds Must Go'. The inclusion of the title struck Griselda as a courteous detail, inconsistent with much else; but perhaps it served to spur David by making Goliath look fiercer.

'I wonder you 'aven't all something better to do on a nice day like this,' the lodge-keeper was saying. Clearly he had allowed himself to be drawn into unwise disputation. He was a mild elderly man with lank hair and an habitual air of having recently been rescued from drowning.

His remark was greeted with catcalls.

'Why don't you join us in fighting the enemy of your class?' enquired a tall prematurely bald young man with spectacles. He carried a battered puppet dangling from a crude gallows, which he had looted, during a university rag, from a Punch and Judy stand. Two or three of his fellow demonstrators began to chant the Internationale.

'My tea's waiting for me, you know.'

At this there was a burst of perceptibly forced laughter.

'I'll send for a policeman.'

'Call out the Cossacks!'

Lena went up to the lodge-keeper and spoke in his ear. He stepped back. Lena raised her hand.

'Sir Travis Raunds is dead. He died this afternoon,' she said in her clear voice. 'So go home.'

There were a few jeers, and a cry of 'Why couldn't you say so?' but the group began to retreat, more or less content in the knowledge that they were alive and that the future was theirs. It seemed to occur to none of them to doubt Lena's statement.

'That was brave of you, Lena,' said Griselda.

'So it was, miss,' said the lodge-keeper. 'But, of course, I 'ad old Cupid up my sleeve all the time.'

'Would Cupid have helped?'

'Torn 'em apart, miss. Cupid only needed a word from me to tear 'em apart. Just one word. That's Cupid.' He indicated a vague black shape which looked too big for the white wooden kennel placed in the lodge-keeper's miniature garden. 'Sir Travis named him after a gentleman he used to know when he was in politics.'

'Good old Cupid.'

It seemed unnecessary to pat Cupid, as he was asleep. He wore a collar with large spikes, like a drawing by Cruikshank; and his muzzle was matted with some sticky substance. When Griselda mentioned his name, he growled in his sleep.

'It's sad news about Sir Travis.'

'Yes and no, miss. Times have changed since the Old Queen's day. Not that either of you young ladies will care about that. But up at the house it's just as if the Old Queen was still with us. Just like Windsor Castle, it is.'

'You don't say so?' said Griselda sympathetically.

'I expect you young ladies believe in being modern and up-to-date?'

'You can tell at a glance,' said Lena.

'It's the best thing. But Sir Travis, he never would see it.'

Outside the park, they found their way without particular difficulty to where they had left the rest of the party.

'You're good at it,' said Griselda. 'You must have what is known as a sense of direction.'

'These little jaunts are symbolical,' replied Lena. 'Instead of leaving the organization to me, who, as you rightly say, am good at it, they will always leave it to Geoffrey, because they like him and because he's no good at it at all, which saves them the anguish of envying him. Not that I greatly care,' she added. 'I really only come to watch.'

'I'm not bad at finding the way myself, you know, Lena. Women often are better at things than men, aren't they?'

'Men have uses, all the same.'

Griselda said nothing; because at that moment the place where they had lunched came into view.

There was no sign of the party. Instead, a troop of Boy scouts were learning about the Arctic.

'Was there anyone here when you arrived?' asked Griselda. 'Sitting on the grass?'

'No one at all,' replied the scoutmaster. 'Only rather a lot of litter, I regret to say.'

A rustle went round the troop at Griselda's good looks and Lena's trousers.

'Come to the pictures, miss,' cried out one of the more precocious scouts.

So Griselda and Lena had to find their way back to London unattended; which they did with much pleasure. The day ended with Lena accompanying Griselda back to Greenwood Tree House for coffee and anchovies. It was after midnight when Lena departed, but there was still no sign of Peggy.

XXVI

Hugo Raunds was not in the Telephone Directory, and even in 'Who's Who' he figured solely as his father's heir, without even an address of his own. To Sir Travis were ascribed four different residences, one in each of the four kingdoms; but Griselda wrote to Sir Hugo at the one she knew. She asked simply if he had any knowledge of the possible whereabouts of a girl named Louise, whom she had met at Mrs Hatch's house, Beams, had since lost touch with, and wished to meet again. 'In the course of conversation she mentioned you several times; so I venture to trouble you.'

One day in the shop a pleasant young man made a really determined attempt to engage Griselda's interest. Entering merely in order to enquire for a copy of *The Last Days of Pompeii*, he had not departed before, in Mr Tamburlane's temporary absence, he had persuaded her to accompany him that evening to the Piccadilly Hotel for drinks.

'We might dance somewhere afterwards.'

'I don't dance.'

'Then we'll go somewhere else and have some more drinks.'

It proved all too true. By the time they had migrated

from the Piccadilly Hotel to Oddenino's and from Oddenino's to the Criterion and from the Criterion to the Bodega, Griselda had begun to feel faint.

'Eat?' said the young man. 'Of course. Come back to my place and my girl will run us something up. She's Italian, you know, or, more accurately, Sardinian.'

He was out of the Bodega (Griselda had felt faint between drinks) and into a taxi with such dexterity that Griselda could not escape without an absurd and embarrassing scene before the cynical eye of the taxi-driver.

'By the way, my name's Dennis Hooper. You've probably heard of me? I should have told you before.'

Griselda hadn't. She said nothing. The motion of the taxi was suddenly making her feel really ill; and also there seemed a case for reticence.

He didn't seem to mind that she hadn't heard of him.

'I bet your name's Anne?'

'How can you tell?'

'Every single girl I meet's called Anne these days. There's a positive Anne epidemic.'

Griselda could for the moment do nothing but groan.

'What's your other name?'

Griselda clutched at a wisp of what she took to be worldly wisdom.

'Musselwhite.'

'So you're Anne Musselwhite. One of the Brigade of Guards people?'

'No.'

'I say, would you rather have gone to Scott's and had

lobsters?'

'No.'

'Not under the weather are you?'

'No.'

'Shall we stop and have a drink? Might pull you round.'

'No, thank you.'

'We're there anyway. There'll be time for one or two quick ones before we eat. We might go somewhere afterwards and dance.'

The taxi drew up at an exceedingly splendid block of flats. Hooper gave the driver a ten shilling note and waved away the thought of change.

They ascended by lift to the top floor. The flat had fashionable furniture, no pictures, and a view.

'Gioiosa! Do sit down.'

Griselda seated herself upon a geometrical sofa, upholstered in a strident, headachy green, and applied herself to watching the rotating dome of the Coliseum through the long low windows.

The Sardinian girl entered. She was brown and luscious, and, bearing in mind the characteristics of her people, could not have been more than fourteen. She wore a black satin dress cut alarmingly low, and no stockings.

'We want to eat. What can you do for us?'

'A spiced omelette with sauerkraut? Some hot meat served in oil?'

'Anne Musselwhite. Which?'

'You haven't any fish?'

'Some potted squille only, signorina. Non troppo fresche.'

'Could I just have a little bread and butter with some warm milk?'

Gioiosa looked at her employer.

'Anne Musselwhite, you've been deceiving me. You *are* under the weather. You must permit me to prescribe. All right,' he said to Gioiosa, 'anything you like.'

'Anything you say, signore.' She smiled bewitchingly and departed.

Hooper produced a bunch of keys and unlocked a vast antique cabinet bearing the Hat and blazon of some fourteenth or fifteenth century Prince-Bishop. He mixed a complicated drink, with ingredients derived from the interior.

'This'll make your blood run cold.'

'No thank you. Could I just sit for a few minutes?'

'Of course. I'll leave it by you.' He drew up a three-legged occasional table in cream aluminium.

'I'm sorry to be such a nuisance.'

'I expect you've been overdoing it in the shop. We'll have to see about that.' He poured himself a big round brandy-glass of neat whisky.

'If I could be quiet for a while, I'll be perfectly all right.'

'I'll leave you by yourself.' She smiled at him gratefully. Taking his whisky he opened a door into the next room. The door was decorated with scarlet zig-zags. In the doorway, Hooper looked back and said 'Darling Anne Musselwhite.' Then he withdrew, shutting the door. Instantly there was the sound of dance music. Hooper's gramophone was such a good model that it might have been in the room with Griselda.

Griselda removed her feet from the carpet (which was covered with representations of the Eiffel Tower in different colours) and placed them on the sofa. The dome of the Coliseum began to rotate faster and faster, and almost at once, despite the music, Griselda was asleep.

She first dreamed that she was climbing Mount Everest with Mrs Hatch, who was dressed as a lama; then that Epping Forest was ablaze and Sir Travis Raunds's catafalque, four times life-size, reared itself incombustible in the midst; and lastly that she was dressed rather mistily in white and had just been married to Kynaston. Kynaston had insisted on removing her shoes in the Church Vestry; was embracing her and about to kiss her. It was, she felt, a perfectly agreeable prospect, because for some reason, not very clear, no responsibility attached to the transaction. But before the transaction was completed, Griselda awoke.

Hooper's arm was round her waist. With his free hand, he was unbuttoning her blouse. Moreover, he had already removed her shoes. Griselda felt it was a situation which Lotus (for example) would have managed better than she.

As she awoke, Hooper sat back a little.

'I do hope you are feeling cured.'

'Yes, thank you.' She was rebuttoning her blouse. 'Well enough to go.'

'But Gioiosa has prepared some food for us.'

'Where are my shoes?'

'Please don't misunderstand me. I'm very fond of you, Anne Musselwhite.'

'Where are my shoes?'

'Sit down and let's talk it over. I'll get you a drink.'

Griselda crossed barefoot to the door.

'You can't very well go without your shoes.'

'I'd rather not. I'll have to explain what happened in order to borrow a pair.'

'Anne Musselwhite, you've got things all wrong.' He was recharging his big brandy glass.

There was a knock at the door. Griselda opened it. It was Gioiosa.

'Ready to eat, signore.'

Looking Griselda up and down, whom previously she had only seen seated, and discovering that she lacked shoes, Gioiosa went into extravagant foreign laughter.

'Grazie, signorina. Non conobbi.'

She was about to go, but Griselda caught her by the arm.

'Lend me some shoes. Your feet are about the right size.'

'*You* wear *my* shoes!' She was giggling like an imbecile.

It seemed hopeless. Griselda dropped her arm and made for the front door. In a moment she was running down the pasage, shoeless like Cinderella at midnight. The carpet in the passage was thick and patterned like a tiger-skin. The walls bore large golden gulls in plastic relief. At the end, an under-porter had been working all day on a defective radiator, and the pieces lay scattered about until he could resume the next day. Some of them had already been kicked quite long distances by passing tenants and visitors.

As Griselda reached the corner where the stair-well began, there was a clatter behind her. She thought that Hooper was in pursuit; then realised that it was only a pair of shoes. She paused and looked back.

'I tell you, Anne Musselwhite, I think very little to you.'

It occurred to Griselda that if she returned to pick up the shoes there might be further trouble.

'If you think it's fair,' went on Hooper, 'to take a man's drink and hospitality, and let him pay for you all round the place, and then give him nothing in return, I for one don't.'

Griselda turned her back.

'Won't you think again? We might go dancing somewhere.'

Griselda's back was negative.

'Oh, go to hell,' said Hooper irritably and slammed the door.

All the same, thought Griselda, it was odd how after weeks and months of only Peggy, she should make so many new friends in so short a time.

Immediately she entered her room, Peggy knocked on her door.

'Come in Peggy. Sit down. Do you mind if I undress?'

'I have never thanked you for the picnic.'

'No need to. I hope you enjoyed it?'

'I found them interesting to observe.'

'Lena said something of the same kind.'

'I thought Lena was more than a little affected, I'm afraid.'

'Who did you *like*?'

'I haven't known them long enough to *like* any of them.'

In view of Barney's attitude, and the lateness of Peggy's return from the jollification, Griselda thought that disappointing.

XXVII

Promptly, and on writing-paper which reminded her of Louise's, Griselda received her reply:

Dear Miss de Reptonville,
   Of course I know Louise. But I don't know where she is. I wish I did. I'm sorry.

Very sincerely yours,
Hugo Raunds.

Kynaston, installed as custodian of the Liberator's immortal memory, moved into an attic flat near his place of work. He had followed *Days of Delinquency* with *Nights of Negation*, but his publishers took the view that the receipts from the former work did not justify further adventures; and he was in a state of melancholy mania.

'Why not try another publisher?'

'They all work in together.'

Although it was obvious that he was still seeing Lotus (on one occasion he appeared with a strange scar on the side of his neck), or she him, he became really industrious in paying court to Griselda. He would not come to the shop, for fear of Mr Tamburlane; but they would meet at the northern end of the Burlington Arcade, and Griselda would take him to Greenwood Tree House for a good meal and in order to listen to his difficulties and advise him.

'If I'm not a poet, Griselda, what am I? Am I any more than a current of hot air?'

Unlike Mrs Hatch, Griselda herself did not care for Kynaston's poems. 'You dance very well. Why don't you try to develop that?'

'I find it empty. As you dance so little yourself, it's hard to explain to you.'

'I suppose so. Have some more stew?'

'Please.'

'And more potato?'

'Please.'

'And more seakale?'

'Please.'

Griselda sat back. Fortunately Kynaston's attacks of self-doubt seldom upset his appetite.

'A piece of currant bread?'

'If you can spare it.'

Later, when they were seated one on each side of the electric heater, and Kynaston had been describing the difficulties of his early manhood, and munching cream crackers, he said 'This is what marriage would be like. I think it would be enchanting.'

Griselda could not possibly go as far as that; but, after her recent loneliness and unhappiness, she admitted, though only to herself, that worse things might easily befall her. Kynaston was not very much of a man, but life, she felt, was not very much of a life.

So before he went she let him kiss her on the eyes,

and even neck, as well as on the mouth. It was one thing about him that he had never attempted to seduce her. She was quite uncertain whether he cared for her too much or too little.

There were several fogs in November, a rare thing in London. On the foggiest morning Mr Tamburlane arrived late at the shop, wheezing slightly but jubilant. He wore a thick scarf in the colours (a little too vivid, Griselda thought) of the Booksellers Association, and a black Astrakhan hat.

'My waywardness has put you to the labour of taking down the shutters, Miss de Reptonville. I can but blame a higher power.' He indicated the fog. 'But your magnificent zeal is to be repaid a thousandfold. Yes, indeed.' He sneezed.

'There's a new edition of the Apocrypha come in,' replied Griselda demurely. 'Shall I arrange some copies in the window?'

'Work,' cried Mr Tamburlane, sneezing again, 'can wait. There are tidings of joy.'

'What can they be? Shall I make you a warm drink?'

'A splendid and original device. Let us split a posset. There's nutmeg in a mustard tin behind the Collected Letters of Horatio Bottomley.'

Griselda set to work in the back room, while Mr Tamburlane sat complimenting her, his legs stretched out to the large gas fire in the shop. Soon the brew was prepared, and Griselda pouring it into large hand-thrown bowls, the colour of nearly cooked rhubarb.

'Miss Otter has news.'

Griselda nearly scalded her uvula.

Ὀτοτοτοῖ Τοτοῖ,' exclaimed Mr Tamburlane sympathetically. 'Let us go further.' He swept across Griselda's feet, and, unlocking a drawer, brought out a bottle. 'We are warned against mixing our drinks, as the idiom is, but I think that on this occasion our common joy will absolve us. Here is finest coconut rum brought direct from the fever belt by one of my clients. It was all he had with which to meet his account, poor fellow. He described it as an antidote against cold feet.'

'Thank you,' said Griselda, taking the glass Mr Tamburlane extended to her. 'What is Miss Otter's news?'

'That,' said Mr Tamburlane swallowing his rum at a gulp, 'I do not know. Miss Otter wrote to me that she will look in this morning to impart it in person. It must be something quite unconventional, because, as you know, this is not Miss Otter's day.'

'And that's all you know?'

'Enough is as good as a feast, Miss de Reptonville. I counsel you to watch and pray. Although unswervingly antagonistic to an anthropomorphic theogony, I often find purgatation in the precepts of the primitives.'

'Some more posset, Mr Tamburlane?'

'Thank you, no. Warmth is already reanimating the various segments of my trunk. Nor, I conceive, should we continue imbibing stimulants until incapacity overtakes us. We should recollect that the hour for toil has but just now chimed; and summon forth our full self-mastery. Or do you differ?' He sat anxiously interrogative, with the bottle clasped motionless in the air between them.

'Far from it, Mr Tamburlane. I agree entirely.'

'What a reassurance that is to me. My inner demon has in it that which could so easily sweep all resistance away like chaff – which indeed on more than one occasion *has* swept it away like chaff – that I fear constantly the thickness of my own right arm.' The bottle still hung in the air.

'I think we have a customer.'

'Then let all be apple pie and shipshape.'

Griselda drained her glass. She did not care for the coconut rum, because it tasted of coconut.

A young man had been standing outside the shop, looking in the window and hesitating. At first Griselda feared it might be Dennis Hooper, come with persuasive protestations of repentance; but it proved to be a young man looking for a chart of the Blackwater Estuary. From his demeanour outside and inside, it was clear that, like many of the customers, he seldom entered a bookshop.

'Charts, Mr Tamburlane?'

Mr Tamburlane ran both hands through his upstanding white hair. 'Try in there, Miss de Reptonville.' Griselda suspected that he had decided entirely by intuition.

'Nothing but almanacs,' said Griselda rumaging.

'I always like to keep a stock of almanacs for past years,' said Mr Tamburlane to the customer in a spirit of affable salesmanship. 'I am, I believe, the only London bookshop to do so.'

The young man simply nodded. He was in a subdued frenzy for a chart of the Blackwater Estuary.

'It's ideas such as that, I always like to think, which set one apart from one's competitors.'

'I want some idea where she dries out,' said the young man anxiously. His eyes followed Griselda round the shop. It was clearly a matter of immense moment.

'I'm so sorry,' said Griselda. 'I'm afraid we've sold out that particular one just at the moment. Shall I order it for you?'

'My dear boy,' said Mr Tamburlane, laying his hands on the customer's arm. 'For a sailor who has youth, there are always the stars.'

Miss Otter failed to arrive.

Griselda, although she had never, except at the very beginning, dared to take that particular ridiculous business in the least seriously, found by midday that she was taking it seriously enough to feel sick.

She had nothing for lunch but bananas and cream, and a cup of black coffee. When she returned through the fog to the shop, she was even more alarmed to perceive that Mr Tamburlane seemed really upset.

'Miss Otter is invariably the very figurehead of punctilio. You could, if I may employ a daring concept at such an anxious moment, use her as a regulator for a clock.'

'Did Miss Otter not mention any time?'

'Tomorrow morning,' said Mr Tamburlane. 'Yesterday, you understand.'

'What about telephoning?'

'Out of the question. Miss Otter will have nothing electrical in the house.'

'Perhaps she dislikes fog and has stayed at home.'

Mr Tamburlane's face lighted up. 'Miss de Reptonville!' he cried. 'I believe you have hit it.'

At a quarter past four, when it was quite dark, a stranger entered the shop and asked to speak to Mr Tamburlane. Griselda showed him into the back room and went on dealing with the arrears of orders sent by post.

About half an hour later, Mr Tamburlane emerged, wearing his overcoat and scarf and looking altogether distraught. 'All is over,' he exclaimed. 'Kindly put up the shutters immediately. Miss Otter has been run over by a postal van. I am informed that it was behind schedule owing to adverse weather.'

'Then,' cried Griselda, 'shall I never know—?'

Mr Tamburlane raised his hand. 'Please say no more, Miss de Reptonville, lest it be taken down and used in evidence against me.'

'Come along, please,' said the visitor.

Griselda looked at his feet, which she had once read was the right thing to do; but could see nothing unusual. 'What is the charge?' she asked.

'That has been under discussion with this gentlemen for the last half-hour,' said Mr Tamburlane. 'It appears that the authorities have visited Miss Otter's house and drawn their own conclusions. Entirely false ones, I am sure I need not add.'

'Come along, please,' said the visitor.

'Cut is the bough that might have grown full straight.' Mr Tamburlane extended both his hands.

'What can I do to help? Please tell me?'

Mr Tamburlane suddenly became transfigured with an idea. 'Officer,' he said, 'may I write a letter?'

'Time we was on our way.'

'Only one line.' Mr Tamburlane looked exactly like half-a-crown.

'Make it short.'

It was very short.

'Miss de Reptonville this is what you shall do. You shall not read this until five minutes after I am gone. Five minutes by any timepiece you choose.' He had rolled the letter into a spill. Griselda took it. The visitor was looking vainly for his half-crown. 'Promise.'

'I promise.'

'Get going,' said the visitor sourly. 'We don't go for your class of offence, you know.'

A woman entered the shop. 'I want a copy of *Reader's Digest* for my little boy.'

Mr Tamburlane put on his astrakhan hat and cleared his throat. 'Tell me,' he said to his companion, 'did you find time to visit Sing-sing this summer?'

When the five minutes were spent, Griselda uncurled the letter. Mr Tamburlane had spoken the exact truth. Apart from his signature it consisted of a single line.

'I hereby give my shop and all its contents to Bearer.'

XXVIII

Griselda made diligent enquiries, partly in the forlorn-est possible hope that she might extract some news of Louise, partly out of gratitude to Mr Tamburlane. But she found all channels blocked; largely, it seemed, at the particular direction of the accused. In the end she realized that in his own way Mr Tamburlane had disap-peared from her life as conclusively as Louise.

Often, however, as she served in the shop, her thoughts turned to him. She was advised in the par-ticular circumstances to adopt another name for the business as soon as possible; and through much of a cold December week, the versatile Lena, clad in motorcyc-ling costume, painted out 'Tamburlane' and substituted 'Drelincourt'. This was because Griselda had invited Lena to go into partnership with her, and had no par-ticular conviction that her own was a suitable name to place above a London shop. Already, after only a fortnight, Lena's knowledge of literature had proved as valuable as her capacity for odd but essential jobs. Griselda had insisted on placing in the window ten cop-ies of *Inhumation* (ordered without Lena's knowledge) on the very first day; and, oddly enough, by the end of the second day all were sold, and another ten had been ordered, to the conspicuous vindication of Griselda's commercial judgement and acquired experience of the trade.

The proposal of Kynaston's which Griselda accepted, was made one snowy night on the Central London Railway, between Oxford Circus and Marble Arch. Kynaston proposed immediately they entered the train, as indeed the shortness of the journey rendered necessary.

'I shall go to Canada, if you refuse,' he concluded. 'The Mounted Police are starting a ballet, and I've been asked to be régisseur.'

There was a tired desperation about him which was very convincing.

'You don't mind that I love someone else?'

'Of course I mind. It's bloody for me.'

'But you're willing to risk it?'

'I don't expect everything.'

Griselda sank her head on his shoulder. But it was Bond Street Station, and she raised it again. It would be pleasant not to have to conduct so much of her emotional life on and near the Underground. She waited for the train to restart. Her heart felt quite dead; like a dry sponge, or a cauliflower run to seed.

'All right, Geoffrey, I'll marry you if you want it so much.'

He said nothing at all and Griselda continued to stare before her.

'Let's make it soon,' she said.

Kynaston still said nothing. From the corner of her eye, Griselda saw that he was quietly and motionlessly weeping. She laid her hand on his. He had attractive hands.

'Thank you, Griselda,' he said at last. 'Could you lend me your handkerchief?'

They had reached Marble Arch. Ascending on the escalator, Griselda reflected that there were said to be wonderful mysteries attendant on marriage. Long before the top, a freezing atmosphere enveloped her from the world outside.

In the Edgware Road it was as if all the air held particles of snow in suspension. None the less, before they reached Greenwood Tree House, they had decided to marry before Christmas. It would, Kynaston believed, require a special licence, which would involve extra expense; but now that Griselda had the shop, extra expense might be less of an obstacle.

At the outer door, Kynaston showed no particular inclination to accompany Griselda upstairs.

'My wretched shoes leak. I must buy some new ones before we marry. This snow could lead to chilblains.'

But Griselda had no wish to be left with her thoughts.

'You can take them off in my room. It's just the sort of thing you've always wanted.'

He did so. His socks were saturated with snow, and his feet were blue. They were, however, as male feet go, attractively shaped, Griselda was relieved to note.

'I can't lend you any socks because I don't wear trousers.'

'I expect they'll dry.' He hung them on the bars of a bedroom chair and pushed the chair in front of the electric heater. At once the socks began to steam profusely and also to fill the room with a faint but individual stench.

'I'll fetch Peggy. She'd better hear the news.'

'Peggy frightens me, Griselda.'

'I expect we shall both find it difficult with the other's friends, but Peggy's got a right to know.'

If Kynaston had asked what right, Griselda would have found it hard to specify. But he merely said 'I'd better put my shoes on.'

Peggy, however, proved to be already in bed.

'Everyone at the Ministry has got a cold. I don't want to take an unnecessary risk.'

'Peggy! I'm going to marry Geoffrey Kynaston.' Griselda came very near to the tone in which such announcements are made.

'You said you weren't the marrying kind.'

'I've changed.'

'Not at all. I never believed you. Remember? I hope you'll be very happy, Griselda.'

'Thank you, Peggy dear.'

'I hope you'll find in him all you wish.'

'Of course I shall. He's in my room now. I hoped you'd be able to join us.'

Peggy smiled with irritating scepticism. 'You can do without me. Just pass me down the bottle of Formamints before you go back to him, would you please, Griselda?'

'Is there anything else I can get you?'

'No thank you. I don't know how you're placed, but

I could borrow my sister's wedding-dress if you'd like it. She was just about your size when she married and I know she's kept it for my nieces.'

There was something about Peggy, fond though Griselda was of her, which tempted to the outrageous.

'Thank you. I doubt whether white would be appropriate.'

But Peggy only smiled and said 'That's for you to say.'

XXIX

A special licence proved unnecessary, but there were difficulties of domicile, and it seemed that for the ceremony the only day convenient to all parties (but especially to the Registrar) would be Christmas Eve. Questioned as to his religion, Kynaston stated that he was loosely attached to the Baha'i Movement; and though Griselda belonged to the Church of England, she had small inclination for the chilliness of so many empty churches on a December morning. The Registry Office, though perhaps little warmer, offered a briefer ceremony, and one free from that undertone of morality still characteristic of so many churches.

As the day drew near, Griselda felt quite resigned. After Beams, her life had subsided into very nearly its former uneventfulness; so that for the present a change of any kind made an unconscious appeal. The only marked modification in her behaviour, however, was that she ceased to buy so many clothes. Also she spent two evenings a week trying to clean and decorate Kynaston's attic flat, which was to be her home until something more suitable could be both found and afforded. Lena assisted: clad in a dun coloured boiler suit, and after a busy day at the shop, she distempered the ceilings in pink and blue, and made water come out of the tap, before returning to Juvenal Court to resume work on her new novel, 'Legacy Grass'. Kynaston came to approve of her more and more until Griselda felt that she ought to feel jealous. Griselda, though good at walking, and good at the design part of interior decoration (she suggested they should try to instal some means of heating the water, even if obtained second-hand), was less good than Lena at implementing her suggestions. Kynaston had become radiantly happy, and restive about his terms of employment.

'After we're married, and now you two have got the shop,' he said to Lena, who was laying a carpet which had been found rolled up behind some old stock in Mr Tamburlane's former office, 'I shall try again with my plastic poses. I often think they're the only thing I've gone in for which has community value. After marriage one must think of that.'

Lena stopped hammering. 'Think of what?'

'Community value. After marriage I mean to be less of a parasite.'

'It's much more important for you to keep Griselda's body happy. Concentrate on that.'

'Ça va sans dire.'

'No man's quite a parasite who can do that for a woman. It's your only hope, Geoffrey.'

'Hadn't we better change the subject? It's in poor taste in Griselda's own home.'

'Griselda's opening a tin. Go and help her.' Lena resumed hammering. The carpet was difficult to penetrate and smelt dreadfully of the East.

As a matter of fact, moreover, Lena was wrong for once. Griselda had heard every word.

She eyed Kynaston across the tin of pilchards. She supposed there might be some joy in the relationship which so many sought for and hoped for and worked for and suffered for. It certainly could not compensate for the loss of Louise, but it might be not wholly barren. Griselda shuddered slightly. It was attractive and Kynaston kissed her.

'Why pilchards, Geoffrey? Why not squille?'

'Because pilchards are cheap.'

'They seem very oily.'

'The fish themselves are quite dry.'

There was no doubt he had a well-shaped body and much patient persistence in pursuit. It was necessary to hope.

On Christmas Eve it was foggier than on the day Miss Otter died and Griselda inherited the shop. Griselda and Peggy took forty minutes to find the Registry Office from Holborn Station; but fortunately (at Peggy's suggestion) they had started very early. Of the two Peggy looked much more like a bride: at extravagant expenditure she had acquired a magenta woollen dress with a salmon-coloured belt. The gesture testified all the more to her warmth of feeling, because, as she explained to Griselda in the Underground, it would be out of the question for her to wear the garment to the office.

The occasion had attracted an excellent attendance from among the friends of both bride and bridegroom (whose friends, as it happened, were largely held in common), and from the people of the surrounding district. Among the latter was even a barrister, on his way from Gray's Inn to Lincoln's Inn, whose large black hat and resonant professional diction enormously raised the tone and spirits of all present. When Griselda arrived, he was explaining that he had just been consulting his solicitor on a normal routine matter and had since been lost in the fog. The contingent from Juvenal Court had shared the cost of a taxi (which the barrister explained was a breach of statute) and stood grouped together protecting the bridegroom. They all wore sapphire coloured orchids paid for by Lotus, who, dressed in black chiffon and a Persian lamb coat, and pale to the lips and ears, was a centre of speculation among all who did not know her. Guillaume wore a fashionable suit hired from a reputable but humble competitor of Messrs Moss Brothers; Florence a pale grey coat and skirt, home-made but none the less well made, and dark stockings sent as a Christmas present from Paris by an old admirer who had fled despairing her marmoreal devotion to another. Monica Paget-Barlow crotcheted away behind the Registry Office font. Freddy Fisher was interviewing the press, who took him for the bridegroom because he looked young and innocent and wore morning dress.

Kynaston entirely resembled Prince Charming in a midnight-blue suit he had salved from an unsuccessful production of a play by Maeterlinck.

As Griselda handed her raincoat to Peggy (she had followed Mrs Hatch's precept and acquired a substantial one), Kynaston stepped forward from his ring of supporters, extended both his hands, and said 'My love! This is our day. Let us not flinch.'

'All right,' said Griselda. 'Shall we start?'

The Registrar's wife ceased her voluntary, and the Registrar himself loomed through the fog which filled the precincts. He was an impressive figure with a cold and wearing a frock coat, at which Griselda stared with interest. It was exactly like that worn by Joseph Chamberlain in Herkomer's portrait, a fine engraving of which hung above the sideboard in her Mother's dining room. Griselda supposed that her Mother might have forgiven her as it was her wedding-day. On the whole, she was glad that the chance did not offer.

The sacristan, a sleek young man in a pepper-and-salt suit reminiscent of Kempton Park, arranged the bride and bridgroom into a procession. At that moment, Griselda's eye fell upon Lena, for whom she had been searching. Lena, in a semi-polar outfit (she was much the most suitably dressed person present), sat in a corner of the Registry Office, obviously trying to comfort someone in distress, whose face was entirely concealed by Lena's handkerchief. The distressed one's clothes at once spoke for themselves, however. Before Griselda lighted up the entire half-forgotten panorama of society at Beams. Horror! It was Doris Ditton.

Now Griselda began herself to weep. The picture of Louise had projected itself with the rest in the so far greater intensity that memory offers than life.

Kynaston held out a twilight blue artificial silk handkerchief which went with the suit.

'Be strong, Griselda,' he said. 'Soon we shall be alone together, and *I* shall be needing *you*.' Lena waved to her slightly, affectionately. Kynaston had presumably not yet identified Doris. Or perhaps she was there by his invitation? Griselda could not see how else she had learned of the event; and had always understood that the bridgroom's guests at weddings consist predominantly of his past passions. Then she realized the answer: Lotus.

'Bride and bridegroom stand. All the rest sit,' bawled the sacristan, his voice filled with the wind off Newmarket Heath.

Kynaston, in the hope of checking her tears, introduced Griselda to a small smooth man in a morning suit made splendid with orders and decorations.

'Colonel Costa-Rica, darling,' he said. 'The Orinocan Commercial Attaché.'

Griselda transferred her handkerchief and extended the appropriate hand. The Colonel fell upon it with his lips. His movement was like that of a closing knife. His cold eyes looked straight through Griselda's handkerchief and into her shivering soul.

'Enchanté mademoiselle. Et très bonne chance.' When he spoke, his lips scarcely moved.

'English is the only European language the attaché doesn't speak,' explained Kynaston.

'Excusez-moi?'

'Yes, certainly. Mais oui,' replied Griselda in reassurrance. The Colonel sat down and began to brood upon the state of trade.

'All set,' roared the sacristan. The bride and bride-groom were propelled forward to where the Registrar stood waiting, his book of runes in one hand, a small flask of eucalyptus in the other; there was a sound of military orders in the fog outside, and of rifle butts crashing on paving stones: and the greatest moment in Griselda's life had begun.

For one presumably experienced in his work, the Registrar seemed strangely dependent upon his little book. That being so, moreover, it was difficult to understand why he had never acquired a larger volume with better print. As it was, the limited natural visibility and archaic lighting (by gas produced from coal) clearly caused him much distress. He peered at the minute screed, varying its distance from his eyes, and every now and then look-ing upwards at the burner above his head with a de-meanour which in another would have passed for dis-taste. Sometimes he stopped for several seconds in the middle of a passage or sentence. Punctuation, indeed seemed a complete stumbling-block. In consequence of all this, however, the literal dreadful moaning of the words merged happily into a synthesis properly evoc-ative of a half-forgotten rite. Behind the Registrar the east wall of the building was crudely painted with ad-monitions headed 'Rules and Regulations Touching the State and Condition of Holy Matrimony,' varied by long closely printed notices signed on behalf of the Home Secretary. The stained glass window above the Registrar's head depicted a bygone Chairman of the London County Council kneeling before the goddess of fertility, represented traditionally. Doris's intermittent sobs offered an emotional continuo. Every now and then the heating system rumbled towards animation. The Registrar forged ahead, his mind on higher things. Regarding the grave mysterious figure, all goodness and wisdom, and his richly significant background, Griselda remembered that this was something she must never forget, even though she had great-grandchildren. Again she shuddered slightly. The congregation sympathetically attributed it to the weather.

Suddenly there was an interruption. The great pitchpine doors parted and someone entered with firm, stamping tread. Griselda could not but look over her shoulder. It was a fine figure of a man in naval uniform. Before seating himself in the back row of chairs (next to Lotus), he caught Griselda's eye and waved breezily. Griselda stiffly inclined her head; then returned her attention to the service. Could this officer be responsible for the martial clatter outside? Possibly he was the next bridegroom, though he seemed elderly.

In the end the Registrar with a final ejaculation of disgust, decided to abbreviate the liturgy; Kynaston produced the ring in excellent order (he had been wearing it on his forefinger); Griselda made a rash and foolish promise; and all was over. The ring was much too big for Griselda's particularly slender finger: it might have been made for a giantess, indeed probably had been.

'Sign please,' said the sacristan producing a mouldering book from under the front row of chairs.

'Have your witnesses managed to get here?' enquired the Registrar.

'They're all our witnesses,' exclaimed Kynaston full of the beauty of the ceremony and gesticulating expansively. Instantly he was deflated. 'Dad!' he cried and looked quickly round him. The naval officer was thrusting forwards through the congratulatory crowd.

'Bravo, my boy,' he cried. 'I never thought you had it in you.' His hand was extended. He was examining Griselda closely and added 'Indeed I never thought it.'

'Hullo, Dad,' said Kynaston. In his blue suit, he looked quite green.

'Take your Father's hand and say no more. Remember I'm waiting to kiss the bride.' He wrenched his son's hand.

'You must introduce me, Geoffrey,' said Griselda hastily.

'My Father. Admiral Sir Collingwood Kynaston. This is Griselda, Dad.'

'Delighted to meet my daughter.' He kissed her overwhelmingly. 'My boy and I have fought like tigers ever since he was born, but that's all over and you mustn't believe a thing he says about me.'

Griselda thought it might be discourteous to say that Kynaston had never mentioned him (as was the case); and all the witnesses were waiting to sign.

'A good hard cudgelling on both sides hurts neither,' affirmed the Admiral, scrawling his name ahead of the rest. 'And the old man's made full amends. Wait for them. Just wait.'

Freddy Fisher took the opportunity to ask for the Admiral's autograph. 'I only collect leaders of the services,' he said.

'Lucky to find one who can write,' replied the Admiral jovially. 'Is that one of your bridesmaids, my dear?' he enquired of Griselda, indicating Lotus.

In the end everyone had signed and the Registrar had come forward with his account.

'Leave it me,' said the Admiral. 'It's only once in a man's life that his boy gets himself spliced and he must expect to pay the piper. Though that reminds me,' he continued, while the Registrar stood respectfully in the background, 'what about you, my dear? Are you an orphan?'

'My Father died of Spanish influenza,' replied Griselda. 'I never knew him. From my Mother I have long been estranged.'

'Lone wolf, eh? See yourself in the same galley with Geoffrey. Never mind. You'll grow. Being a widower I'm always persuasive with women of my own generation.' He made a handsome settlement on the Registrar, who became profuse with improbable felicitations before retiring into his vestry.

'Now then,' said the Admiral. 'Just you see.'

The sacristan threw back the big shining doors and Griselda saw. Outside, drawn up in the fog, were two lines of bluejackets. As the doors opened, an order rang out, and they crossed carbines.

'I really must protest,' said Guillaume, his face grey with inner conflict, 'at the use of force. Surely the occasion is sacramental?'

The Admiral only beamed at him. Then he glared at Kynaston.

'Well, my boy, get on with it. Give her your arm, like a man. If you don't, I shall.'

The reconciliation between father and son seemed already strained.

Kynaston was white to the finger-nails. For a moment there was silence, broken by one of the bluejackets tittering.

'No, Dad,' cried Kynaston. 'I refuse.' He gathered strength. 'Come on Griselda. Let's find another way out of this place.'

'Oh, well done,' said Guillaume under his breath. Florence drew closer to him.

The admiral seemed unexpectedly taken aback. 'You can't refuse,' he cried in a shrill voice. 'I've ordered luncheon for everyone at the Carlton.'

'Sorry, Father,' replied Kynaston. 'Griselda and I have another engagement.'

Peggy had drawn back some time ago, embarrassed by the Admiral's display of emotion, and had somehow got into what seemed mutually satisfying intercourse with Doris, who was regarding Kynaston's heroism with soft wondering tear-soaked eyes. By this time all the strangers had withdrawn to form a crowd outside.

The Admiral looked with some anxiety at the guard of honour. Clearly he felt that the situation could not be much longer continued without becoming legendary on both lower and upper decks for years to come.

He glared at his son. 'Boy,' he said sotto voce, 'I have only one thing to say. Be a man.'

'That's just it, Father. I am a man.'

'Oh I say,' interposed Freddy Fisher, who had lost sympathy with Kynaston. 'Surely you can compromise?'

Outside, the Petty Officer cleared his throat. The men were tiring under the strain of the crossed carbines.

The admiral wheeled. 'Dismiss your men.' Then amid the necessary bellowing and stamping, he cried to the party 'Those who wish for luncheon may follow me. There are cars outside;' and, ignoring the newly married couple, he left the building.

There was another pause.

'Go on,' said Kynaston. 'Have lunch. Griselda and I will see you later.' Lena's eyes were moving round the group. The sacristan was waiting to lock up.

'I would rather beg my bread on the Victoria Embankment,' said Guillaume. He was in a passion of indignation. The guard of honour could be heard marching away. Soon the fog hushed them.

'Please go and enjoy yourselves,' said Griselda.

A motor-horn blared commandingly. Florence looked out into the murk. 'That lawyer's got in,' she reported.

Among the rest of them Guillaume's opinion seemed to prevail. Even Freddy Fisher, though horribly disappointed by the turn of events, abided by an unconscious loyalty, to none could clearly say what.

After another minute or two the cars drove off; the

Admiral in the first of them, with his only guest; the remainder empty.

Griselda felt still further cut off from the world which had been hers until she visited Beams; a feeling enhanced by Peggy coming up to her, thanking her for the wedding, wishing her happiness, and then departing, her new dress hardly displayed, clearly much upset. Doris, after quietly congratulating the bridal couple, departed with her.

XXX

They lunched at the Old Bell Restaurant, recommended by Barney, who now appeared. He had been delayed by the completion of a commission, his work being much in demand about Christmas time.

'You can depend on a Trust House for a sound middle of the road meal,' he said. 'Besides there's a dome of many coloured glass: the finest thing of its kind in London.'

In the Ladies' Room, two things happened. Griselda found that she had already lost her overlarge ring (and Kynaston, of course, had been unable to afford an engagement ring: indeed there seemed, in retrospect, to have been no very clear period during which Griselda had been engaged). Then Lotus pinned her in a corner and said 'Remember.' It was just like the ghost of Hamlet's father. Griselda wondered what would come out of it all.

At luncheon (where Monica would eat nothing but salad) Barney enquired after Peggy; Lana, ostensibly for Barney's information, told the story of the Admiral's intervention; Kynaston kept feeling for Griselda's hand; and Freddy Fisher became drunk with extraordinary rapidity. Lotus seemed increasingly out of it. Griselda wondered whether she was contemplating a final disappearance to a wealthier milieu; then supposed that she could not be, in view of her reminder in the Ladies' Room. Lotus's beauty and passion and sense of dress would make her rather a forlorn figure in any modern environment that Griselda could conceive. After a while, Lena, who, unlike Freddy, was drinking heavily, removed her polar outfit, and emerged in her usual shirt and trousers. As well as drinking, she was talking continuously, and without adapting her talk to the particular listener. Griselda looked at her a little doubtfully. Lena often seemed hightly strung for a business partner.

Luncheon ended with Carlsbad plums in honey, halva, black coffee, and (at Lotus's expense) Green Chartreuses all round. There was some disputation, more or less affable, as they allocated among themselves liability for their respective parts of the bill; during which one of the business men who constituted the main element among the customers, approached Griselda and insisted on presenting her with a large bunch, almost bouquet, of Christmas roses.

'You look so happy,' he said, 'that I should like you to have it.' Since the beginning of their meal, he had spent his luncheon hour searching the cold streets and stuffy shops. Instantaneously and for an instant it almost made Griselda feel as happy as she looked.

Then Barney was making a speech, and all the waiters and some of the bar and kitchen staff, had entered the room to listen to it. Lotus sat sneering slightly, which only made her more seductive than ever; and indeed it was not the best speech which even Griselda had ever heard. The business men listened like professionals, and at suitable moments led the applause. The speech ended by Barney announcing that now they would leave the happy couple alone together; at which, despite the hour, there was a pleasant round of cheers. Barney then spoke to a waiter, who flashed away. In a moment he was back and speaking in Barney's ear.

'I have ordered,' said Barney, 'a taxi; and what is more, paid for it. It is yours to go anywhere not more than ten minutes away, or a mile and a half, whichever is the less.'

Everybody leaned from the windows of the Old Bell and cheered as the happy pair entered the taxi, which, having been decorated with white streamers at lightning speed by the driver, was already surrounded by a cluster of strange women, haggard as witches with Christmas shopping.

'Best of luck,' screamed Freddy Fisher and threw a toy bomb which he had acquired next door at Gamage's for the purpose. Considering its cost, it was surprisingly efficacious.

'Where to?' enquired the driver.

There seemed nowhere to suggest but back to the attic flat.

XXXI

Griselda wondered when the mysteries would begin.

It seemed not immediately. In the taxi, Kynaston concentrated upon his achievement in routing and evading his father (which had, indeed, impressed Griselda considerably); and in the flat, having changed his suit, he continued alluding to the same subject. He described the wretchedness of his childhood for more than an hour and a quarter, a topic with which Griselda was fairly sympathetic; then unexpectedly said 'I think we'd better go to the pictures. I feel we should celebrate, and all the cinemas will be shut tomorrow.'

Griselda quickly made tea (neither were especially hungry after their platesful of venison at luncheon) and they found their way through the fog to a double-feature programme which did not come round again until past nine o'clock. Most of the time Griselda sat with Kynaston's arm round her. She found it pleasant, but detrimental to concentration upon the films. However, it being the programme immediately before Christmas, the films were undemanding.

'Let's go to Lyons,' said Kynaston. 'You'll have plenty of opportunity for home cooking in the years ahead.' He smiled at her affectionately. Griselda smiled back, though suddenly she had wondered what the food was like at the Carlton.

At Lyons, however, the big new Corner House at St Giles's Circus, the food was, as usual, unlike the food anywhere else, though the ornate building was full of fog, through which the alien waiters called to one another in little-known tongues above the tumult of the orchestra. Griselda and Kynaston ate Consommé Lenglen, turkey and Christmas pudding, followed by portions of walnuts; so that it was nearly eleven before they left.

When they emerged, their heads spinning with Viennese music, the fog was so thick that the busmen had gone on strike, leaving their vehicles standing about the streets and blocking most of the other traffic. In some of the buses passengers bearing holly and rocking-horses, were defining and proclaiming their rights; in some, mistletoe was being hoisted; and in some, tramps were beginning to bed down for the holiday. Every now and then a bus became dark, as its battery failed or miscarried. Over all could already be felt the spirit of Christmas.

'Let's look for the tube.'

But when they found it, the Underground had ceased to run. Across the entry was a strong iron gate, bearing the notice 'Special Christmas Service', surrounded by little figures of Santa Claus.

'Let's walk. Do you mind, Griselda?'

'Of course not, Geoffrey.'

'Fortunately I'm good at finding the way.'

'I can't see my feet.'

Allowing for errors of direction, and the further time consumed in retracing their steps, the walk took until a quarter to one. By the time she reached their attic flat, Griseida's legs were cold, her respiration clogged, and her spirits chastened.

Kynaston left her alone in their bedroom (where his single divan bed had been supplemented by its double) to undress. Almost at once she was in bed. Rather charmingly, Kynaston then appeared with a glass of hot milk and some bread and treacle.

'Would you like a hot water bottle?'

'It's lovely of you, Geoffrey, to work so hard, but I don't use them.'

'I do.'

'That's all right.'

Kynaston disappeared again and was gone some time. After the hot milk, Griselda felt not anticipatory but comatose. Ultimately Kynaston returned. He wore pyjamas. He must have changed in the sitting room.

He crossed to Griselda's bed, where she lay with her eyes shut.

'You look tired, darling. I suggest we just sleep. There's all day tomorrow.'

Griselda opened her eyes. 'Yes, darling, let's just sleep.' He kissed her lips fondly.

All the same it was disappointing. Griselda could not resolve how disappointing.

Kynaston put out the light.

'I think we'd better keep to our own beds. For to-night. Else we might spoil things. Because I'm sure you must be cold and tired.'

'I agree.' But Griselda was now perfectly warm and, for some reason, much less tired.

She rolled round and round in her bed several times.

Then without warning in the darkness Kynaston said 'Are you a virgin?'

And when Griselda had explained the position, he said 'I expect we'll be able to manage;' then sighed and began to snore.

On Christmas Day Griselda became quite fond of Kynaston. He performed unending small services, and seemed to be filled with happiness every time she smiled. He spent the morning writing a sonnet, while Griselda made a steak-and-kidney pudding. In the afternoon he attempted to codify some new plastic poses, while Griselda mended his clothes. At about the time of the King's broadcast, however. Griselda became aware of an undefined, unacknowledged strain. At dinner it seemed to have affected Kynaston's appetite: a very unusual circumstance. Griselda herself continued more cheerful than she had expected. Kynaston's slight nerviness seemed to make him more attentive than ever, almost anxiously so; and the immediate future aroused interest and curiosity.

After dinner, Kynaston began to read *The Faery Queen* aloud. Fortunately he did this very well. Every now and then he broke off while Griselda made some more coffee in a laboratorial vessel of glass and chromium which Lotus had given them as a wedding present. On one of these occasions Griselda noticed that Kynaston's hand shook so much that he spilled the coffee into the saucer.

'Is anything wrong, darling? You're shaking like a leaf.'

'I'm not used to so much happiness.'

'Does happiness make you tremble?'

'Of course. Now I'll go on reading.'

His explanation was convincing but unsatisfying. Griselda felt that happiness precluded while it lasted the thought of its own fleetingness. Kynaston, moreover, every now and then between stanzas, flashed a look at her which was positively panic-stricken.

After several hours of reading, and several rounds of coffee in the pretty shepherdess cups which had been Peggy's wedding present, Kynaston reached the lines:

> '"Or rather would, O! would it be so chanced,
> That you, most noble sir, had present been
> When that lewd ribald, with vile lust advanced,
> Laid first his filthy hands on virgin clean,
> To spoil her dainty corps, so far and sheen
> As on the earth, great mother of us all,
> With living eye more fair was never seen
> Of chastity and honour virginal:
> Witness, ye heavens, whom she in vain to help did
>   call!"'

At this Kynaston broke off, thought for a moment, while Griselda continued mending a sock, then, with glassy eyes said 'Darling. Would you care to take off your sweater and skirt?'

'Of course, darling. If you wish.' Griselda laid aside the sock and complied with Kynaston's suggestion.

He looked at her doubtfully, his eyes still glassy. 'You won't be cold?'

'That depends.'

'You mean on how much longer we go on reading?'

This seemed not to require an answer, so Griselda simply smiled.

'I'll finish the canto.'

Griselda sank to the floor and sat close to the heater. Lena had given her a quantity (much greater than Lena could afford) of attractive underclothes as a wedding present, and she felt that she looked appealing as long as she could keep warm. Kynaston resumed:

> '"How may it be,' said then the knight half wroth,
> 'The knight should knighthood ever so have
>   spent?'
> 'None but that saw,' quoth he, 'would ween for
>   troth,
> How shamefully that maid he did torment:
> Her looser golden locks he rudely rent,
> And drew her on the ground; and his sharp sword
> Against her snowy breast he fiercely bent,
> And threatened death with many a bloody word;
> Tongue hates to tell the rest that eyes to see
>   abhorred.'"'

At the end of the canto, Kynaston looked at the floor and said: 'Magical, isn't it? And so modern.'

'How much more is there?' asked Griselda. She liked *The Faery Queen*, but was increasingly troubled by the draught along the floor.

'We're less than a third through. There are six books. Spenser actually hoped to write twelve. Each is concerned with a different moral virtue. We've only just begun Book Two. On Temperence.'

'I remember,' said Griselda. 'What's Book Three about?'

'Chastity.'

Griselda's bare arms were beginning to make gooseflesh.

'Shall we go to bed, darling? It's past midnight.'

Kynaston nodded. Griselda put away her pile of socks. Kynaston crossed the room like a man heavily preoccupied, and replaced *The Faery Queen* on her shelf. Then, pulling himself together, he said 'Shall I bring you some hot milk? To make you sleep?'

'I don't know, darling. Should you?'

Kynaston turned, if possible, a little paler.

'Or should we both have a stiff drink?'

'Would that be a good thing?'

'I'd like you to have what you want.'

'I want bed. I'm frozen.'

'I'm terribly sorry. Really I am.'

'I didn't mean that at all.'

The sudden turning on of the light emphasized the quantity of fog which had entered the little bedroom. Griselda realized that it was the only day for many mouths on which she had taken no exercise. With shaking hand, she cleaned her teeth, and fell into bed exactly as she was. She lay in the foggy freezing room (for the heater had not yet begun to take effect) with the light on, waiting for Kynaston.

He took much longer to appear than on the previous night. When he entered his face was set in a way which recalled to Griselda his repudiation of Lotus and his defiance of his father. Without a word he turned off the light and the heater, and climbed into his bed. He had not even bidden Griselda good night, or kissed her.

In the foggy darkness there was silence for a while. Then Kynaston said 'Shall I turn on the heater again? We might leave it on.'

'We can't afford it, darling.'

'Of course I'd rather not get up, but I don't want you to be be cold in bed, darling.'

'I don't want to be either.'

This time there was a really long silence. Griselda, who was positively rigid with wakefulness, wondered if Kynaston had fallen asleep. Then she recalled that when asleep, he snored. Suddenly he spoke. 'Griselda.'

'What is it darling? I was thinking about *The Faery Queen*.'

'On the subject of any physical relationship between us.'

'Living together as man and wife?' Griselda elucidated helpfully.

'I imagine all that's of secondary importance to you.'

'Why?'

'Because you have always said you don't love me.'

It was odd, Griselda reflected, how few people seemed to know the condition of being to which she would refer that word. She supposed she knew, and would always know, something that few knew, or would ever know. She felt to Kynaston as she had once felt to Mrs Hatch: very superior. Though she had lost, she had loved. All the same it was difficult to explain to Kynaston that lack of love as she understood the word, did not necessarily imply precisely proportionate lack of love as Kynaston understood it.

'I married you.'

'Yes.' He sounded as if it was a case of forebodings being fulfilled.

'I knew what I was doing, Geoffrey darling.'

'Of course, darling . . . I'd better go on with what I was saying.'

'I'm sorry not to be more helpful.'

'No, it's I who am sorry. You're utterly in control.'

'Go on, darling. What do you want to say?'

He gulped; and sucked at the bedclothes. 'First, it's marriage. At least I think it is. You know how it is with men?'

'Not very well, darling, I'm afraid.'

'A man sees marriage in terms of affection, domesticity, and inspiration.'

'I understand that.'

'With me it's particularly true. I need a woman – a woman of character, like you, Griselda – to mould my life.'

'I remember your saying so.'

'You've seen Lotus. You understand that there's been something between us?'

'I guessed there had.'

'You don't mind?' It was as if he hoped she did.

'You say you love me.'

'Passion's possible with Lotus, great drowning seas of it, but none of the other things.'

'Whereas with me—' A hard shell was beginning to enclose Griselda's entire body; beginning with her still cold feet.

'With you the situation is further complicated by what you said last night. Whatever Lotus is like in other ways, she is good at making things easy. I hope you'll let me put it clearly. Because I love you so much.'

'Do you mean, darling, that you married me just because I *don't* love you?'

'Of course not, darling. I'm utterly determined to *make* you love me. I don't think it would help for us to begin with a physical misunderstanding.'

That, however, was what they did begin with, Griselda, her new shell hardening and tightening all the time, had supposed that now for certain she would be spending the night alone, and an uncertain number of future nights, until (she surmised) she broke down in health or espoused a good cause. But, instead, Kynaston almost immediately entered her bed and gave her ample and unnecessary proof that his hints of unease and inadequacy to the circumstances were firmly grounded. Things were not made better by a continuous undertow of implication that it was all to please

331

Griselda. At the end, there was very little mystery left, and less wonder.

After similar experiences at irregular and unpredictable intervals on twenty-eight occasions, Griselda, when a twenty-ninth occasion offered, felt positively but indefinably unwell. It would be deplorable, she spent much of the time reflecting, if, moreover, nature, despite counter-measures, took her course. She began to wonder more than ever whether she was truly suited to marriage.

Energy, thwarted of satisfactory direct outlet, expended itself obliquely, as is the way in marriage. Griselda began to apply herself more steadily and more forethoughtfully at the shop; and also to see that Kynaston applied himself as efficiently as his temperament and his job permitted. Soon the shop became the subject of a note in *The Bookseller*, and Colonel Costa-Rica was holding before Kynaston the possibility of a position, at higher pay, in the Orinocan Intelligence Service. Not only did they become richer, their increase in income being coupled with a diminished desire to expend; but they began to scent the first faint sunrising of social approbation renewed.

Before long Kynaston was losing interest in both poetry and his plastic poses, in favour of a projected Anthology of Curatorship, for which he hoped to obtain a Foreword from the Editor of *Country Life*. Sometimes they found themselves invited to visit homes of repute and to mingle on equal terms with the enbosomed families. More and more the shop stocked books which might sell, instead of minority books. Lena, over whom, of course, hymeneal happiness had yet to hover, regarded this last tendency disapprovingly; though the proceeds conveniently augmented the slight returns from her own new book. A climax was reached when Kynaston received an invitation to stand in the Labour interest at the Parish Council Elections. He declined, because he deemed politics to obstruct full self-realisation; but he declined politely, conscious that, far more than any other party, the Labour party gives careful heed to the morals and probity of all it permits to join its pilgrimage.

When she had been married nearly a year, Griselda one morning realized with surprise that Lena, to judge by some remarks she made, regarded her state with envy.

'But, Lena, you don't have to marry a man in order to enjoy him.'

Lena leaned back against the counter, her hands in her pockets. 'There are times, Griselda, when your superficiality is equalled only by your smugness.'

She had never before spoken so to Griselda, though given to the style when speaking to certain other people. Griselda had observed, however, that Lena's censoriousness, though seldom judicious, was seldom wholly undeserved.

'Am I becoming smug, Lena?'

'I apologize for what I said. I'm a bitch.'

'But am I becoming smug?'

'As a matter of fact, you are.'

'What should I do about it?'

'I wish I knew.'

Before the matter could be taken further, they were interrupted by the arrival of a thousand copies of a book describing the atrociousness of the new German government.

Not the least remarkable change in Kynaston was his sustained firmness in dealing with the problem of Lotus. Quite soon Lotus was reduced to supplicating Griselda: a procedure which Griselda considered superfluous and irrelevant, though, with a perverseness new to her nature, she did not say so to Lotus.

'You gave me your word,' cried Lotus, her beauty rising from her tears, like Venus from the flood.

And instead of simply pointing out that she had in no way broken it, Griselda replied reflectively 'Things are never quite the same after marriage as they were before it,' and offered Lotus another glass of lemon tea.

After weeks of apparent rebuff and equivocation Lotus tumultuously capitulated at the end of February.

'You've won him and I've lost him,' she said to Griselda over morning coffee. 'You've been stamping out my body like wine beneath your little feet. I need renewal. I always find it in the same place.'

'Where's that?'

'Sfax.'

In due course, a picture postcard of a grinning Arab under a palm tree laden with dates, confirmed Lotus's decision; but Griselda wondered what in Kynaston's life had replaced the satisfactions, however limited, which, even by his own account, Lotus had given him. She looked at the sky of Sfax, almost unnaturally ultramarine, at the camels on the horizon, at the Wagons-Lits official in the foreground; and supposed that Kynaston must at last have found a purpose in life. Really it was most unlike him.

About a week after Lena's outburst in the shop, Griselda received a visit from Guillaume. It was a Saturday afternoon; and Griselda was lying on her back, gazing at the ceiling, and eating Pascall's crêmes-de-menthe. She and Kynaston had not yet found a better place to live; indeed lately the search itself had flagged.

'Sorry Geoffrey's out. How's Florence?'

Guillaume was wandering about the small sitting-room collecting cushions.

'Losing weight just a little, I'm afraid. She strains you know. I try to open her eyes to the wonder of life, but I doubt if the brightness of it all is ever wholly clear to her.'

He filled an armchair with his accumulation and sank his large body slowly into the midst of it.

There followed a long silence. Guillaume looked like a dingy Mother Goose.

He restarted the momentum of intercourse. 'I thought I'd take a chance of finding you in.'

'Have a crême-de-menthe?'

'May I take a handful?' He nearly emptied the small green tin. 'I'm engaged on research at Soane's. The work of years. Probably my very last chance. The final

335

brief passage before the volume closes.'

'Surely not?'

'I'm a disappointed man, you know, Mrs Kynaston.' He smiled like the last sunset of autumn. He had difficulty in extracting the sweets entirely from their papers, so that every now and then he ejected a tiny moist scrap which had accidentally entered his mouth.

'Florence told me.'

He seemed disturbed. 'That she had no right to do. Even a failure has his pride.'

'I shouldn't have mentioned it. Where is it that you've failed?'

'Can you look at the world around you and ask me that?' he replied. 'On the one hand the dream. On the other the reality. And I started with such hopes.' He was feeling for his pocket handkerchief. Griselda feared that he was about to weep, but he only sought to remove some of the stickiness which his large moist hands had retained from the sweets.

'Take only one case,' he continued, 'Take the state of affairs in denominational schools. Little children exposed naked to the blast of bigotry. Take the mines. Do you know that the faces of miners are black all the time they work? Men born as white as you or I. Take the so-called catering industry. Have you ever worked for twenty-four hours on end in an underground kitchen? Do you know that the world's supply of phosphorus is being consumed at ten or twenty times the rate it's being replaced? Look at the cruelty and waste involved in the so-called sport of polo alone! If you live in Wallsend, you have to walk ten miles to see a blade of grass. Is anything being done to harness the energy in the planets? Even though there's enough to extirpate work everywhere. Think of the millions deceived by so-called free insurance schemes, paid for out of profits!'

'I see what you mean.' said Griselda.

'And in other countries things are worse. What have you to say about the Japanese? Or the Andaman Islanders, who pass their entire lives in a prison camp? Or the so-called freed slaves in Liberia?'

'Perhaps we'd better stick to England. At least to start with.'

'There's a great danger in parochialism. The aboriginal Tasmanians discovered that.'

'How?'

'Very simply. They were trapped, killed, and eaten by men of more progressive outlook.'

'I think there is a lot in what Lord Beaconsfield said.'

'Of course there is,' said Gullaume unexpectedly. 'But did he put it into practice?'

Griselda was far from sure. But almost certainly Guillaume was thinking of some other remark of the sage's. In any case, he resumed speaking immediately.

'Though who am I to throw the first stone?' he enquired. 'William Cook, the failure. You didn't even know that my real name was William?'

'It would never have occurred to me. I suppose you disliked being called Bill? I know I should.'

'In those days no one would have ventured. I was a man of spirit then. I knew Hubert Bland quite well: and

Hyndman too. No. I chanced my name, Mrs Kynaston, solely in order to appear to advantage with women.'

'I'm sure you did impress them.'

'Not one. I might have saved myself the cost. Never has one woman truly opened her heart to me, although my heart finds room for the whole human race.' He looked into Griselda's eyes and coughed back into his mouth a crême-de-menthe which had involved itself with the lump in his throat.

'You have Florence. She's devoted to you.'

'A mere Ahaviel. A simple handmaiden,' he replied irritably. 'If I could have made my own, utterly my own, a woman of spiritual power, comparable with mine, mountains would have moved.'

For some reason this remark annoyed Griselda. 'I think Florence is one of the nicest people I've ever met.'

'Nice is the just word,' he replied bitterly. 'But you speak to a prophet. My responsibility is wide. I seek the divine flame, not soapsuds.'

'I won't have this,' said Griselda quietly and putting on her shoes. 'I am fond of Florence. You're lucky to have her.'

'Florence is Florence. Naturally no one estimates her more justly than I do.'

'She is beautiful and intelligent and devoted and faithful and kind. Kind people are rare. As a prophet you ought to know that.'

Guillaume eyed her through the gathering October dusk. 'I understand why you set store by at least one of those qualities.'

'I set store by all of them.' Griselda suspected another attempted seduction.

'We need not pretend. Your business partner still lives at Juvenal Court, you know. Florence has known Lena for years.'

Griselda thought quickly and clearly before deciding what to say next. Then she decided.

'I'm sorry I can't offer you tea. I've arranged to join Geoffrey.'

'Like everybody else, you under-estimate me. Had you been taking tea with Kynaston, I should not have chosen today to visit you.'

Griselda had not expected that either. But for reasons she had not yet had time to determine, Guillaume's surprising remarks had the effect of clearing rather than unsettling her mind.

'I'm afraid I must ask you to go. Please give my love to Florence.'

'I am quite used to eviction and condemnation, as to many other unpleasant things. I should be a poor creature if by now I had not my philosophy, strong as iron.' Laboriously he rose from his cache of cushions, like the nook of an animal about to hibernate. Still sucking and spitting, he crawled across to the window and stared into the encroaching night. Griselda stood by the open door, waiting.

'I was absorbing the peace of the lamplighter at work,' said Guillaume after a while, 'like a glowworm. Or, perhaps more nearly, a firefly.'

'I often watch him,' said Griselda, who had never previously noticed him.

'"Like a good deed in a naughty world." You are sensitive to the beauty of words?'

'Of course. I own a bookshop.'

'It would be pleasant to live so high up.' Guillaume sighed and looked about in the twilight for his hat.

'Here.' Griselda extended the object. It was a close replica of that worn by Mazzini when in disguise.

'Good-bye,' said Guillaume, assimilating and retaining her hand. 'I grieve for you.'

'Quite unnecessary,' replied Griselda, struggling slightly.

'You mustn't deny me that single luxury.' He kissed her heavily and adhesively upon the brow and went away, reeking of charity and peppermint.

Griselda drew the curtains, turned on the lights, and prepared for herself a satisfying, solitary tea, including cucumber sandwiches, and custard creams, new and crisp. For the first time since before Christmas, she felt able to regard herself and find all her faculties present and functioning. Before long she wondered whether it was not even more than that: whether she was not in process of restoration against the consequences of losing Louise. It might be that her marriage to Kynaston had been required to achieve that.

The only awful thought was that Guillaume's hints, bearing in mind Guillaume's nature, might have been untrue.

XXXII

Griselda thereafter took particular trouble to be kind and understanding to Lena, despite provocations which steadily increased.

One morning, as the anniversary of her wedding drew near, Griselda sat in the little office after the shop had closed. She was writing and addressing Christmas Cards, designed by herself. Lena had been supposed to be keeping an appointment of some kind, but at the last moment had decided not to go. She was wandering about the shop examining the stock with dissatisfaction.

Just as Griselda decided that she was not called upon to send a specially designed Christmas Card to Mrs Hatch, Lena called out 'Griselda. May I talk to you? Or do I interrupt?' She was seated on top of one of the shop ladders.

'Of course you don't interrupt. I've hardly spoken to you alone for weeks.'

'I think our books are frightful. There's an entire shelf of Warwick Deeping.'

'It's right up under the ceiling. No one can see it.'

'And under it Jeffrey Farnol.'

'That's just old stock.'

'And under that J. B. Priestley.'

'We've got to live.'

'I'd rather live honestly.'

'Come down and talk about it.'

Lena descended and entered the office. She had taken to wearing dresses; which did not suit her personality. Griselda reflected with interest upon the deterioration in her own clothes since marriage.

'I want to hand back my partnership. With thanks, of course, Griselda.'

'I can't do without you.'

Lena upturned the wastepaper basket, and sat upon it. The floor was now covered with the transactions of the day.

'I'm going to live abroad.'

'Where?'

'Somewhere warm.'

'North Africa?'

'Possibly.'

'Dear Lena. Of course, it's a man?'

'The feeling when you haven't got one is exceeded only by the quite different feeling when you have. But you don't know about that.'

'You don't like it?'

'Not this particular example of it.'

'Then why leave the shop?'

'I told you. I don't like the books we stock. The books we have to stock. I admit that. I still don't like them.'

'Is it that he still chases you?'

'Mind your own business, Griselda.' Then she added 'You'll be much better without me.' Griselda had never seen or even imagined her so distressed. She spoke very gently.

'It's Geoffrey, I think.'

Lena shook her head.

'I recognized him from your description.'

'It's over, Griselda. At least for me. I'm not sure about *him*, I'm afraid. I feel a pig, pig, pig.'

'You needn't. I believe I'm grateful to you. Anyway I know very much how you feel. I feel some of it myself. Please don't feel it any more. It's quite unnecessary. I do know.'

'You're good to me Griselda.' She looked at the pile of Christmas cards. 'Shall I stick on stamps?'

Griselda smiled and nodded. Soon Lena's tongue was inflexible with mucilage.

'May I stay in the shop?'

'I can't do without you.'

XXXIII

Griselda felt more than ever that marriage did not suit her. She supposed that she should have a plan to extricate herself; since resignation, the other possibility, had never suited her either. The trouble was that Kynaston was clearly coming to depend upon her more and more. Worse still, his marriage had enabled him to acquire and develop a variety of social and professional responsibilities and entanglements, which he would be wholly unable to sustain unaided. Griselda found difficulty in deciding how far these were expressions of Kynaston's personality, previously kept latent by restricted conditions, and how far mere substitute outlets for energy diverted by marriage from true and individual aims. Things were not made easier by Lena's normal defence mechanism of aggression turning against herself, and manifesting as acute guilty embarrassment, whenever she came into contact with Kynaston. This led to Lena absenting herself from the shop whenever she thought Kynaston might appear; and to Kynaston making sour remarks about Lena whenever opportunity offered. In the end he suggested that he himself might take Lena's place.

'I could begin by organizing a display of ballet books. Give the entire shop over to it, I mean.'

'It wouldn't be fair on Lena, darling. After all she's done nothing wrong.'

One day in November Griselda received a letter from Lotus. It was on a large sheet of paper in a large envelope, possibly because Lotus's handwriting was so large; but the contents were brief. It simply invited Griselda to luncheon at Prunier's the same day. It was the first she had heard of Lotus since the postcard view of Sfax. Apparently she was now staying at the Grosvenor Hotel.

Lotus was very brown, a little plumper, and even better dressed than usual. But her big green eyes were deep rock pools.

She lightly touched Griselda's hand, swiftly looked her over, and led the way without speaking to a reserved table.

'Is it true?' Her voice seemed to Griselda softer and more stirring than before she left England.

'Which particular thing?'

'That Geoffrey loves Lena, of course.'

'In a way.'

'The only way?'

The waiter brought Lotus a large menu. Lotus, without consulting Griselda, ordered at length for both of them in rapid convincing French. The waiter, who was a Swede, departed much impressed.

'Saves misunderstanding,' said Lotus. 'But you haven't answered me.'

'Is it necessary? You seem to know.'

'Of course I know. Of course it's not necessary. Things like that are always true. I knew it inside me. But

I wanted to hear you say it. I needed to touch bottom.'
Two very large small drinks arrived.

'All the same how *did* you know? Does Geoffrey write to you?'

'Write to me! He never even thinks of me! Never once since I went away.'

'Have you been in Sfax all this time?'

'Sfax failed me.'

'Where else have you been?'

'Twice round the world.'

Mussels arrived.

'I wish I had been once round.'

'The world's become very crowded.' She was consuming mussels with enviable grace and firmness. 'I've been in Johannesburg for the last six weeks. Buying clothes and buying men. Then throwing them away again. I couldn't go back to Sfax while the hot weather lasted.'

'I thought Sfax was always hot.'

'It's still hotter during the hot weather. After what you've told me I leave again tonight. I'm living on Victoria Station, you know. I sit all day at my window watching the boat trains and wishing myself beneath their wheels.'

'You mean you still love Geoffrey?'

'He is my god. I know that now.'

'Take him with you Lotus.'

'Please don't laugh at me.'

'He's yours. I don't want him and nor does Lena. Take him.'

'You offer to sacrifice your whole life to my great

love? You are pure, Griselda. You will go to heaven.'

Coquilles arrived. Two each.

'Of course, I'm not sure that he'll go. He's become a little set in his ways.'

'What am *I* now? Tell me, Griselda, where should we go, he and I? If I accept your sacrifice, that is. I feel you know both our hearts. Tell us where we should be happy.'

'I don't think Geoffrey's good at being happy. Men aren't, do you think?' The shells were rattling about on Griselda's plate, making a noise like dead human hopes.

'Then we'll be splendidly, radiantly miserable. But where?'

Griselda considered the maps of the continents in her school atlas. Australia, of course, was out of the question.

'I suggest the Isle of Wight. I've never been there, of course; but I believe it's full of picturesquely wicked people.'

'An island!' cried Lotus. 'Like George Sand. And Geoffrey like Chopin. He could play mazurkas to me. We could throw away our clothes and dance. And aren't there coloured cliffs?'

'And a Pier. It's nearly a mile long.'

'And great birds flying into the sun.'

'And palm trees.'

'There were palm trees at Sfax.'

Before the arrival of the bouillabaisse it was settled.

'Where is Geoffrey?' asked Lotus. 'I must find him immediately. The Grosvenor's gone and let my room to a parry of nuns.'

'I'll take you. He's still with the Orinocans. There's a reception this afternoon. The President's in England.'

Lotus's eyes were misty and mysterious. 'No formality, Griselda,' she said, clutching Griselda's hand across the table. 'Geoffrey and I will creep away like children; hand in hand into the dusk.' Griselda was fascinated by the solid banks of emeralds in her bracelet. They were so nearly the colour of her eyes.

The Liberator's birth-place was en fête. All the windows were shut and fastened, and the lower ones additionally protected by closed iron shutters. There were swags and clusters of artificial flowers in the national colours; and a huge entirely new flag swirling in the November breeze which set the teeth of the spectators on edge with the chill foreboding of even worse weather inescapably ahead. Up the steps to the door was a red carpet showing even yet, and despite hard scubbing, marks left by the blood of an earlier notability. Above the line of the cornice could be detected the glint and reassurance of steel helmets. The shivering crowd was laced with detectives, chilled to the bone and waiting for trouble. One or two common constables stood grumbling about their pay and working conditions. They were conscious of being outnumbered and outclassed. Preliminary entertainment was provided by a small brass band which was accompanying His Excellency on his travels. As a compliment to England, they played the same tune again and again, being the only English tune they knew except only 'The Holy City', which they had learnt in-stead of 'God Save the King.' It was 'Poor Wandering One'; and, what is more, no royalty was being paid to Mr D'Oyly Carte.

Lotus and Griselda arrived by taxi four and a half minutes before the climactic moment. Lotus ordered the taxi to wait, despite dissent from a section of the crowd which had been there since dawn and now found its view obstructed. Fortunately, however, the taxi-driver was very old and queer, and fell into a deep sleep every time his vehicle became inanimate. Lotus was shaking all over with nerves. Her face was so thickly veiled as to be quite invisible in the dim taxi; but her sable coat scented the stale cold air with wealth and the anticipation of desire fulfilled. The taximeter was de-fective and apppeared to be running downwards instead of upwards. Every now and then there was a little crisis, when a spring seemed to go; but each time the invin-cible machine recovered itself and recorded a sum smal-ler than ever. The watchers on the pavement went on complaining unpleasantly, but took no further action. Griselda found it impossible to withhold admiration for Lotus's Johannesburg hat. Griselda herself wore a large black velvet beret, à La Bohème.

'Where is he?' asked Lotus in a low voice, further muffled by layers of expensive veiling. 'When shall I see him?'

'I expect he's inside. They may have lighted a fire as the President's coming.'

'When he comes out, what do you advise me to do,

Griselda? I trust you absolutely.'

'Wait until the end of the ceremony. Geoffrey usually makes himself some toast before he leaves. You can help him with the sardines.'

'Will it be long?' Lotus's lovely voice was throbbing.

'We'll see. Here's the procession.'

The common constables had been active and were thrusting people back behind invisible lines. Soon Lotus's taxi was isolated. Griselda found it rather exciting. She supposed that Lotus and she must be taken for persons of privilege. Doubtless Lotus's veil was responsible. She resolved to acquire a veil herself as soon as Geoffrey was off her hands. The watchers on the pavement could be heard expressing further resentment as they were lined up behind a huge pantechnicon which, having missed the diversion notices, was waiting for the crowd to clear, while the driver looked for a public house. The constables were quipping and appealing obliquely to the crowd's common humanity in order to reconcile them.

Then from the other direction a scout from New Scotland Yard roared into being on his splendid motor bicycle; and some way behind him came a funeral Daimler, bearing a tiny silk pennant. Without a sound the Daimler ceased to move; the footman opened the door; and, as the crowd cheered half-heartedly, eight men alighted, in various different kinds of overcoat. Simultaneously the front door of the house opened with a deep clanking, as of heavy chains falling on to a deck; and Colonel Costa-Rica in a pale blue uniform and a feather at least two feet tall, descended the steps to greet the First Citizen of his homeland. After a moment's confusion, the band rushed into 'Sheep may safely graze' which had been adopted as the Orinocan national anthem. Their performance would have been better if they had not been so unaccustomd to prolonged damp cold.

Then Lotus gave a suppressed cry. Behind the Colonel, Kynaston had appeared. He wore a frock coat, which Griselda supposed must be retained by the Embassy for such occasions; a discreet rose in his buttonhole; and pale grey spats. He carried a silk hat almost as tall as the Colonel's feather; but could have done with a suitable overcoat. Griselda was surprised she had not before noticed that he was gathering weight. He looked anxious but determined, as at other turning points in his career at which she had been present Lotus clung to Griselda's hand. Rapture made her speechless.

Among the men getting out of the car Griselda recognized the Under Secretary for Foreign Affairs, a raw youth whom she had met at the All Party Dance. She remembered him as suffering from a conclusive impediment in his speech. Now he was followed by a tottering figure from his Department, and by the Orinocan Ambassador, who looked as pleased and as unchallengeable as if he had just captured the national meat-packing contract (as was quite possibly the case). The Ambassador was accompanied by a Chargé d'Affaires, indistinguishable from Mr Jack Buchanan, and by the Military Attaché, who, though a small man, based his style on Field-Marshal Göring, thus being entrusted with as many personal confidences as professional. Behind this brilliant figure, appeared the chef de cabinet and the President's aide-de-camp, the former somewhat younger than the latter, which was opportune as the two looked so South American as to make distinction between them otherwise difficult. Griselda would have expected the President to appear first, but, in fact, he appeared last: possibly in consequence of having been the first to enter the well filled vehicle. He was a commonplace stocky man, in movement staccato from years of watchfulness, and with a head like a small round cannon-ball. His sharp nasal voice could be clearly heard, carried on the chill moist air as he addressed his entourage. He seemed dissatisfied with something. Griselda knew from Kynaston that he was of Irish extraction, a fact which he concealed under the name of Cassido.

Despite the autumnal weather, Griselda enjoyed looking on from the sanctuary of the cab. Indeed she found many of the conditions perfect for witnessing a spectacle of the kind. It was almost cosy. Lotus, however, had begun to pant slightly, filling the enclosed space with delicate vapour filtered by her veil. Quickly, as Colonel Costa-Rica was saluting, she lowered the window of the cab and, putting out half her body, ecstatically waved her handkerchief, executed for her by Worth's South African branch. The draught in the cab was really appalling; and Griselda, moreover, was reduced to looking out through the unsatisfactory little panel at the rear.

The cab being, like most of its kind, old and almost in pieces, the sudden frenzied lowering of one of its windows was audible above 'Sheep may safely graze' and the fury of the President. The distinguished visitor still stood with his back to the saluting Colonel, so that Kynaston, waiting to be presented, permitted his attention to be drawn by the obtrusive clatter. Through her tiny window Griselda saw him go very white and drop his silk hat.

Lotus uttered a cooing cry of reunion. The President, his round Irish face black with passion, had begun to wave both arms above his head and to jump up and down on the pavement. Then there was a shot. The Military Attaché, secure in his diplomatic immunity, was effecting a coup d'état.

Griselda saw the President jump higher than ever. Clearly as yet he was little, if any, the worse. Kynaston was stooping for his hat, which had rolled down the red carpet. Then there was a second shot and Kynaston disappeared. By this time one of the common constables, who a second before had seemed to be standing a long way off, had covered the ground and, disregarding international law, thrown his arms round the Attaché's middle. Colonel Costa-Rica, supposing all to be over with the Father of his People, continued at the salute. Then, looking much mortified, he lowered his arm as unobtrusively as possible. The President was intact, though in a worse mood than ever.

*

History, or such of it as was under proper direction, related that a young foreigner privileged to work at the shrine of the Liberator, had had the honour of offering his life to save the life of President Cassido. Even a gringo, indicated history, was thus exalted after only a single meeting with the Liberator's great successor.

Occasionally Griselda wondered, not without remorse and self-questioning, whether Kynaston had not preferred death to Lotus; but on the whole she was convinced that his end had been sadly but entirely accidental.

To Colonel Costa-Rica it is to be feared that the incident presented itself mainly in the light of another contest with an obstructive charwoman upon the subject of once more cleaning up that unlucky carpet.

Part Three

XXXIV

One day between Christmas and Near Year Griselda and Lena were dusting some of the stock. The shop had just opened. They worked along the upper shelves taking out the books one at a time, dusting their top edges, and replacing them. Every now and then there was a long pause while one or other of them investigated a volume entirely new to her.

The door opened and a tall man entered in a Gibus hat and a black cloak covered with snow.

'Good morning.' said Griselda from the top of her ladder. She had just been dipping into Pears' Cyclopedia.

'Please don't come down,' said the visitor. 'I'll look round, if I may.' He removed his hat. He had curling black hair, parted down the middle.

'Certainly,' said Griselda. 'Won't you take off your cloak?'

'Thank you.' He looked up at her. He was very pale; with large but well-shaped bones, and black eyes.

'There's a stand in the corner. Under the bust of Menander.'

'I didn't know there was a bust of Menander.'

'It's conjectural.'

'Like so much else.'

Griselda thought he almost smiled.

He removed his cloak. He was wearing evening dress with a white waistcoat; and across his breast ran the bright silk ribbon of a foreign order.

He hung up his coat and hat, and began to examine the books. He went along the shelves steadily and methodically, noting every title and frequently extracting a book for similarly exact scrutiny of its contents. Some of the books he bore away to Griselda's desk, where he had soon built a substantial cairn. Griselda and Lena descended alternately to serve other customers. Many of them seemed surprised by the distinction of the stranger's appearance.

Before his circuit of the shop was three-quarters completed, he came to rest by the desk. 'Alas, I must go. You see: I am awaited.' He extended his hand towards the wintry morning outside the shop window. The snow clouds were so heavy that it hardly seemed day; but as Griselda followed his gesture, she saw that the dim and dirty light was further diminished by some large obstruction.

'I'll make out a bill and then pack up the books in parcels.'

'Please don't trouble. My coachman and footman will load them into the carriage.'

He went to the door and spoke briefly to someone outside.

A man of about thirty, with very long side whiskers, entered, and began to bear away armfuls of books. He wore a beaver hat, a long dark green topcoat with a cape, and high boots. Clearly he had been sitting on his box in the snow while his master shopped.

'Don't take them before Miss de Reptonville has accounted for them.'

Griselda put some shillings in the pounds column and Lena slightly damaged the dust-jacket of *The Light of Asia*; but both took care to display no surprise.

'Ask Staggers to help you, if you wish.'

'No necessity, sir. One more trip and I'll finish. Staggers needs to hold the umbrella between the door and the carriage.'

'Of course. Most proper.'

Griselda, being unproficient at arithmetic, could only hope that the grand total could be substantiated. It was certainly the grandest total since she had entered the shop.

The customer produced an unusually large cheque book from a pocket inside his cloak and wrote out the cheque in black ink. Griselda saw that the cheque, which was on a small private Bank previously unknown to her, bore the drawer's coat of arms and crest. One glance at this last and she had no need to look at the signature.

The customer was regarding her. 'I received your Christmas Card. Thank you.'

'I was grateful for your letter.'

'Nothing would have pleased me more than to have been able to help you' He spoke with much sincerity.

An invisible hand lightly squeezed at Griselda's throat.

'I must give you a receipt.'

She was unable even to stick on the stamp symmetrically.

'Please introduce me to your friend.'

'Of course. Please forgive me. Both of you. Lena Drelincourt. Sir Hugo Raunds.'

Lena descended. She looked a little startled. Their visitor removed a white kid glove, more than slightly discoloured with his recent work, and put out an elegant and well kept hand.

'I like your shop. I used to know Mr Tamburlane quite well. I shall hope to visit you again. May I?' It was if he were a caller rather than a customer.

'As soon as possible,' said Lena.

'Lena writes.'

'Of course. Her three books are by my bed, and I admire them more at every reading.'

Lena went slightly pink and looked charming.

'Good-bye then, Miss de Reptonville.'

Griselda took his hand. It was firm and dry and cool. She looked him in the eyes. 'There's no news?'

'No news.' He still held her hand. 'I hope I need not say I should have told you?'

'No . . . I couldn't help asking.'

He said nothing for a moment; then silently released her hand. All the while he was returning her gaze. Lena was looking on flushed and fascinated.

'All packed up, sir,' said the footman from the exactly right distance between the group of them and the shop door.

'I'm coming. You can tell Staggers to get back on his box.'

'Very good, sir.'

Their visitor put on his cloak. He had reached a decision. 'I propose,' he said, 'to ask you to come and stay with me. Both of you.' He seemed to speak with hesitation. 'But naturally only if you wish to do so. Please say nothing now. There will be a formal invitation; which if you wish to decline or ignore I shall entirely understand.'

At this moment Griselda recalled old Zec's curious behaviour at the All Party Ball when Hugo Raunds was mentioned.

'We'd love to come,' said Lena casually.

He made no reply, but bowing slightly and saying 'Your servant, ladies,' departed into the London snow.

Griselda and Lena followed him to the door. His carriage was an immense affair, with the familiar crest upon the door and at the base of the massive brightly polished lamps. Drawn by two proportionately immense black horses, with wild eyes, nostrils steaming like volcanoes, waving manes, and long undocked tails, it was governed by an immense coachman, so rugged and round and red as to overawe all possible comment. His red hair stuck out horizontally from beneath his huge tilted beaver. His red beard was snowy as Father Christmas's. His red ear was curiously round, like the top of a red toadstool.

As the equipage drove away into the thickly drifting snow, Griselda and Lena perceived that on the opposite pavement, previously obscured from them by the bulk of the carriage itself, had accumulated, even in the teeth of the weather, a small cluster of passing Londoners. Rage and contempt were in every face and posture. Griselda had seldom seen any gathering of people so much under the influence of their emotions.

XXXV

Griselda had told Lena about Louise and said that she had mentioned the family which dwelt in the house they had entered on the day of Kynaston's final picnic. Now she told her about Zec and his wife, whom for a long time she had forgotten; and of Louise's words 'Hugo is a very *secret* man.'

'You mean,' said Lena, 'that after Mr Tamburlane you've had enough of secret men?'

'Not altogether that. I don't think Hugo Raunds is like Mr Tamburlane, do you, Lena?'

'Not altogether, I should say.'

'I just thought that if we're going to stay with him – are we, by the way?'

'It'll mean coffins for beds and tooth mugs in gold plate.'

'If we *are* going to stay, perhaps we could find out just why people don't seem to like him.'

'I don't know that that's any great mystery,' said Lena. 'If you think what people are like. Still I agree we might dig about.'

But it was hard to know which piece of ground to turn first; so that by the time the invitation arrived, they had discovered nothing more about their host whatever.

They were invited to visit a house which seemed to be in the Welsh Marches; and no term was set to their stay. The brief letter ended with the words 'Come and see for yourselves. Then please yourselves.'

'Hell of a journey in February,' remarked Lena, 'and, I should say, doubtfully worth the expense seeing that we can't both leave the shop for more than a day or two. Still, better than that mausoleum in Essex doubtless. I suppose I shall have to freeze in a skirt all the time as it's a country family?'

'Louise said that Hugo Raunds lived entirely for clothes.'

'I can imagine what that means. Brittle women in models.'

'Surely not in Montgomeryshire?'

'Unlike us they travel wrapped in mink in centrally heated Rolls-Royces.'

'Shall we not go?'

Lena thought for a moment. Then she said gently 'You go, Griselda. They'd only eye me.'

'I won't go without you.'

'It's much the best thing. You could do with a holiday, and I could look after the shop. Stay a long time if you find you like it. As long as you want to. You're beautiful and it's a kind of thing you need. One kind of thing. Sometimes, anyway. So, please.'

'You need a holiday too.'

'Less than you.'

Griselda put her arm round Lena's shoulders.

'You're good to me, Lena, I'm grateful.'

'You gave me half a shop. *I'm* grateful. I'll look you up a train to Montgomeryshire.'

Of course Griselda had to change at Shrewsbury, but she had never expected to have to change at Welshpool as well.

Darkness had descended long before she arrived. The minute but not inelegant Welsh station seemed high among the mountains. A small but bitter wind crept murderously along the single platform. There was one oil lamp, and otherwise not a light to be seen anywhere. Griselda was the only passenger, but two figures awaited her on the platform.

One was clearly the station factotum, though his aspect, demeanour, and even uniform seemed of an antique type. He came forward, touched his cap, and, though able to speak little but Welsh, bade Griselda Good evening, and took her bag. After a wait of only some seconds, the engine whistled, and the train drew out as if glad to be away.

The second figure was a woman. She was closely muffled in a hood and wore some long garment reaching to the ground. Her perfume hung on the cold air. She extended her gloved hand and, having confirmed Griselda's identity, said 'My name is Esemplarita. I look after things at the Castle. Hugo asked me to apologize for being unable to meet you himself. He turned his ankle yesterday fencing.' When Griselda had greeted her and expressed her regret about her host's misadventure, the woman continued 'We have to go down a narrow path to the lane, where the carriage is waiting. But Abersoch will go first with the lamp.'

Abersoch lifted the single lamp from its bracket and led the way.

'You go next,' said Esemplarita to Griselda.

They descended a cinder way which zig-zagged down a high bank to a tiny sunken lane below. At the bottom of the path Abersoch's lamp fell upon a small black cabriolet with a gleaming horse.

'Good evening, miss,' said another Welsh voice from the box.

Abersoch opened the door and handed up Griselda's luggage, which the coachman placed in a high-sided cage on the roof.

'Your ticket if you please, miss.'

Griselda had to grope by the light of Abersoch's lamp, but in the end she found it and delivered it up.

'Not all of it, miss,' said Abersoch. He bisected the ticket and gave her half of it. 'You may be wanting to go back.'

'Thank you,' said Griselda smiling: 'So I shall.'

'It's entirely up to you, miss.'

Griselda stepped into the carriage. The interior was pitch black and filled with Esemplarita's scent. Esemplarita followed her in. There was scarcely room for two on the seat. Abersoch shut the door and again touched his cap, the light falling on his face as in an old-fashioned coloured drawing. The carriage began to move.

'I'm afraid the road is atrocious almost all the way.'

To Griselda this seemed to be true.

After a considerable period of compressed jolting silence, while Griselda tried to think of something to say, Esemplarita took up the conversation. 'I believe you don't know Hugo very well?'

'No. He's really a friend of a friend of mine.'

'I know. Your friend gave Hugo a good account of you.'

'When?' Griselda's heart was beating among the beating of the horse's hooves.

'Some time ago. As you know, we're not in touch with her at the moment. But I wanted to speak of something else. You have heard, of course, that Hugo's life – and the lives of all of us – differ from the lives people lead nowadays?'

'I was told a little – by the friend we have in common. A very little. I have noticed – some small differences. I know almost nothing.'

'The Castle is, so to speak, enchanted. Your friend gave Hugo to understand that you might like to know about it; to see for yourself.'

'She was kind.'

'The opportunity is mutual. We want suitable people to visit us.'

'I see.'

'There are very few suitable people.'

'Can you define?'

The carriage had plunged across what Griselda took to be a series of deep diagonal ruts frozen to the unyieldingness of stone, before her companion answered 'It cannot truly be defined. You will soon begin to see. There is only one thing.'

'Yes?'

'Your friend commended you for your acceptance of what life can offer. Your lack of surprise. You understand that?'

'Yes.'

'Lack of surprise is taken for granted at the Castle. That is what I wanted to say.'

'I see . . . I love your scent.'

'Thank you.' Then she added kindly 'That is the sort of thing not to be surprised about.'

For some time they compared tastes in books and music. Then the carriage stopped.

'The Castle gates,' said Esemplarita.

Griselda could hear the clanking and grinding as the lodge-keeper opened them. Remarks were exchanged in Brythonic between him and the driver. Then the carriage proceeded on a much better surface. Griselda could hear the gates closing behind her.

The distance up the drive seemed very long. Griselda and her companion turned to the subject of edible fungi: how to find and prepare them, and which of them to eschew. Esemplarita explained that she had known nothing of these matters until she came to live at the Castle, but that now they had fungi with almost every meal.

In the end Griselda felt the carriage following a huge arc, as if going round the edge of an immense circus ring. Then it stopped again and the driver was opening the door.

Griselda realized that the Castle was not, as she had supposed, mediaeval, but Gothic revival at the earliest. The long front before her was decked with three tiers of lighted windows. Clearly Sir Hugo was entertaining largely.

When the coachman had rung the ornate bell, the door was opened by a footman. Griselda entered, followed by Esemplarita. The coachman was getting down Griselda's bag to give to the footman.

The big Gothic revival hall was hung with paintings, and lighted with hundreds, possibly thousands, of candles, in complex candelabra descending from the ceiling, and storied brackets climbing the walls. There was an immense carpet, predominantly dark green: and involved painted furniture. At one end of the hall was a fire which really filled the huge grate and soaked all the air with warmth. Round the fire was a group of men and women. They sat or lay on painted chairs and couches and on the predominantly dark green floor. Griselda thought at first that they were in fancy dress. Then she turned and saw that Esemplarita was dressed like them. She remembered that she must not be surprised.

Instead she smiled. She felt as one returned to life She was relieved of care and accessible to joy.

Esemplarita went round introducing her. Several of the names were known to Griselda. If she was not surprised, neither, it was clear, were they.

Then she heard herself greeted. She stood with her

back to the the blaze, a huge portrait of Jeanne de Naples above her head, and saw her host standing at the foot of the wide staircase. He wore a dressing gown in mulberry silk and leaned on the baluster. Behind him stood a figure Griselda recognized. It was Vaisseau.

'Are you pleased?'

'It is beautiful.'

'It is doomed of course.'

'Of course.'

'You are smiling.'

'I am happy.'

The men and women round the fire had kept quite silent during this colloquy. Now a tall woman came to her and said 'Would you like to change? There's no need if you'd rather not. But if you'd like to, I could help.'

'Thank you,' replied Griselda. 'I'd like to.'

Envoi

Before many days Griselda found that happiness unfitted her for the modern world; and, though the master of the Castle, as she knew, often travelled, as on occasion did most of the others, decided to give her half of the shop to Lena, who, despite the warmest of invitations, persisted in her attitude that Wales was a waste of oracles and oratorios.

Griselda was happy, though cognizant that sooner or later the spell would be broken by public opinion and Order in Council; but whenever there was mention of Hero and Leander, about whom one of the others was writing a poetic drama, and indeed whenever her thoughts were idle, she knew that if only Louise were there, then indeed would she be whole.